I0615997

The Rebel Christian Publishing

ISBN: 978-1-957290-56-0 (eBook)
Print: 978-1-957290-57-7

This is a work of fiction. Any references to historical events, real people, or real places are used fictitiously. Names, characters, and places are products of the author's imagination. Inclusion of or reference to any Christian elements or themes are used in a fictitious manner and are not meant to be perceived or interpreted as an act of disrespect against such a wonderful and beautiful belief system.

Cover designed by Valicity Elaine

The Rebel Christian Publishing LLC
350 Northern Blvd STE 324 - 1390
Albany, NY 12204-1000

Visit us: http://www.therebelchristian.com/
Email us: rebel@therebelchristian.com

Contents

Exodus V
1.. 1
2.. 8
3.. 20
4.. 29
5.. 36
6.. 46
7.. 56
8.. 66
9.. 77
10.. 88
11.. 102
12.. 114
13.. 124
14.. 134
15.. 145
16.. 155
17.. 161
18.. 172
19.. 179
20.. 189
21.. 199
22.. 211
23.. 221
24.. 233
25.. 244
26.. 255
27.. 263

28 272
Finish the series... 280
ACKNOWLEDGEMENTS 282

Trilogy Order:

Decipis

Exodus

Eternus

Exodus

Book II in the Treachery Trilogy

By Valicity Elaine

A Rebel Christian Publishing Book

1

Adrian

Connor and Delilah are having sex. I can hear them in the bedroom down the hall—Mya's *father's* bedroom. Aside from that being creepy as all get out, it's also nauseating. They've been going at it every morning for the last few weeks. They think no one knows. Technically, they're right about that. No one except *me* knows because I'm the only one who goes out scouting this early in the morning.

We've divided up our chores and responsibilities; cooking, scavenging, cleaning, keeping watch, emptying the bathroom buckets, boiling water. There's a lot to be done just to stay alive. It takes up every second of every day. Bone-grinding work, meticulous attention to detail, high anxiety, overwhelming stress levels. We need food. We need water. We need to stay hidden so foreign soldiers don't track us down and kill us. Or looters don't find us and take our supplies. And then kill us—or kidnap us and do whatever the heck they want with us.

I don't really blame Delilah and Connor for finding relief in each other. I just wish they would keep it quiet.

I'm tiptoeing through Mya's kitchen so I can leave through the side entrance. My scouting shift doesn't start for another hour, but I always leave early so I can go for a jog first. Of course, neither Delilah nor Connor has ever noticed this. They finish up their morning dance routine and then stumble down to the basement where everyone else is asleep like nothing ever happened. Since I'm not there when they go downstairs, they probably assume I'd only left moments earlier, while they were getting dressed, and hadn't heard a thing.

I wish that were the case.

As it stands, I leave the house with Connor panting in the background, and I run like mad just to clear the sound from my head.

We are animals... Animals disguised as humans. And we do animalistic things to survive, to keep going, to maintain some semblance of sanity. I run until my legs go numb, Delilah and Connor rut until they can't breathe, Jupiter has gotten into the habit of painting her nails with Mya's leftover polish from her bedroom. And Mya...

I grunt aloud as her face pops into my head. I don't want to think about Mya right now, but like most things in my life, I can't help it. I can't control this—this *thing* I feel for her. Or the way she feels about me. All I can do is hope, but hoping is pointless. Who wants to hope when you can *make* things happen? Instead of wishing and praying.

Mya's found a way to cope with Julius. They've buddied up well these last three months. And here I thought their little fling wouldn't last a week. But Julius beat me at my own game. He's been a perfect little prince since the day we first arrived here. Since they made up for the awful fight they had on the road.

I thought I'd found a weakness, a crack between them I could expose and use to my advantage. But I was wrong. That argument hadn't weakened their feelings toward each other, it made them stronger. So much stronger that I half expect to wake up and hear *them* in Mya's bedroom one morning. But I know better than that. Mya's a Christian. She wouldn't taint her body the way Connor and Delilah have.

Which means there *is* a crack I can expose. Mya doesn't mind keeping herself pure, but I wonder how Julius is holding up. He has never had a serious relationship for as long as I've known him. Some weekends, he enjoyed a different girl each day. One of the perks of being the captain of the track team.

There is no way the leader of the Kappa Pi Fraternity Brothers is fine with having a sexless relationship right now. But what am I supposed to do about that? Strip down and give him a lap dance myself?

I shake my head, jogging down a dark alleyway. Whatever will happen between Julius and Mya will peter out soon. I know it will. Until then, I've got to keep my own head straight. I can't afford to think about romance right now. I'm three months late on tracking down my family. The only thought in my head should be of my twin siblings.

Danya. Dinara. I wonder if they're alive. I wonder if they're waiting for me.

I slow to a stop and heave for air, holding onto the brick building beside me. My chest hurts, but the pain has nothing to do with running. I can't stop the panic that shoots through me right now. My knees knock so badly, I stumble to the side. My hands go clammy with sweat, my eyes sting with unshed tears. I can feel anxiety building in my torso like a raw scream waiting to be released. With a gasp, I double over and bite my lip until it bleeds, trying hard not to make a sound.

This neighborhood has been thoroughly swept by our group—we haven't seen a guard around here in weeks, so I know it's safe to go for a run here, but I wouldn't take my chances at *screaming*. Still … that may not be up to me. I can't control myself right now. I feel like I can't even *breathe*.

I'm having a panic attack.

I … I've been having them a lot lately. They started a few weeks ago, and I don't know why.

I'm so scared right now. All I feel is **fear**. Inexplicable fear that sends nails of anxiety raking down my back. I choke out a sob and tear my shirt from my body as a wave of heat flashes through me. I'm soaked with sweat.

Why… The thought surfaces through the murky waters of my conscience. *Why is this happening to me?*

It takes another few moments for the attack to pass. I squeeze my eyes shut as the last rocky waves of the storm calm and then fade away. By then, I'm on my knees in this dirty alley. Shards of broken glass poke at my flesh, the grime on the brick building beside me smudges onto the tips of my fingers as I grip the wall and struggle to my feet. Blonde bangs stick to my forehead in sweaty misery. I brush them back with a dirty palm and take a deep breath.

"Get it together," I tell myself, and then I take off running again.

The wintery Arizona air is only a balmy 50 degrees Fahrenheit, but it still turns the sweat on my skin into a deep

4

chill. So, I pick up the pace. I sprint through the back alleys because I know we've cleared them, but once I've finished my usual route, I feel a lingering sense of anger inside me, so I keep going. I know I should slow down and start my scouting shift, but I can't focus on keeping watch when it feels like my skin is being peeled from my bones.

I can't stand whatever this is. Whatever monster of worry has taken root inside me. It's turned me into a shivering mess, and it's making me weak.

I veer off my usual jogging trail and find myself moving toward the outskirts of the city. I run until my legs threaten to give out, and even then, I only slow down because something catches my attention.

A tiny pyramid in the distance.

I'm standing at the edge of the city, near a major highway exit and a wide street that leads to a strip containing a mini mall and a host of other stores I've never had the luxury of shopping at. I don't care about the mall or the stores. I care about the pyramid I see set up between two abandoned trucks.

As I squint at the figure, I realize what I'm looking at.

A tent.

I haven't been to the outskirts of the city in a long while, but I know for a fact that tent wasn't there the last time I was in this area. A tent is a home. A home means someone is living there. Someone who could be our enemy.

Maybe that anxiety attack fried my brain, but for whatever reason, I decide the best thing to do is get a closer look. So I take off at a slow jog, breathing deeply so I don't exhaust myself before I get there.

This tent could belong to soldiers. It could belong to survivors who'll shoot me on sight, just like those thugs on the

5

highway did. Or it could belong to people like me and Connor O'Reilly, or Bunny.

Once I make it to the tent, I learn that it belongs to no one. It's abandoned.

The layer of dust all over the blankets and sleeping bag isn't what makes it obvious the camp is abandoned, it's the sign posted on the tent entrance. A sheet of paper with bold red letters that read:

ABANDONED BY ORDER OF 5TH BRIGADE. SURVIVORS RELOCATED TO ORLY CENTER.

There's a seal on the bottom right corner of the page, but I don't recognize it. I mean, a seal from the US Army would have an eagle on it, right? Maybe some stars and stripes?

I shake my head. I'm not patriotic enough to know random facts like that. I don't even know if the US Army *has* a seal. Whether it does or not, someone sealed this letter and stuck it to this tent post. Someone from the 5th Brigade. And then they relocated the owners of this tent to a place called Orly Center.

Is that a survival shelter?

My breath catches in my throat, and I crumple the letter in my fist without thinking. It's an uncontrollable reaction as excitement shoots through me. *This is it!* Whoever found this tent was a soldier, and they escorted the survivors to a shelter. To Orly Center shelter.

What if that's where my family was taken? What if Mya's father is there? Or even Julius's foster mother? No, I don't like the guy, but even Julius deserves to know if the woman who raised him is alive. She *could* be alive. She could be waiting for him at Orly Center.

Wherever that is.

The place sounds vaguely familiar but, more importantly, I've never seen this *seal* before. It must mean something. It's the first clue we've gotten about our families since we settled down at Mya's house. We haven't had much time to search like we'd originally planned, but it's never too late to start. Now that we're finally learning to survive and getting our feet under ourselves, it might be time to set out and do what we initially said we'd do.

It's time to find my siblings.

We've already waited too long, but survival isn't an overnight task. Each day was its own challenge in that house. Sorting our supplies, sticking to our rations, looting for more food, keeping watch, avoiding soldiers, coping, mourning, just trying to get along and not lose our minds. Not to mention Connor's leg. He'd been shot a few weeks earlier, before I arrived back with Mya and the rest of our group. He couldn't walk, which meant we couldn't leave until he was all healed up. Even as he got better and returned to his normal self again, we kept making promises to set out, to find our families, to leave this place. But three months passed in the blink of an eye.

Now, we can't wait any longer. We *won't* wait.

With a smile, I fold the paper up and carefully stash it in my back pocket. Then I turn and take off running, sprinting madly, but for an entirely different reason.

2

Mya

"The water is boiling," I whisper as the pot begins to sizzle.

Julie quietly leans over to empty the packet into the water. I watch him stir in silence, enjoying his concentration. So much has changed in the last three months. We're all living in my house together, we're all surviving together, and we've somehow managed to make it work. But our change is deeper than that.

Julie and I have gotten close. Closer than best friends. Neither of us has ever said the word *boyfriend* or *girlfriend*, but we can't deny the connection we have anymore. So we don't try to.

Adrian was right when he said we should start over, leave all our drama behind. Give ourselves a fresh new beginning. We needed that, truly. Julie and I deserved a fresh start, an honest chance to see what could happen between us. So far, things have been good.

We try to spend as much time together as we can, exploring this strange new territory. But with our chores split up and everything else on a strict schedule, sometimes it's hard for our paths to cross, despite the cramped quarters. Most of us sleep, eat, and work entirely on rotation.

My father built an incredible shelter in our basement, but he'd built it for our family of three. He was kind enough to anticipate taking in a straggler or two, so there's enough supplies down here for five, but our group is seven strong. That's two extra people. Two extra rations we don't have, two extra beds we don't have, two extra butts to wipe with toilet paper we don't have. Things are stable, but not for much longer.

In this stressful madness, Julius and I started over. In a way, I feel like we had no choice. I was driving myself insane with worry over my father. How could I sit here making grits for breakfast while my dad might be out there starving?

Everyone else in our group is worried too. We all have family out there. But we're not staying in their abandoned homes. Their families are far off, only reunited in their dreams. But my father is all around me. I see him in the pictures on the walls, and I wonder if he's still smiling. I smell him in the dusty spare clothes left in his room, and I wonder what he's wearing. I see him in the blankets we snuggle under at night, and I wonder if he's warm when he sleeps—or if he's sleeping in a coffin now.

My father could be suffering while I'm making breakfast with the supplies he left behind. The pain of my guilt and worry is sometimes enough to bring me to my knees, and it was in this deep pool of misery that Julius found me.

He knows my father. He's the only one who truly understands what I'm going through because he was there almost every step of the way. Julius knows I can't look at Connor when he wears my father's red flannel shirt because it was his favorite. He knows why I always add an extra bit of honey to my oatmeal no matter how low our rations get because that was the way my father prepared it for me. And he knows the hospital bed in the basement isn't another mattress to sleep on. It's a reminder of how much I've already lost, and how much more pain could be waiting in my future.

When Adrian told us to start over, I practically ran into Julie's arms. They were the only arms that felt right. The only arms I knew and understood. Arms that felt as warm and familiar as my father's. Arms that'd held me at my mother's funeral. Arms that pulled me out of the black hole I'd gotten trapped in when the grief of her death overwhelmed me. They pull me out of that hole every day now. Reminding me that my father could still be alive. Reminding me there is someone else who needs me. Another parent to still live for.

Maybe Adrian was who I wanted, but right now, Julius is the one I need. And I think he needs me too. Because as much pain and misery Julius sees in me, I see the same in him too. We're both down to one parent. We're both swimming in the same pool of sorrows. But we're swimming together, kept afloat by the memories of our shared childhood and the hope of a shared future. The Hands of God are around us—I know they are. We'll get through this together. It's the only way we know how.

I glance at Julie now as he stirs quietly, wondering why he's willing to give up so much for me. He hasn't mentioned searching for his foster mother at all. But I know he misses her.

I know he wonders about her as much as I wonder and worry about my father. But all of his attention has been on me. Helping me cope. Helping me heal. Promising to help me search for my dad.

Maybe that's why I've been tangled up in this complicated relationship with him. Turning him away would make me feel so guilty. It would mean trampling on all the sacrifices he makes for me every single day.

Julie typically takes a late watch shift so he's dead tired in the morning, but since I'm on the first meal shift, he wakes up early and helps me with breakfast. He does it with a smile and dark circles beneath his eyes. When I tell him to get more sleep, he insists he's okay and silences my protests with a kiss. That's one way to shut me up. I can't worry over his sleepy face when I know I'm secretly giddy over the few minutes of privacy we're able to steal away sometimes.

Technically, we're not completely alone. Jupiter and Bunny are still snoring on the hospital bed and a cot in the corner of the room, so the kissing never lasts long. But Adrian is out on his scouting shift and while Julie helps me out, Delilah uses that time to sneak upstairs with Connor O'Reilly. So we're as alone as we can be for now.

I should complain about Delilah sneaking off since she's supposed to help me with breakfast, but I don't mind her absence. Julie and I have gotten close, but I haven't forgotten how close he'd once been with *her*. Technically, I don't have anything to worry about. Delilah's been hooking up with Connor for weeks now. He's got the sunrise shift for keeping watch, so their rotations overlap for about an hour. Instead of keeping an eye on the house, Connor spends the last hour of his shift with Delilah, who should be spending the first hour of *her* shift helping me with breakfast. They think they're slick, sneaking off like that, but it's so obvious. The only reason I don't say anything is because I want more time with Julius.

I stare at him as he focuses on stirring the pot of grits. We're using a camp burner, down to just a few cannisters of butane gas now, but he swears he's got a cooking method that'll save our gas, so I lean closer and try not to ogle him. I can't really help it. Despite our living conditions, Julius is still handsome.

His hair is longer now, dark wavy locks grown past his ears. We have razors and combs and even shampoo, but Julie's chosen to forgo the clippers. I like his hair like this, it makes him look a little older. A little more mature. Or maybe it isn't his hair, maybe he *has* matured.

Everyone's grown up a bit—we've had no choice—but maturity looks good on Julie. It's taken him from my boyish best friend to a man I can't ignore. I shouldn't be this crazy about him, not with how turbulent things had been before this. But ... that was different. That was when Adrian was a problem. But he isn't anymore.

Yes, I liked Adrian too. But he's the one who told us to start over. I'd been stuck in a love triangle. I *had* to make a choice. One of them was going to end up hurt. I'm sorry it was Adrian, but Julie and I needed this. If I had chosen Adrian, I would've lost Julius completely. I couldn't survive him walking out of my life. So, I gave this relationship a chance, and it's working.

"Hit it!" Julie says, snapping his fingers.

I quickly flip the camp burner off and watch as Julius tilts the pot and starts stirring more vigorously. It's just a pot of instant grits, but he's determined to save us gas, which means cooking as much as we can without using fire.

"The residual heat should be enough to keep the grits cooking while I stir," he explains, squinting at his pot. "But I've got to move fast, so they don't lose their texture." He's breathing heavily now, perhaps taking this a bit too seriously, but I'm hungry so I just let him work.

"Almost done?" I ask after another minute of stirring.

He nods. "Grab the bowls."

With Delilah and Connor still busy, I've only got to serve breakfast for five—but Adrian is missing too. His sleeping bag is already rolled up and resting neatly beside the pile of his personal belongings. He left early this morning, even though his shift doesn't start for another hour. He's been doing that for a while now, and sometimes I can't help but wonder why.

I shake my head, adjusting my grip on the stack of bowls in my hand. I don't like to think about Adrian. If I do, my mind will wander in a thousand different directions. I'll wonder why he never wants to eat breakfast with the group. I'll wonder if he hates being in the house when he knows I'm here with Julius. And I'll wonder why he wakes up and leaves early while Delilah is still upstairs.

Maybe he joins her and Connor. Or maybe Delilah has him all to herself, two guys every morning. All before breakfast.

"Mya!" Julius's voice is as loud as he'll let it be with Jupe and Bunny still asleep. Still, the sound of it snaps me to attention and I quickly turn back to join him.

He glances up at me with a frown. "Couldn't find the bowls?"

"We didn't wash dishes last night," I mumble in reply. It's not the reason I took so long, but it is true. Our water supply has been running low, so we've been washing dishes every three days now, reusing whatever isn't grimy enough to make us sick by cooking in it. The grits pot had a sticky layer of baked bean syrup in it before Julie started breakfast. We didn't bother wiping it out before adding the food—plain grits are awful, hopefully the residual bean syrup added some favor.

"Right," Julius replies, spooning grits into the bowls I'd collected. "We've got enough though."

"Yeah, four bowls." I swallow.

"Wish we had five."

"Why?" I hope he doesn't hear how defensive I sound, but I think he does because he hesitates before answering.

"Delilah usually comes down a little late."

I press my lips together and turn back toward the rack of supplies. "I'll grab one more then."

"Don't. She can just reuse one of ours. We don't want to use any dishes if we don't have to." Julie frowns at the line of bowls on the floor; he's filled two of them with grits so far. "Actually, we can share a bowl to save dishes too."

"Really?" I squeak out.

He smirks. "I don't know why we never shared before; it's not like we haven't done other things together."

If my skin wasn't so brown, I'd be beet red right now. I can hardly look Julius in the eye as he pours the grits into one more bowl and then chuckles. The sound sends little ripples of joy zinging right through my gut.

Julie is right. We have done other things, but not *that* thing. Not yet. Not until…

I sigh. *Until what?* We get *married?* There is so much about that idea that makes my heart seize in my chest. How could we even get married? Are there any priests around who could

14

marry us? Where would we get a marriage license? Do we still need one?

Even if we could get our hands on all of that… Do I *want* to marry Julius?

It's way too early to tell. Right now, entertaining any thoughts of marriage would be foolish. We'd be getting married to have sex. But I don't want that. I want to marry someone because God has given me a partner to share that intimacy with. Not because he makes my toes curl.

But he *does* make my toes curl—he makes me feel all kinds of things I hadn't known I could feel with him. But beneath that girlish butterfly joy, I feel something else. A deep sense of worry. Worry that something is off between us. Something is lurking at the edges of this barricade we've built around ourselves, searching for cracks.

Are there any?

Every day it gets harder to say no. That sounds so confusing, doesn't it? I keep saying we've started over, we've given this relationship a chance, and that it's working out. But that's just it. It's what I keep *saying*. Over and over. Because if I don't repeat this to myself every day, I will have to tell myself the truth. That I let go of someone whose feelings for me were true, all so that I could chase after someone who was only looking to win a competition.

That's the darkness I fear; one day Julius will wake up and realize he never truly liked me. I mean, how could I ever believe he did anyway? He was my best friend, sure, but he was also captain of the track team and a leader of the Kappa Pi Fraternity. He had no reason to fall for a nerdy freshman girl who spent her Friday nights at Bible study instead of college parties.

But he *did* fall for me…

After realizing I'd fallen for someone else.

So that's my nightmare. A horrible dream that this was all just another game for him, a competition for my heart. But he won the competition. I've chosen Julie. Now I've got to make it work.

Jupiter groans as she wakes up and rolls over.

"I'll go feed the kiddos." Julius takes their bowls and walks over to the two sleepyheads.

Out of everyone here, Bunny and Jupiter have been adapting the worst. Bunny is bad at everything, and Jupiter is slowly falling into a dark hole of depression. She's barely eating anymore, only speaks when necessary, and seems to have lost all interest in finding her family. I know we've delayed the great search, but we haven't given up. There's a difference between delayed and discarded. Jupiter doesn't see it that way.

I'm worried she's going to wither away before we leave this place, but some of my anxiety dampens when she takes her breakfast without hassle and starts eating. I let go of a breath I didn't even know I was holding. Jupiter is my closest friend here; I need her to be strong.

Julie wipes his hands on his pants as he returns to sit across from me on the floor. My gaze immediately focuses on him again, abandoning Jupiter and Bunny as they gobble down their food behind us. "Ready to eat?" Julie says. He holds out his hands toward me; they're big and calloused, there's even a scar across his palm now. We've all got scars and scabs from the fighting we've done.

People lost their lives for us to get here. Everything started with the power outage on our college campus, and then things got worse as our supplies dwindled. We stayed because we thought the National Guard would eventually show up and help us. But that never happened.

By the time we realized help wasn't coming, multiple students were dead—most of them killed by other kids. We left with the clothes on our backs, literally running for our lives. The scar on Julie's palm is a sign of our victory. We made it. We're still here. And we're going to keep moving forward. I almost want to take his hand and kiss it, instead, I hold Julie's hand and close my eyes.

There's another reason I've enjoyed this fresh new start with my best friend. He's gotten closer to God.

Months ago, Julius didn't even believe in God. Now he won't eat without me praying first. I can't stop myself from smiling as he closes his eyes and waits for me to say grace. This side of him is like a dream come true.

"Lord Jesus," I whisper, "thank You for this food. Bless it to strengthen us and nourish us. Please help us find more to replace it. In Jesus' Name I pray, amen."

Julius whispers *amen* and then grabs the bowl. I wait for him to eat his half, but he shocks me by trying to feed me a spoonful.

"What are you doing?" I jerk away from him.

He cocks his head to the side. "Feeding you."

"I'm not a baby."

"You're my baby." He winks—and before I can even comprehend his words, someone makes a gagging noise over my shoulder.

I turn around to see Delilah descending the stairs into the basement. She's barefoot and wearing an oversized t-shirt, her blonde hair swaying around her hips.

What great timing.

"Get a room," she says in her husky morning voice.

"You're one to talk," I mumble.

"What'd you say?"

I shrug one shoulder. "You know your little rendezvous with Connor isn't a secret, right?"

Delilah is silent for a heartbeat, like maybe she *hadn't* known the secret was out, but she recovers with a smirk as she walks past me and heads to the bathroom down the hall.

"You're welcome to join us if you want."

"No thanks," I say, rolling my eyes.

"That offer wasn't for you."

I glance up to see Delilah looking at *Julius*. He averts his gaze, fiddling with his stupid spoonful of grits. I wait for him to tell her that he isn't interested—that he's busy with his *baby*—but he doesn't. He just sits there like an idiot as Delilah grins at him.

"I'm up for anything, Caesar," she practically purrs. "God knows you aren't getting any action from your Bible study partner."

My cheeks burn with embarrassment.

"Aren't you going to shower?" I snap.

Delilah laughs and then shimmies out of her oversized tee. That's when I realize she's wearing *nothing* underneath. She stands in the basement entirely naked, not an ounce of shame in her as she tosses her tee into the hamper by the bathroom.

I have no idea what to even say. No one does. We all watch in silence as she strolls to the shower room, hips swaying.

I … I don't want to look, but I can't stop myself from glancing at Julius. My worst fears are confirmed when I see him watching her.

"Nothing like a good wash after great sex," Delilah says, closing the door behind her.

Only then does Julius snap out of it. Like an alarm has gone off in his head, he finally looks at me and his eyes widen in shame.

Bunny groans and tosses his blankets away. "I'm leaving," he announces.

"Where are you going?" Jupiter asks.

"To find Connor. I need details." He takes the stairs two at a time, leaving us in an awkward silence once the basement door shuts.

"That was interesting," Jupiter mutters.

Neither I nor Julius responds. Julie won't look at me anymore. He keeps his gaze focused on his breakfast, moving his nasty, bean-syrup grits around the bowl. His avoidance makes me angry. The way he gawked at Delilah makes me angry. The fact that he didn't even try to hide his attraction to her makes me want to smack that bowl out of his hands.

Delilah called me his *Bible study partner*. I don't know why that makes me feel embarrassed, but it does. She belittled me right in front of Julius and he didn't say a word. He *still* won't say a word.

I push to my feet and start toward the stairs. *Then* he finds his voice.

"Mya, wait—"

"I'm going foraging," I say, cutting him off. "You can clean the dishes yourself."

3

Caesar

"I can't believe this has been going on for *weeks*," Bunny whines.

We've been doing our chores for the last hour, cleaning the sheets, clothes, and blankets while the girls handle scavenging or scouting. Normally, I don't mind cleaning with the guys, it beats sitting upstairs and staring out a window with a pair of binoculars like Delilah's doing on watch right now. But today I'm tired of my friends.

Delilah has been the topic of discussion this entire time. It's about to drive me crazy, but Connor O'Reilly seems immune. He doesn't mind any of Bunny's invasive questions, in fact, he grins as Bunny whines again.

"You've been sleeping with her for weeks and I never knew!"

Connor lets out a chuckle as he beats his blanket with a tennis racket from the garage. We don't have enough water to wash our clothes and sheets, so we hang them up and whack them until they smell like the outdoors instead of sweat and tears.

"You weren't ever supposed to know," Connor says, grunting with exertion. "Just be thankful for what you've learned so far."

"So, we aren't getting any details about Delilah?"

Connor drops his racket and wipes sweat from his brow. He's tired—we all are—but I can tell the job is starting to get to his leg. He got shot just before our team grouped up together; apparently some crazy travelers on the road tried to kill him and Adrian but they ended up getting away. Adrian tended his wounds until we all met up and chipped in to take care of each other. His leg is fully healed now, but it isn't good as new. He walks with a limp and can't stand or walk for very long without complaining of muscle cramps or a terrible ache that takes hours to pass.

I stare at his leg now as he shifts his weight from one foot to the other, trying to find a better stance to take before he lifts his racket again. Part of me wants to tell him to stop, but the truth is that we've got to get this done. The girls are busy with other duties; Mya and Jupiter are out scavenging, and Delilah is on the second floor keeping watch from the upper windows. If Connor doesn't finish his chores, someone else will have to pick up the slack. Probably me.

I like Connor, but not enough to watch him rest while I beat his sheets for him.

"What do you want to know?" he asks Bunny, exhaling heavily.

21

The kid practically salivates as he gets this faraway look in his eyes, drifting into his imagination. "Are those her real boobs?" he finally says.

I roll my eyes as I fold up the blanket I'd been working on.

"What do you think?" Connor replies.

"Come on!" Bunny says miserably. "You're the only one getting any action around here. I need to know."

"Why don't you ask Caesar?"

I'm in the middle of hanging a sheet from the clothing line we've set up in the garage, but the sound of Connor's question catches me off guard so badly, I end up missing the sheet and clipping my finger with the pin.

I curse and stick my finger in my mouth. "Ask me what?"

"About Delilah." Connor makes a face. "Weren't you two hooking up back at the university?"

Bunny snorts. "Who *wasn't* Delilah hooking up with? You might have a disease, Connor."

"I don't know why you risk it," I mutter.

Connor glowers. "She's available. It's just sex."

"She's not available to *me*." Bunny pokes his lower lip out like a child.

"No one is available to you," Connor teases.

"Caesar, you'll tell me something, right?" Bunny goes back to salivating as I take my second attempt at hanging this stupid sheet. It's one of the white ones from the hospital bed in the basement, still stained red from when Connor's leg bled out on it.

I know he's the reason for the stains, but when I look at the sheets, I can only think of Mya's mother. She died of cancer when we were in high school. She's the reason the hospital bed and all the medical supplies are in the basement in the first place. Mya's paranoid father was a doomsday prepper and had singlehandedly built the fallout shelter we're currently staying in. He stocked it with tons of provisions and advanced medical supplies because he thought his wife would live long enough to need it.

She didn't.

We've been the beneficiaries of the supplies she never got to use. I'm grateful for everything that was left behind for us, but the sight of these stained sheets makes my stomach churn. I can't stop seeing Mya's mother in my head, taking slow painful breaths, smiling through her sickness. She was friends with my foster mom, and sometimes I would see her when I visited Mya. But now… She seems like a memory so far off, her image in my head is more like the remnants of a bad dream than a reality I lived through.

I can only wonder how Mya is dealing with all of this. And then I remember her mother is already dead. It's her father she's worried over now. But we're *all* looking for our families, left wandering in the nightmares of the unknown.

"Caesar?" Bunny pokes me in the side, and I pin the stupid sheet in place and blink at him.

"What?"

"Details. How good was it to hook up with Delilah?"

I have to stop myself from rolling my eyes. I can't believe we're still talking about this.

"It was sex. Like Connor said. Felt good for an hour, then it was over."

"That's it?" he groans.

"What else do you want me to say?"

"I want you to say what she's like!"

"She's very flexible," I say, taking an angry whack at the sheets. I wish I was hitting *myself* instead. Delilah is the reason Mya's pissed at me right now. She got undressed in front of *everyone*, right after insulting our relationship. And I couldn't do anything except sit there and stare like a virgin high schooler.

Or like Bunny.

I'm not even sure which is worse, at this point.

"Why do you even care?" I snap at him. My tone wipes the smirk right off his boyish little face. Bunny is blonde and pretty and the sight of his sadness almost tugs at my heart, but I'm too annoyed to care about offending him. He's pushing a very sensitive button right now. "You're not sleeping with Delilah, so it isn't your business. Stop being a child."

The garage falls silent until Connor whistles. "I think you touched a nerve, Bun."

"I'm only asking about Delilah because we all know your girlfriend is—"

I point my racket at him. The motion is so fast, his curly bangs move back from his face as the air brushes over his cheeks. "My girlfriend is *what?*" I dare him.

I can't even enjoy the childish excitement I feel at finally saying that word out loud. I just called Mya my *girlfriend*— Bunny called her my girlfriend first because he sees how close we've gotten. *Everyone* sees it. That's how much I love her. It's obvious enough that we can't hide it anymore. And I'm glad.

But there are problems between us. Weeds have grown in our paradisical oasis.

We haven't touched each other. I promised her I wouldn't. Not until she was ready. Not until she wanted me to. I know she's Christian, but ... I mean ... The world has fallen apart. I thought that part of her faith wouldn't count anymore. What are we supposed to do, anyway?

I want sex. I *need* it. I'm not a saint like Mya. I can't wait like this. I don't *want* to wait. But I want to *try* because I care about her. Because I *love* her. I thought my love for her was strong enough to overcome my shallower side—and it has been so far, right up until Delilah pranced around the basement with her booty out and left me with my jaw on the floor.

I don't know how much longer I can take this. But I'm not going to let Bunny get away with taunting me for it. I already screwed up by letting Delilah disrespect our boundaries, I can't let it happen twice in one day.

"Whatever I do or don't do with my girlfriend is none of your business," I tell Bunny.

He swallows and nods, glancing at the racket held a mere hairsbreadth from the tip of his nose.

"Don't ask about details again. Not with me and any other girl. You got it?"

He opens his mouth to reply, but no sound comes out. Instead, Bunny's words are cut off by a sharp whistle from outside. It's a high-pitched noise that lasts about two heartbeats before cutting off abruptly. We stand in silence for another second, and then we hear it again.

"Sounds like Adrian's back." Connor sets his racket down.

I lower mine from Bunny's face, frowning in confusion. "He's back early."

That makes everyone pause. Instead of rushing out to greet Adrian, we all stare at the entrance to the mudroom, listening to the sound of Delilah's feet as she descends the stairs and moves toward the backdoor. In the silence, I can hear my heart beating. It's a strong, sturdy sound. A good rhythm. A healthy pace. But it starts to increase as I listen to Adrian's heavy footsteps march through the door and then stop in the living room.

"He goes out scouting every morning for three hours. That's his normal shift," Bunny says, eyes glued to the mudroom door. "Why is he back early?"

I let out a sigh. "Because he saw something. And he needs to tell us."

Despite how vital this information is, none of us move. We don't want to move because that would take us closer to the secret news Adrian has to tell us.

If there's one thing I've learned since the grid went down, it's that secret news is never good. Not for us, at least.

I set my racket down and turn toward the door, smiling as I hear another whistle from outside. This one sounds like the call of a bird, a short shrill sound that repeats three times. I know it's the girls before Bunny even says, "The gang's all here."

"Let's go then." Connor walks toward the mudroom door, and it swings open before he even reaches for the knob.

Adrian's massive form darkens the doorway. His gaze lands on all of us and no one at the same time, but his voice reaches every corner of the room. It's dark, grating. Two little words fire from his lips like gunshots.

"Get inside."

His authoritative tone makes me angry, and that anger gets worse when I see Bunny and Connor move toward the door like obedient pups. Everyone around here follows his orders like he's in charge, which, technically he *is*—but that's only because he's still got that gun. He took it from his own home when he returned to town before us, and he's been waving it around ever since. That's the only reason everyone in this stupid house listens to him.

"We're in the middle of doing chores," I say, feet planted firmly. I know it's dumb to start an argument right now, especially when it's so painfully clear that Adrian has something important to tell us, but I was already irritated before this—now I'm itching for a fight.

Adrian's gaze sharpens. "I just returned from a scouting trip. I saw something we need to discuss."

I shrug. "Just tell us now."

"Or I can tell everyone inside." He turns away, dismissing me. "We're having a meeting."

I suck my teeth. "Since when—"

"Are you guys coming?"

The sound of Mya's voice makes my anger shrivel inside. It's replaced by a heart pounding anxiety as she pokes her head around the corner. Our eyes meet with a jolt, and I lose all coherent thoughts.

We haven't spoken since she stormed out of the basement earlier. With the way her brows lower, I get the feeling she doesn't want to speak again.

"What's taking so long?" Mya questions.

"We're trying to have a meeting," Adrian answers, "but Julius is busy with his chores right now."

"Maybe Delilah can help."

Her words carve a hole into my heart, but I don't have time to respond. Mya's gone, briskly pivoting, and walking back into the house before I can form my next thought. The only thing I register is the smirk on Adrian's face as he follows my girlfriend back inside.

27

4

Adrian

I don't know what happened while I was gone, but the basement is full of tension now. And bodies. We all clambered down the stairs once I finally convinced everyone that we needed to have an emergency meeting. Normally, we're not all down here at the same time. There isn't enough room to comfortably hold everyone. The girls are relatively small, but all the guys are athletes. Julius and I are both over six feet tall, and even though Bunny is laughably short, he's still muscular and built like a runner.

Basically, the guys take up too much room, so I promise myself to make this quick as I stand in the middle of the basement and wait for everyone to settle down. Connor and Delilah are sitting together on the hospital bed, Bunny stands beside the bed, trying not to stare at Delilah. Jupiter is leaning against the rack of canned goods, and Julius is beside her. Glaring at me.

29

I can't tell if he's angry I embarrassed him earlier or if he's pissed that Mya is standing beside me and not him. It's obvious some sort of drama went down while I was on my morning run, but I don't have time to analyze the situation. Any other day, I'd gladly leap at the opportunity to expose the cracks in Mya's relationship with him. It's been long overdue that she wakes up and comes back to me. But this is important. Mya will have to wait. I'll deal with her later.

"What's so important?" Julius says, his voice is a contained snarl, but I keep my tone calm when I respond, if only to agitate him further. Julius is a spoiled man-child. The only thing he hates more than someone stealing his spotlight is not having a spotlight at all. Ignoring him is the best way to truly get under his skin.

I take a breath. "I saw something while I was out on my scouting shift this morning."

"A soldier?" Bunny asks. "We haven't spotted soldiers in weeks."

"No," I answer.

"Other survivors?" Jupiter butts in, and I shake my head.

"I saw a tent near the outskirts of the city."

"Why were you on the outskirts of the city?" Julius snaps. "That's way beyond your perimeter."

I pause. Julius is right, the outskirts of town are beyond the scouting perimeter. I hadn't thought of a good reason to explain my location because I thought everyone would be more concerned with what I'd found, not why I'd been there in the first place. And also … I didn't know how to tell them I'd ended up there because I had a panic attack and was trying to outrun my fears and troubles.

"What's so special about the tent?" Mya asks.

I glance over at her, and she gives me an almost imperceptible nod. She asked that question to save me, not just to gather information. If we were alone, I'd kiss her. I'd probably do a lot more than that, but as it stands, I simply clear my throat and shift my weight from one foot to the other.

Get it together, I tell myself—something I've been saying a lot lately. For a lot of stupid reasons.

"The tent had a letter posted on the entrance." I dig the sheet of paper from my pocket and pass it to Mya. She pretends not to notice my hand shaking.

"What's it say?" Bunny asks impatiently.

Mya reads aloud, "Abandoned by order of 5th brigade. Survivors relocated to Orly Center." Her face wrinkles as understanding hits her, then she snaps her gaze up to Julius. That stings. Mya's immediate reaction is to look at him, like he's her source of comfort. Her focus.

"What does this mean?" Jupiter asks.

"It means we finally know where to start looking for our families," I say.

"I've never heard of Orly Center." Mya passes the paper around, returning her vision to me.

Julius is her source of comfort, but I'm clearly her source of wisdom. Whenever she doesn't know what to do, whenever she needs answers, she looks to me. I can live with that.

"It's an entertainment complex in the mega mall outside the city," I reply.

"The mega mall that was built last summer?" Mya asks, squinting in thought.

I nod. "It's pretty new."

31

"How do you know about a mega mall out here in Wakedon?" Julius questions. "You live in Phoenix, over an hour away."

I give him a flat face. "That's not very far. And plus—the mega mall popped up in a lot of job searches when I was filling out applications."

Julius snorts like the prick he is. "Filling out applications for the *mega mall?* What do you wanna be, a grocery store bagger?"

"It doesn't matter what he wants to be," Mya snaps, shocking both of us. "The world is dead."

The two of them glare at each other until I clear my throat.

"I did bag groceries at a store before all this crap went down. I was so desperate for work; I went to two interviews at Orly Center because I needed money and was willing to do whatever it took to get it." I sigh. "I lived too far for them to hire me without reliable transportation. But I'm glad I went to the interviews anyway because now I know how to get us there."

I smile, thinking of all the times in my life that I complained about needing money and having to work so hard to get it. Being so broke made me bitter, but it was that need for money that pushed me to Orly Center. In our group, I'm the only one who's been there. I'm the only one who can lead us there.

Now I feel like all that struggling I experienced as a teenager was some sort of gift all along. That's what Mya would call it, at least. A blessing in disguise. Part of God's plan. All that religious mumbo jumbo. But even an atheist like me can't pretend it's so silly anymore.

Did I have to be so broke? Did I have to go hungry more nights than a kid ever should? No... But maybe that sort of starvation was the only thing that would make me hungry enough for money that I'd search for a job over an hour away. Now that search is beneficial. Now I can see the part it played in the bigger plan for my life.

I glance at Mya, hoping she can see my conviction. She smiles at me, but I know she has no idea what I'm thinking. I'm thankful for her smile anyway.

"We're going to Orly Center," I tell the group. "That's where we begin our search for our families."

"What about those of us who aren't from here?" I can't tell if Bunny looks annoyed or worried. We all know he's from out of town, but he's never voiced any concerns with finding his folks. I assumed that was because he figured finding them was a lost cause. I don't even know if I can find my *own* family and they didn't live far from here.

"Where do we begin our search for families outside of Wakedon?" Bunny asks.

"Well—"

"We should split up," Delilah cuts me off, making everyone stare at her in stupefied silence.

"Split up?" Connor finally says. He takes a step away from her, frowning. "What are you talking about? We need to stick together. We'll find everyone's families, eventually."

"Eventually," Bunny repeats.

"My family isn't from Wakedon either." Connor jabs his chest with his thumb.

"Yet, you're oddly calm about not finding them."

"Listen, you little rat—"

"Guys," I hold up my hands to get their attention. "We cannot afford to fight like this."

33

"This is why we need to split up," Delilah says. "We're not all friends with each other. We can only get along so much for so long."

"These quarters are seriously cramped," Jupiter mumbles.

"And travelling in a large group can be dangerous," Delilah adds.

"But your family is from Wakedon," I remind her. "Why do you want to split up?"

She pauses long enough for me to figure it out. It also helps that she sneaks a sideways glance at Julius. It's a well-known secret they had something going on back at campus—honestly, Delilah is the type of girl to have something going on with anyone who's willing—but I get the feeling she had real emotions for Julius. Obviously, those emotions were not reciprocated.

That's when it dawns on me. It's a little devious, but I've seen people do worse. Delilah wants to split up Julius and Mya, even more than I do.

Julius isn't from Wakedon either, so if the group splits based on location, Julius will leave. Delilah would stay here with Mya too, but that doesn't matter to her. As long as he isn't with Mya, she'll be happy.

"I don't want us to split up," Delilah finally says. "I'm just trying to think of everyone here. We all want to see our families."

"Then we should stick together," I say firmly. Delilah tries to cut in again, but I'm done letting her sow these bitter little seeds. If she wants to break up Julius and Mya, she'll have to find another way. Splitting up means I'll have to leave too, and I'm not doing that.

34

"Orly Center could have information," I speak over Delilah's last feeble protest. "If it's truly a refugee camp, there may be soldiers who can tell us where other camps and shelters are located. We can't afford to split up now. This is a huge break for us."

I glance around the room, watching everyone come to the same conclusion. They all know I'm right. We don't even have to take a vote on it—Delilah and Bunny are the only ones who would disagree with this plan, and they're clearly outnumbered. So, with a smile on my face, I take a deep breath and make the announcement.

"Start packing up the supplies. We'll need scouts to begin planning a route, and we'll need to arrange our security measures. If everything goes well, we'll set out in three days."

To no one's surprise, they all nod in agreement.

5

Mya

My hands shake as I roll up a dirty t-shirt and stuff it into my backpack. It's happening. Tomorrow, we're finally leaving. We're going to find my father. This is what I've been praying for. But something about it doesn't feel so exciting, something about all this feels scary.

Flashes of the university plague my mind as I try to cram clothes into my bag. I can't think straight. I can't get myself to focus. Every time I close my eyes, I see the chaos I barely survived, and I wonder what my father has been through. I wonder if he found a group of people he could trust and hunkered down like me. Or maybe he was stabbed in the back like Coach Noble.

Noble was murdered in cold blood, and all I did was turn and run.

What if my father isn't okay? What if he's needed me all this time?

I drop the pair of pants in my hand and cover my mouth as a sob swells in my throat. It leaks between my lips as ugly and hot as the tears that suddenly streak my cheeks. I have no right to cry, but I can't stop the sorrow that grips me. It's like a coffin and I'm trapped inside, banging against death's door. But death is a punishment too sweet for a daughter like me. I've abandoned my only family and spent this time with stars in my eyes, dreaming of kissing a boy who puts more effort into fighting with his rival than making things work with me.

"I'm a monster…" I whisper.

"Mya?"

I whirl around to find Adrian standing in the doorway to my bedroom. The basement has become one large bedroom for everyone to share, this is the only place I have a sense of privacy in the house. Jupiter and Bunny are busy sorting canned goods downstairs. Julius is hanging laundry in the garage. Delilah and Connor decided to scout our starting route for tomorrow, which means they're hooking up in an abandoned house somewhere until lunch. I don't care about their promiscuity, I'm just happy for the privacy—except I'm not alone anymore.

Adrian has appeared in my doorway like a ghost, moving across the floor before I can even register his presence, let alone try to hide my tears.

"What's wrong?" He frowns like he can somehow beat up the misery I feel. "Did something happen?"

I shake my head. Sniffle. Scrub my cheek with the back of my hand. I feel a little snot draw across my chin and hope he doesn't notice. Honestly, his eyes are glued to my own, drilling holes through my skull like he's trying to will the truth from me.

37

"Nothing happened," I say honestly.

He cups my chin and lifts it, forcing me to meet his gaze. "Mya, you're crying."

"We've all cried a little. Right?"

He glances away and I realize I've touched a tender spot.

"Do you miss them too?" I whisper.

"Every day."

He doesn't even need me to explain who I'm talking about. I know about his family, his twin brother and sister who depend on him for everything. Adrian talked about them all the time when we hung out in high school. That's what made it so easy to fall for him. His love for his family made me envious, in a good way. Instead of loathing how my family crumbled with my mother's sickness, Adrian's passion made me appreciate the time I had left with my mom. It made me yearn for a family of my own one day.

As much as I relate to Caesar for the childhood we share, I can relate to Adrian for the protective fear he has for his loved ones. Julius fears for his mother too, but he hides that fear. He buries his worries beneath his feelings for me, focusing on finding my father instead of thinking of the woman who raised him. Adrian doesn't hide anything. I can see his worries in his eyes as he sighs and pulls away. I can feel his fear in his voice when he says, "I miss them so much it hurts."

His shoulders slump, like the world just dumped his failures onto him. Failure to protect. Failure to provide. Failure to rescue the only ones in his life who matter. I share that failure. It hurts like a raw, bloody wound.

"Are you worried?" he asks me.

"More like overwhelmed. I just don't know what to expect. I don't know if I should get my hopes up—if I even *deserve* to have hope."

"We all deserve hope," he says quickly, and I get the feeling he's talking about himself. "Hope is all that some of us have."

"I'm sure your family is okay, Adrian."

"Same for you."

I swallow. My throat feels sticky.

"You taught me about hope." Adrian's voice is so quiet, I squint in response, unsure if I've heard him correctly. He's staring at the floor like a tamed wolf, humbled but still wild and unpredictable. I have no idea how to approach him right now, but if I don't say something, I'll lose this moment forever.

"I didn't teach you about blind hope. I taught you to place your hope in *God*. To trust that Jesus has your back, no matter how bad things look."

"Is that really the sort of hope you have?"

I nod without hesitation. "That's the *only* hope to have."

"Then why do you think you don't deserve it?"

My brain freezes.

"If Jesus really died for everyone, then *everyone* gets to hope in Him, Mya. Don't give up on your father. If God loves you, then He'll protect your old man. I believe that."

I almost laugh. "Imagine getting a lesson about hoping in God from an atheist."

Adrian goes quiet. "Would ... Would God really have *my* back? Even if I don't believe in Him?"

"You do believe in Him. Otherwise, you wouldn't care if He had your back."

He seems to chew on this, nodding slowly and scratching the silvery blonde stubble on his chin.

"Even if you didn't believe," I say, "I think God would still protect you because I've asked Him to."

Adrian's eyes snap up to meet mine. "You pray for me?"

I nod timidly. "All the time."

"I thought you stopped when—"

"I've never stopped," I blurt, cutting him off. I don't want to hear the rest of his sentence. I don't want to think about the boy between us. Not right now. For just a few moments, I just want it to be Adrian and me.

"What do you pray?" Adrian asks.

My answer is immediate. "That you would see God's Hand of protection wrapped around you all this time. That you would acknowledge Him in your life, and maybe ... Give your life to Him."

He steps toward me again, closing the little space that'd kept us apart. I keep my gaze leveled because he's so close, if I look up, he could easily lean down and kiss me. I want him to. I'm a terrible girlfriend who wants to be kissed by another boy right now. But I'm not terrible enough to act on it. So, I keep my chin tucked against my chest as I whisper, "That's what I pray."

"You still care about my soul." Adrian's voice is deep. I feel it rolling through every part of his body, hear it rumble in his chest, fill his throat and tumble from his full lips. The sound is warm as coffee and smooth as cream. I have to step back and hug myself to keep from reaching out and touching him.

"Of course I care," I admit.

He nods. "Does my salvation make a difference to you? Is it still ... a factor?"

I know what he's really asking, which is why I remain silent. Adrian has always liked me. He's asked me out before, and aside from the fact that he's four years older than me and our relationship would've given my overprotective father a heart attack, I rejected him because he isn't a Christian. I've done a lot of things and made a lot of romantic mistakes, but being unequally yoked is not one that I plan to add to the list.

Sure, Julius isn't the greatest Christian in the room—in any room, really—but he believes in God. He wants God in his life. That's more than I can say for Adrian, and until that changes, it will always be the brick wall between us.

"Adrian, I—"

"Don't answer," he says quickly. "A girl with your kind of faith... I already know what the answer will be."

I sigh slowly.

"I didn't come here to talk about God anyway. I came to ask you something, Mya."

I blink at him, totally shocked. Adrian and I have barely spoken since we got here. Now he's asking about his soul, nearly kissing me, and has some secret question for me. This is so much more drama than I signed up for.

"Yes?" I say cautiously.

"Delilah wants the group to split up," Adrian explains. "We've agreed to stay together until we reach Orly Center, but whatever we find there could point each of us in different directions. We might actually end up splitting up."

"Yeah..." I whisper. That possibility has crossed my mind more than once. I'm not even friends with everyone but I don't want our group to separate. We've been through so much together. Survived together. Now we're travelling again, and no one knows if this will be the end of us. I don't want to think about it, but I suppose it's got to be addressed at some point.

41

I'm just not sure why that point is now. Right here. With Adrian.

I look at him expectantly, and he takes a very uncharacteristically nervous breath. Adrian has always been in full control of himself. Totally focused. Totally calm. This anxiety is odd, but I know pointing it out will only make him clam up and leave, so I don't say anything at all. I wait for him to come to me when he's ready.

After another moment of silence, he does.

"If the group splits up, will you come with me?" he asks.

My eyes bulge.

"I can protect you, Mya. I'll keep you safe. I'll help you find your father. I won't ever leave you."

"Adrian…" it's the only word I can say, and it tumbles from my mouth like a desperate plea.

This isn't the first time Adrian has asked me to run off with him. I turned him down before because I wasn't ready to leave campus so hastily. But also because I wasn't ready to leave Julius. I'm still not.

I shake my head. "What about Julie?"

He sighs. "Mya—"

"You know I can't just leave him behind, and not just because of our relationship. He's still my best friend, Adrian. That's never going to change."

"Fine. He can come too."

That shocks me into silence.

"I've always had feelings for you. You know that. I crossed the state for you, Mya, when I should have continued walking and searching for my family instead. I came back. But I'm not complaining because I'd do it again."

"*Why?*" my voice trembles.

"You know why…"

"Adrian—"

"I love you, Mya. I don't know why, but I always have." He offers a weak smile. "That's never going to change."

I wipe my eyes, unsure where these sudden tears are coming from. You don't get to cry when you're breaking someone else's heart. Over and over again.

"I'm not asking you to love me back, Mya. I'm just telling you how I feel and asking you to let me have some sort of place in your life. You don't have to answer now," Adrian says. "I just want you to think about it. Can you promise me you'll do that?"

As he patiently stares at me, I think about Julius. I see his smiling face, and then I see the look of embarrassment he wore the other day when I caught him ogling Delilah. There are cracks in our seemingly perfect relationship, but does that give me a free pass to run off with Adrian?

It wouldn't really be running off, though…

Adrian said Julie could come along. He said he isn't even asking me to love him back. I think that's fair. I think that gives us room to maintain some sort of connection that won't require me to betray Julie's trust. I can make this work. I can be friends with Adrian.

I tilt my head to nod. "Okay," I whisper. "I'll think about it."

"Thank you."

I let go of a huge breath, feeling my shoulders ache with tension. "I need some air," I say softly, then I move to step around Adrian and dash out into the hall. I half expect him to grab me and stop me, but before that worry can take root in my head, I open my bedroom door to find Julius standing right outside and all my thoughts vanish.

"Julie!" I blurt, shocked by his presence. How long had he been standing there? Did he hear anything inside?

He glances up through the open door, looking right over my head and into the room. I know he sees Adrian inside, and I know how this must look to him. But I hadn't done anything wrong in there. I'd felt wrong things. I'd made room for wrong desires to enter my heart. But I hadn't acted on them. In fact, I'd agreed to be *friends* with Adrian.

Yet … I feel guilty when Julius looks down at me. I can't even maintain eye contact.

"Were you looking for me?" I say quietly, dropping my gaze to my dirty socks.

"Yeah," he replies. "I need help chopping wood for us to take with us."

No, he doesn't. This is Julie's way of asking me to speak in private. It's a code we developed a little while ago when we wanted to sneak off and enjoy a moment alone—outside this crowded house. We could only ever sneak off during the day because no one chops wood *at night*, but still, that little request has given us so many afternoons together. I almost smile at the warm memories his request stirs up. I remember napping together in an abandoned house up the street. I remember sharing a meager picnic of peanut butter sandwiches and two rare bottles of apple juice. And I remember Julius kissing me like a lover once we'd finished our food. His mouth had tasted of peanut butter, his breath smelled of apple juice.

That day, I let him slide his hand under the dirty dress I'd worn to the picnic. My stomach had filled with butterflies at the guttural sound he'd let out in response. He'd taken that

44

dress off me that afternoon, and we'd stopped short of sex., both of us left panting, blinking at each other in nervous glances. I hadn't regretted it for a second, but I knew it was wrong. I knew we'd gone *way* too far. And now I wonder if these are the repercussions.

Am I being punished for my bad behavior?

God, I'm sorry, I whine inside, hoping for mercy as I nod at my angry boyfriend.

"Sure. I'll meet you out back," I tell him.

Julius turns and leaves in silence.

Adrian finally emerges from my room a moment later. "You don't have to mention this to him," he says as he walks by. "That conversation was only meant for you."

I don't have to say anything... But I should.

No matter how large the cracks are in our relationship, Julius is still my boyfriend. He's the one I chose. Not Adrian. I owe it to him to explain this whole situation. I owe it to him to be loyal in my heart, not just in my actions.

So instead of making any more promises to Adrian, I swallow my nerves and walk down the stairs and out the front door. I need to meet Julius. I need to do whatever it takes to make this work between us.

6

Caesar

I've only been standing in this room for five minutes before I hear Mya's soft footsteps. Her head appears first before she climbs the rest of the stairs. We're in an attic on the other end of the street, but the house is large enough that I can see Mya's home from the window. It looks so small and insignificant from here.

I feel warmth blanket my side and I realize Mya is standing next to me, staring straight ahead. Her hair is neatly braided into two large plaits that fall past her shoulders. She looks so cute, but I can see the worry on her face. It matches my own expression.

I have no idea what I interrupted when I walked up to Mya's bedroom, but the look on her face when she saw me outside made it clear that I'd interrupted *something*. She was in her room alone with Adrian. I have no idea for how long. I have no idea why.

"You came," I say, still staring out the window.

"Of course I came."

"You seemed busy."

She doesn't respond.

"We need to talk," I tell her, and to my surprise, she agrees.

"There's so much to unpack," she whispers.

"Is it Adrian?"

"Is it Delilah?" she counters.

Touche.

I don't have a right to be jealous over whatever happened with Mya and Adrian when she caught me staring at another naked woman. We both messed up. We both brought extra baggage into this relationship that we clearly weren't ready for. But we're here now. We want to make this work and I think the only way we can is to wipe away the past. Get rid of whatever lingering feelings and desires we might have for anyone else.

I don't know about Mya, but the only way I can wipe away Delilah is with her. So, when she turns to face me, I lean down and kiss her.

She lets me, meeting my lips with equal fervor. It's a shock but also something that sends fire straight to my groin. We've had our passionate moments, but Mya's a good girl at heart. Any time we spent exploring each other was met with a week of deep remorse and depression. Eventually, I got so tired of convincing her we'd done nothing wrong that I just stopped trying to be passionate toward her. I stole a kiss here and there, but nothing like the fire that'd burned between us in the first month of our relationship.

This house—this attic—is the place we'd meet to be alone. I know she must remember all the afternoons we spent here. I remember. I could never forget the warmth of her brown skin, the sound of her voice in my ear, the tingling of her breath on my neck. But I'll also never forget the look of guilt she'd wear whenever she'd pull away and stop me before things went too far.

She's wearing that look now as she stops to breathe, pressing a hand to my chest. I capture her hand and kiss her palm, then I tug her toward me and slowly lower us both to the floor. Mya tries to slow things down again, pulling away to speak—

"Julius, hold on—"

But I silence her with a rough kiss, pinning her hands over her head and groaning into her mouth. She doesn't fight me anymore, not until she feels my hand slide beneath her shirt. That's when she brings her knee up and almost hits me in the groin. I roll to the side and lie on my back, staring up at the ceiling, blinking, breathing, wondering what the heck is going on between us.

"I thought this is what you wanted," I tell her once I've caught my breath.

She sighs and lies down beside me. "You know it's what I want. More than anything."

I swiftly roll over so I'm on top of her, pinning her to the dusty floor. "Then take it, Mya. It's yours."

"You know I can't."

"You love me—"

"I also love *God*, Julie."

"So do I."

I think.

"It's just..."

I don't know.

I take a breath and hope I don't ruin our relationship by saying this. "You remember what Delilah said about us before."

The look on Mya's face is a terrible mixture of pain, anger, and shock. "Of course I remember. She basically made fun of us for not having sex."

"Right."

"But our relationship isn't built on sex, Julius. I love you for other reasons than the way you make me feel inside."

"You don't know what I can make you feel inside," I say, watching her closely.

She blushes and looks away, but she's still trapped beneath me, so I get to watch as she tries to hide her cute embarrassment. "Julie—"

"Delilah has a point."

"What are you saying?"

"I'm saying... I love you. But ... maybe there are things you're willing to sacrifice that I'm not."

"Things like what..."

She already knows. I *know* she knows, but I reach for her hand anyway and lean forward to kiss her gently. Once she starts to relax, I lower her hand and place it on the stiffened bulge in the front of my pants.

Mya freezes.

Now she knows what I'm talking about. Without a doubt.

"Julius," she whispers.

"I want this Mya. I want *you*. And I'm willing to wait, I really am. But ... Can you at least tell me when you'll be ready to take the next step with me?"

"It isn't that I'm not ready, Julius," she says. "You know I'm Christian."

"Of course I do—"

"And you know the Bible is *clear*. Sex outside of marriage is a sin. I can't betray the Lord."

I swallow as I shift off of her and sit on the floor. "I thought this is what you came here for."

"I came to fix our relationship."

"And this is one way to do that. It's the only thing missing between us."

"The only thing missing is respect for God's Word." Her statement comes out in a shaky voice, like she's holding back tears.

"Mya..." I whisper. "I thought I could wait. I thought that didn't matter to me. But..."

"But what?" I see the tears in her eyes, and I know I've broken her heart.

"But maybe it does matter," I say miserably.

"Julius... You can't be serious. You're just letting Delilah get to you." She pauses, waiting for me to respond—to deny her accusation.

I don't speak.

She lets out a noise that might have been a sob or a scoff. I can't tell.

"I shouldn't be surprised," she says venomously, "you've always been a man-whore."

I jerk back at her words, like she's just slapped me in the face. "And you've always been an emotional whore," I say in a salty tone.

She blinks like she truly has no idea where that came from.

"I've messed around with a lot of girls, but I've never had multiple women claiming they *love* me. Fighting each other over me."

Mya glances away, and I hit the gas one more time.

"What happened in your room? With Adrian."

"He asked me to leave with him if the group split up." She glares at me. "And I told him I couldn't leave you behind."

"Oh…" I deflate.

"Did you think I'd say yes? Did you think an *emotional whore* would run off the first chance she got?"

"I'm *sorry*," I mutter. "But honestly, I have no idea what to expect from you, Mya. Sometimes I can't tell if you're holding back because of God or something else."

She looks at me in confusion. "Do you really think I'm using God as an excuse to not sleep with you?"

"Are you? If I asked you to marry me right now, would you say yes?"

Her answer is a growl. "I would absolutely say no. Because you'd only be asking me so we could roll around on the attic floor! Not because you *love* me, Julius!"

"But I *do* love you!" I nearly shout. "That's why I want this!"

Mya stares at me with a hard look on her face. When she speaks, her voice is just as rigid. "If you loved me, you wouldn't mind waiting."

I run my hand through my hair, and we sit in a stiff silence for longer than necessary. Neither of us knows what to say. Neither of us *wants* to say anything. The only sound in the room I can hear over my pounding heart is the occasional sniffle from Mya. I'm not even sure I feel bad for making her cry. It's not like I said something horrible to her. I was just being honest. Waiting for marriage is hard for me, and I don't know if I can do it. Am I such a monster for admitting that?

Am I wrong for coming to my girlfriend for help, instead of mindlessly acting on my baser needs?

This is something Mya can't understand—it's something she isn't *willing* to understand. As soon as I open that door, she shuts down and hits me over the head with her leatherbound Bible.

God says its wrong, so I can't do it. That's it. No other explanation. No other sense of sympathy for someone who might have more questions.

I get it. Blind obedience to God is perfect obedience. He's GOD, He doesn't have to explain Himself. When He speaks, you should follow blindly because He's LITERALLY always right. But I'm not arguing that He's wrong. I'm not even asking for an explanation. I'm asking for Mya to just hear me out. To understand where I'm coming from. To *help* me.

I let go of held breath and lick my lips. "Mya," I say slowly. "I know you don't want to hear this, but I think maybe Delilah was right."

She starts shaking her head.

"Just hear me out," I insist. "Maybe she wasn't *right*, but she did expose the cracks between us. I want sex. You don't. Whether we like it or not, sex is an issue for us right now and we need to address it—no matter how uncomfortable it makes us."

She turns to face me, a sincere look on her face, like she might really be trying to understand me. "You're wrong, Julius. I do want sex. But I love God enough to honor His instruction on how sex is to be enjoyed."

I sigh. "So, I'm weak because I don't love God as much as you do."

"No. That's not it. Falling short of the glory isn't a matter of how much you love God, sometimes it's simply a matter of strength. You don't have the strength to wait. I'm not always sure I do either, but I trust that God will give me the strength because I *want* to wait. I think that's the difference between us, Julie. You don't want to wait."

"Is it so bad that I don't?"

"No. To be honest, I think most Christians wish that God would change His mind about that rule." She laughs. "But He hasn't, so I've got to honor it. I *want* to honor it with someone else who wants to as well. So, the question right now is; are you that man? Will I be able to honor God in my relationship with you?"

The question of humanity.

One of the greatest reasons Mya didn't want to date me was because of my lack of faith. Because we were *unequally yoked,* as she put it. Once I started trying to follow God, she softened toward me. Obviously, I'm happy Mya changed her mind and gave me a chance, but I have to admit that I never understood why it mattered if I believed or not.

Wasn't it enough that I *respected* her beliefs? Did I really have to *share* them too?

Whenever I voiced my concerns, she gave me the same excuse she did for pretty much everything. God said its wrong so I can't. There was always some Scripture to back up her decision, but since I never understood those scriptures, I chalked it up to religious brainwashing. Old fashioned morals. Outdated ideals.

But now I get it.

Being equally yoked is more than just finding someone who'll sit through Sunday service with you. It's about this conversation right here. Will Mya be able to honor God in her relationship with me? Or will every part of our connection be some sort of emotional battle? A struggle to maintain her purity because I don't take it as seriously as her. A fight over what's right or wrong because I think her opinion is just religious brainwashing.

I want Mya. But I don't want that sort of rocky relationship.

When I don't answer her question, Mya sniffles and wipes her eyes. I think we both know what this means for us, but I try to hold on anyway.

"I don't want to let you go, Mya," I whisper.

"Then don't," she says through tears.

"How about this…" I pause to clear my throat, hoping she doesn't hear the tremble in my voice. "Adrian says it'll take a few days to get to Orly Center. Once we're there, we'll find out if the group needs to split up."

Mya nods, unsure where I'm going with this.

"Think about everything we discussed today. Think hard on what you want. On *who* you want. And when we get to Orly Center and decide where we're going next, I'm going to ask you the same question Adrian asked."

She gulps, blinking back more tears. "Julius…"

"I want you so bad. But I don't want you to feel like you have to choose between me and God. That isn't fair to you."

"You can honor Him *with me*," she pleads, but I shake my head.

"I don't think I can, Mya."

I don't even know if I *want* to. But I don't say that. Mya's in enough pain, she doesn't need to know I'm losing faith in the God she loves so much. Especially not over something so shallow as sex.

What am I supposed to do? Go bang Delilah and repent afterward? Should I get my fill of sex and *then* give my life to God? I could never show my face to Mya again if I did that. At some point, I'll have to learn self-control. I just don't know if I can learn that lesson with Mya.

"Julie," Mya says again. "Please don't do this."

"Just think about this discussion, okay? Think hard and then focus on what really matters."

"*You* matter—"

"So does your father."

That seems to sober her, seems to remind her why we're going to Orly Center in the first place. She sucks in a gasp and wipes her eyes in silence. "Okay..." The word is a whisper, but it's strong and sure. "When you ask me that question at Orly Center, I'll give you an honest answer. I promise."

7

Adrian

We set out at the break of dawn. Mya's father had a few solar-powered flashlights in his impressive basement, so we could have left earlier, but I don't want to use those unless we absolutely must. Light is easier to see in the dark, using the flashlights—or even starting a fire—could alert soldiers to our presence.

The group didn't like my decision to leave the flashlights off. It means we can only travel while the sun is up, but I'm not letting up on this one. The world is in shambles right now, anything, especially the *bad* things, could happen. I've learned that firsthand.

On the way to Wakedon, I saw a woman raped in the middle of the street right beside the dead body of her child. The men who held her down and forced her legs open were soldiers. The gun that put a bullet through her child's skull had been a military issued weapon. Those same soldiers chased me through the neighborhood and would have killed me if God Himself hadn't intervened. But soldiers aren't our only enemies.

I haven't forgotten the chaos I went through just after leaving the university. Connor was shot, some of the other students were killed. The people responsible for that violence were not in uniform. They were people just like us. Survivors.

I fear those people more than I fear the men who held that lady down. Because soldiers can be cruel, but even they have a protocol and punishment for breaking it. But there are no rules for the average citizen anymore. Governmental forces are gone. Police don't exist. It's just us, hoping we can make it to Orly Center in one piece.

So far, things have been uneventful. It's the middle of the afternoon, so we're all tired and sweaty, but no one has spotted any soldiers and no drifters have spotted us. We've made good use of the backroads which took us out of our way, but we all agreed the highway would not be the safest option. At least no one fought me on that.

The gun I took from my stepfather's safe is tucked into my waistband, it's the only thing keeping me in charge. But it also keeps me sane. If anything does happen, I know I'll be able to do something about it. I won't have to watch or hide while another innocent woman suffers, while a child is murdered, or while my friends are mowed down like escaping cattle. This journey changes everything, whether we find our families or not, we're not going back to Wakedon.

Then again… Where will we go? What happens when we make it to Orly Cetner and realize our families aren't there? What happens next?

I don't want to think about that. I just want to concentrate on making it there and then decide when the time comes. For now, I'm focused on making sure Bunny doesn't overheat because he's barely eating or drinking lately. I'm focused on keeping the head count every few hours because Delilah and Connor keep looking for ways to sneak off and I'm afraid they won't come back. I don't care if they want to leave, but Connor is carrying the most water of everyone. If he leaves, so does two-thirds of our hydration.

I'm also focused on Mya.

It seems like the drama never ends with her, but I can't help but notice the stony silence between her and Julius. They haven't even made eye contact since we left the house this morning, let alone spoken to each other. I know I probably had something to do with that. Julius saw me inside Mya's bedroom. He knows something happened in there between us. It was just an innocent conversation, but still. Just knowing that conversation was with *me* probably started a fight, and here we are. The two lovebirds aren't speaking again and I'm not sure I care anymore. I've planted the seed in Mya's head, she knows how I feel, and she knows I'm going to address those feelings again soon.

Like I said before, once we make it to Orly Center, everything changes.

"Adrian."

I glance to my left to find Connor O'Reilly staring at me, a serious look on his face. There are dark circles beneath his eyes and hard lines on his face, like he's aged twenty years over the last three months. I bet we all look old and tired like that, but I can't say for certain. I stopped looking in the mirror over a month ago.

"What is it?" I grunt, stepping over a giant prickly weed growing between a crack in the sidewalk.

"We need a break. We haven't stopped since we set out."

I don't want to break yet. Over half this group belongs to the track team, if we grin and bear it, we can push for another few hours at least. Walking and running is what we're built for. The girls will complain, but they'll get over it. This is what needs to be done to survive.

I almost say all this to Connor, but when I look back at him, I catch a glimpse of Mya from the corner of my eye and my heart softens. She looks just as beat as Delilah and Jupiter—not to mention Bunny who's so weak he might as well count as a child tagging along. Who even rescued this guy and brought him with us?

"Fine," I say, slowing to a stop. There's an abandoned sandwich shop with an attached gas station ahead. I point to it. "We've got about a mile until we hit that rest stop; let's make it there and then break for an hour."

Everyone collapses once we're inside the sandwich shop. I take this time to do a head count and then watch as Connor passes out the water and Bunny separates everyone's rations. Today we're eating jerky and water. If we make good time, we can set up the burner we brought for dinner and cook a family size can of beef and barley. There's even a scary can of *bread* none of us have been looking forward to eating but what choice do we have now? Food is food. I'll take anything.

With my own strip of jerky in hand, I take slow bites and pull out the map I made before we left. I returned to the Wakedon welcome sign two days ago and copied the map onto a fresh sheet of paper. It isn't very good, drawn with permanent marker and a shaky hand, but it's better than nothing. I'd already memorized most of the map anyway, but Orly Center is in a part of town I've been to only twice. I want to be extra cautious.

According to our crappy map, we should hit Orly soon. If I were alone, I could make it to the center and back twice in one day, but I'm not alone. I'm travelling with a bunch of tired and nearly broken people who are one bad argument away from hating each other.

We have to take our time. We have to be careful. We have to keep watch. And we have to keep our spirits lifted. Travelling carelessly is one thing, but travelling angry is another monster entirely. That's when backstabbing happens. That's when lies, betrayal, and deceit replace loyalty and trust. I can't have that, not when we're this close.

Get it together, I tell myself. But that's not enough; I have to keep *everyone* together now, so when Connor reaches for Delilah's hand to walk her out back for a bathroom break, I clear my throat and stop them both.

"Connor, I need you to walk the perimeter."

He swallows, throat bobbing. "Yeah, yeah. Just let me make sure Lilah is fine first—"

"This can't wait. An ambush can happen at any moment."

"Then you do it," he mumbles, but it's just a mumble. Before I can reply, he drops Delilah's hand and stomps out the front door.

"Julius, care to join him?" I request kindly—too kindly for him to say no. Without a word, Julius marches out the front door behind his angry friend.

60

I could've let Connor and Delilah go, they are literally the only people here who still get along, but I need everyone focused. How on earth they manage to find the energy to hook up so often is beyond me, but that can't happen so much anymore. If they're sneaking off for a good romp, then who will watch the perimeter, scavenge for supplies, and guard our things? No more slacking from those two. Not until we know what's going on.

I turn to Bunny and Jupiter. They're the worst of our group; *Useless* and *Depressed* are my nicknames for them. Jupe is sitting on the floor picking at the leather of her sneaker, Bunny is sucking on his jerky, watching Delilah longingly.

"Would you two mind looting? There might be supplies here," I say.

Both of them look at me with dead expressions. They *look* dead. But dead people can't argue, so with only a grunt in response, they both get up and find their way to the back rooms to dig for supplies.

"I still gotta pee." Delilah hops from one foot to the other.

"I have to go as well," Mya admits.

I sigh.

Julius and Connor are walking the perimeter, Jupiter and Bunny are scavenging inside. I'd wanted to stay here and watch our supplies, but it should be safe with the others so close.

"I'll walk you both," I finally say, moving toward the door.

I walk the two ladies to the edge of the parking lot where some thorny bushes have overgrown. It won't be great coverage but that doesn't stop Delilah from yanking down her clothes right in front of me. She squats and starts peeing before I can even turn around. Mya, on the other hand, waits for Delilah to finish and then walks around the other side of the

61

bush to pee, even humming loudly to cover the sound. How cute.

Delilah wipes her hands on her jeans as she walks to stand beside me. "No toilet tissue?" She raises her blonde eyebrows.

"Mya has it. You could've asked for it."

She shrugs. "We're all dirty. Who cares, at this point?"

Umm, I do. But I don't say that. I just fold my arms over my chest and stare back at the gas station. Connor and Julius are walking side by side in the distance, both of them sending furtive glances our way.

"Why'd you separate us?" Delilah asks, watching them beside me. Mya hums in the background.

"You guys need to slow down with all the … *dancing* … you've been doing lately."

"Screwing," she corrects. "You can call it what it is. We're all adults here."

"There's no need to be so vulgar, Delilah."

"What are you, *twelve*?" She chuckles. "Did the little preacher turn you out too? She's got everyone wrapped around her finger."

I don't respond.

"Seriously, I've never seen so many sexy men lose their minds over a woman who won't even let them touch her."

I sigh very slowly, turning to look Delilah in the eye. I know she's pushing my buttons on purpose. I know she just wants to get a rise out of me, but I don't care. I'm not too proud to put her in her place.

"Maybe that's why we've lost our minds," I say calmly. "Because she's actually a challenge."

Delilah …. Looks hurt. She presses her lips together and shifts away from me like I've just said the worst thing in the world to her. I shouldn't feel bad, but I do. She's slutty, but I guess that doesn't mean she has no feelings. Besides, it's not like I don't know why she is the way she is. She might sleep around but the only person she's ever truly wanted is Julius. And she can't have him because of Mya. So, she seeks attention from everyone else to make up for not getting it from the one man she wants.

In a way, Delilah is just like me. We both want someone who doesn't want us back because they're distracted by someone else. They're distracted by each other.

A breeze blows through the parking lot, and I feel the bite of the Arizona winter. It isn't a fatal bite, but it's chilly enough to make me cram my hands into the pockets of my hoodie.

Delilah hugs herself and angles her body away from me, still looking offended.

I try to change the subject. "I think something happened."

Delilah stares at me.

"I think something happened between *them*," I say quietly, listening to the sound of Mya's humming. "I think they broke up or something."

I don't know why I chose *this* as our new topic of discussion, but I can't stop myself now that the gossip is out there. I need someone else to confirm my suspicions, to tell me I'm not imagining things.

"They haven't even looked at each other all day," I say to Delilah.

She nods, smirking. "I might have had something to do with that."

I raise my eyebrows.

"Julius saw me getting undressed, and now he's going crazy for sex. Of course, the good little Christian girl won't give it to

63

him, so…" She shrugs and giggles, clearly pleased with what she's done to their relationship. Then again, I don't think she seriously expected them to break up all because Julius saw her naked. Delilah is hot, but she isn't *that* hot. But Julius has always been *that* kind of guy. I'm honestly surprised he lasted this long without getting anything special from Mya. He must really love her. Well … if he *really* loved her, he would've stayed with her.

"Are you sure they're done?" I ask Delilah, but before she can answer, Mya appears behind her with a very embarrassed smile on her face. She can't even look us in the eye as she shrugs, stubbing her toe in the dirt.

"All finished," she mumbles.

"That took forever." Delilah rolls her eyes.

"Sorry. I—I had to do number two."

I almost snort. "Did you save any tissue for the rest of us?"

"Don't make fun!" she says, giving me a playful shove.

"Let's go before it starts to smell." Delilah strolls away and we follow in silence, but just before we reach the door, I hear Mya say beside me, "If you want to know something about my love life, just ask."

I stare down at her, stunned. I thought she couldn't hear me over all the humming she was doing. Suddenly, I wonder if she was pooping at all, or just eavesdropping.

I nod slowly. "Mya, I'm sorry. I was just—"

"I'm not angry," she cuts me off. "I think it's obvious something happened since we clearly haven't been talking to each other lately. I just…" She shakes her head. "I don't want everyone gossiping about it. That's all."

"I won't bring it up again. I promise."

She surrenders a weak smile, weaker than the one she wore when she confessed to doing *number two*. "Okay. Thank you."

"You're welcome," I say.

This is exactly why I wanted to stay focused and stay out of the drama, but it's too late. I've been caught red-handed. But does this really change anything? My goals are still the same. I want Mya and now I know for a fact I have a real chance at making things work with her.

Don't screw this up, I tell myself as I enter the sandwich shop again. Make it to Orly first, and deal with everything else second.

8

Adrian

The next building we find is an elementary school. The group is elated, but I'm just worried about how large it is and how difficult it will be to guard the entire building. Or sweep it for drifters and soldiers. Anyone could be hiding inside. Anyone could be lying in wait.

Connor takes off at a jog once we're closer, crossing the parking as he lets out an excited, "Yippee!" His hooting gets everyone else energized, and the group starts to run behind him, one by one. Even Mya bops by me at a jog, shooting me a smile before she continues to the front doors.

I stand in the middle of the parking lot, staring up at the large building. It looks like it was old and raggedy even before the power went down, but that's not what holds my attention. As I stare at the classroom windows, all I can think of is Cross North University and the madness we barely escaped just three months ago. I wonder if tragedy befell this school too. I wonder if students turned on teachers. If friends betrayed friends. Did everyone make it out of there alive?

The question stirs up that awful fear inside of me and I feel my heart rate pick up in response. I clutch at my chest, trying to ward off the panic attack, but this is something I can't control. The anxiety latches onto me and squeezes the breath from my lungs. I feel like I'm choking to death right there behind my friends, but they're too excited about a new place to explore to look back and notice.

It's better this way. I'd rather suffer alone, if that's an option. So I turn around and set my hands on my knees, blinking away the nervous sweat that runs from my forehead into my eyes. I see tiny black dots decorate my vision, as annoying as little gnats I can't shoo away. All I can do is wait. Suffer and wait for this agony to pass. Wait for air to fill my lungs again, wait for my heart to slow down before it bursts from my chest, wait for this sudden headache to pass.

I squeeze my eyes shut and Dinara's face appears in my mind. I can see her blonde hair and her wide blue eyes. I can see her toothy smile and how it makes her cheeks bunch in joy. I hold on to that joy, that happiness, and I pray that it's real.

A clammy coolness washes over me, and I feel my hoodie stick to my chest from all the sweat. I fan myself as I begin to calm down, standing upright and stretching out my back. I can hear my friends behind me, some of them have propped open the school doors and are laughing like this is all normal and fun.

"Adrian!" Connor calls me. "Come inside! This place is cool!"

I turn and wave. "Be right there."

Connor is right. The school looks decent inside, despite the dust and crud from people looting or fighting here. The classrooms are small enough to have been used as bedrooms, I can tell from the abandoned sleeping bags and rolled out mats we find in some of the rooms.

"Anything to loot?" I ask as Connor guides me to the gymnasium.

"Nothing so far. Place is picked clean."

I grunt, walking beside him. I'd love to have found some new supplies or food, but if the place is already picked clean then there's a smaller chance of running into other scavengers. I guess it's a fair trade.

We walk into the gym to find our friends setting up their tents. Actually—Delilah and Julius are setting up tents, leaning toward each other and chatting closely, totally unaware of the rest of their friends who have gathered in the far corner of the gym in a tiny huddle.

I frown. "Have they found something?"

Connor doesn't reply, and I glance over at him to see him glaring at Delilah and Julius Caesar. I seriously do not have time for his petty jealousy.

"Connor!" I snap.

He blinks at me.

"The rest of the group—did they find something?"

For the first time, he notices our friends and he frowns too. "I thought the place was clean when we first entered."

"Did you sweep it?"

"Well..." he scratches the back of his head and I know the answer already.

"You have to follow the safety protocol—"

"Dude, the place is safe!"

I stomp away, ignoring his footsteps as he jogs to catch up to me. When I reach the group, Bunny looks up and steps aside. Mya and Jupiter both gasp, but then so do I when I peer down at the sleeping bags they've found.

There are two bodies curled up in the bags.

"How?" I say in a whisper, eyes darting around the gym. They land on Connor with a snap, and he sheepishly raises both his hands. "I thought this place was safe?"

"It is—"

"We just found bodies here, Connor!" I yell.

Julius and Delilah finally leave their little world and stare over at us from across the gym.

"This is why you follow the safety protocol. You should have swept the building before setting up camp."

"They're dead," he repeats. "They can't pose a threat if they aren't breathing."

I kneel and peel back the flap of one of the sleeping bags. It sticks at first and I put in more effort, covering my face when the flap rips away. It'd been stuck to the body from a thick layer of dried blood, but now that the bag is open, a foul smell fills the air around us. My friends begin covering their noses too. Connor starts to cough.

"They're decaying," I say, staring at the body. It looks like a man, dark hair, pale skin. His throat has been slit. "This man didn't die of starvation. He was murdered by someone."

Bunny kneels beside me and slowly peels back the flap of the other sleeping bag. The body is in the same condition, except this one is an Asian woman.

"These bodies don't pose a threat," I say, glaring at Connor as I rise to my feet, "but someone else does."

69

"Those bodies are rotting, like you said," Connor reminds me, "that means they've been dead a while."

"Doesn't mean the murderer has left yet. But maybe we'd know if you had swept the building like you were supposed to when we first arrived."

Connor wisely remains silent, so I turn to the others, "Pack up. We're leaving."

"Can't we just sweep the building now?" Connor says desperately.

I ignore him as I storm by, not waiting for the others to catch up. I've still got my backpack on, so I don't need to pack up my own things. But Delilah and Julius have set up one tent already and had begun unpacking another.

"Don't bother," I wave at them. "We need to take all this down."

"Why?" Delilah sets her hands on her hips. "We just put it up."

"We found bodies."

She stares in shock. Julius blinks at the rest of our friends, searching their worried faces for confirmation. "What kind of bodies?" he asks.

"Throats slit. Been dead a while."

"That doesn't mean any soldiers are here right now, though. Right?"

I kneel to untie the rope keeping Delilah's tent in place. "Connor didn't sweep the building. We don't know who's here."

"I don't want to sleep in a place with dead people." Lilah starts helping me pack.

The group moves in panicked silence, cramming their things back into their bags. It takes us all of ten minutes to meet by the gym entrance. I take another head count, and then lead us out. No one speaks as we move swiftly through the halls, more alert than we've ever been before. I can see the fear in everyone's eyes as I glance back and give the signal for them to follow me to the door. Delilah is nearly freaking out, Jupiter is wiping tears from her eyes, and Bunny looks like he's about to wet himself. The only people wearing stony expressions are Julius and Connor—though Connor only looks angry because he knows this is all his fault.

"Stay close," I whisper, turning the corner, then I pause.

There's a man waiting at the front door.

He isn't tall or strong or well built. He doesn't even look healthy. His skin is caked with dirt and his hair is stuck to his face with sweat and grease. I can't tell if he's tan from the sun or tan from all the grime. But the dirt doesn't matter, the only thing I pay close attention to is the knife he's holding in his hand.

He points it at me. "Big group."

"More of us than you."

"What do you want!?" Delilah shouts behind me.

I turn around to tell her to be quiet, but the knife guy beats me to it. "Make her shut up."

Delilah starts crying. I hear Connor's voice trying to soothe her, but she isn't listening.

"We're gonna die," she whispers, then sniffles and whispers it again. "We're gonna die."

"Did you kill those people we found?" I ask the man.

He keeps his eyes on Delilah over my shoulder. Licks his lips. I take a step forward, regaining his attention. "Did you kill those people?"

"Don't matter."

71

My eyes narrow.

"Ain't no law says killin' is illegal no more. You feel me?"

This isn't a legal matter. I don't care what the nonexistent law says anymore, this is about what's *right*. Did those people deserve to have their throats slit in their sleep?

I raise my hands defensively. "We're just trying to leave."

"We don't want any trouble!" Delilah screams, and I hear Connor tell her, "Let Adrian handle this!" Julius starts whispering too, everyone trying to keep this from escalating.

"You're scaring my friends," I say calmly.

The man focuses on me again.

"Why don't you put the knife down?"

He lifts it higher, but it's still pointed at me.

"We just want to leave," I repeat.

"Gotta pay the toll first," the man says, then he chuckles and I see the gap between his stained teeth. "They didn't pay the toll."

So, he did kill those people... Has he been living in this school? Surviving off supplies he's taken from travelers by trapping them inside and then forcing them to pay a toll. Or just slitting their throats while they slept and taking whatever he wanted.

If we hadn't found those bodies, we could have ended up just like them tonight.

Thank God, I think to myself, unwilling and too ungrateful to call my words a prayer. *I'll pray if You get us out of this...* I know it's stupid to bargain with God, but when you don't have faith, all you can offer is desperation. *Help us and I'll start praying, I promise. I promise I'll get it together. But I can't do that if I'm dead!*

The man waves the knife and I snap out of my silent pleas. That's when I begin to feel thankful. He has a knife, but I have a gun. I could curse myself for not having it out already, but all I've got to do is yank it out of my waistband and fire before he swings. I don't think I'm close enough for him to get me before I can pull the trigger.

"What's the toll?" I ask the knife man, trying to distract him.

He licks his lips, they're chapped and the bottom one is split in the middle, dried blood staining the skin. "You got medicine?"

That's an interesting request. We do have medicine, there was plenty in Mya's basement because of her mother's illness. Painkillers, alcohol, first aid. We took a little of everything in case we'd need it.

I give an honest nod. "We've got medicine."

Kinfe guy points at me, stabbing the air between us. "Give it here."

"Delilah," I call.

I hear her begin to sob behind me.

"Give the nice man your bag."

"I'll bring it to him—" Julius's voice is calm and comforting, but the knife guy interjects.

"No, I want her to do it."

I can't let Delilah get too close to this guy, he could grab her and hold her hostage, then take *all* of our supplies by force.

Delilah approaches on wobbly legs, tripping and wiping her weepy eyes. She tries to hold in her sobs, but it's clear she's a broken girl. Hiding out in Mya's basement is one thing, but being held at knifepoint by a dirty lunatic who licks his lips as you walk toward him is another thing entirely. I half expect Delilah to faint before she makes it to the guy, but she stays on her feet. One step at a time. When she's within arm's length, she takes off her backpack and holds it out.

The man doesn't take it right away. He's too busy admiring her pretty face, licking those spitty lips, and using his free hand grope himself. He reaches down and grabs a handful of his own crotch and even *my* skin crawls in response, but I don't focus on how gross he is. Instead, I focus on moving my hand behind my back as slowly as I can, taking advantage of this distraction.

"Set the bag down," the man orders Delilah.

She obeys.

"Now open it and set the supplies on the ground."

She starts to kneel, but he stops her.

"Bend over."

Delilah pauses, her eyes filling with fresh tears. To her credit, she doesn't fall apart, instead she does as she's told and bends over to unpack the bag. We all watch in an uncomfortable silence as the man stares at her bottom while she sets aspirin and bandages on the ground. The man is so engrossed with his imaginations, he doesn't notice me pull my gun—until it's too late.

The lecherous grin on his face is wiped away by shock when he hears me cock it. Now his eyes are on me, but I don't give him the chance to speak. I fire before he can react, and his body hits the ground as Delilah screams.

She runs forward, away from the knife guy and both Connor and Julius are there for her. I roll my eyes at them, unsure if they're being kind or desperate. I know Julius and Mya have been distant but watching him play hero for Lilah is just annoying.

Fortunately, I don't have to watch this for long. The next moment, I hear a screech—like a door has opened somewhere else in the school—and I hear pounding footsteps. On instinct, I step over the knife guy's body and run out the front door.

There's a woman running across the parking lot.

I lift my gun.

"You're going to shoot her?" Julius appears beside me.

"She was probably working with that guy," I grunt, trying to focus on my aim.

"She's running away."

"Or she's running to find the rest of her group."

"You don't know that!" Julius snaps.

"You're right, I don't know. And I'm not taking any chances."

I try to aim again, but Julius keeps talking and I can't think beyond the fact that each step this woman takes is one more step away from us. One more chance for me to miss this shot.

"That guy asked for medicine. She could be the reason why—that means she's sick."

"Sick people can hurt people too. Or did we imagine those bodies in the gym?"

Julius sucks his teeth and takes off running. He aligns himself with the woman's path, so I'd have to shoot through him to get to her. What a jerk move. I don't even know what he plans to accomplish here. But he runs like fire, his legs eating up the pavement in haste. He's not as fast as he was at school—because only one of us continued daily runs for the last three months—but it's clear he's going to catch her.

"Captain of the track team," Connor says beside me, almost in awe. Even Delilah wipes her tears as she watches Julius run, smiling a little.

He grabs the woman by her elbow, and they tumble to the ground in a pile of limbs. I'm sure they're both scratched and scraped up, but the tussle that follows doesn't last long. The woman only screams and slaps Julius hard across the face. He takes the hit like a man and subdues her easily, pinning her arms behind her back and shoving her into the concrete. Once he's sure she's secure, he glances back at us.

"What do we do now?" Connor asks me.

I grunt. "I guess we tie her up."

"Is she going to be our hostage?"

"Well, she ain't gonna be our friend."

9

Mya

The woman hasn't spoken to us. All she's done since we captured her is cry. We've kept her hands bound and have led her on a rope as we've walked, but no one is sure what to do with her. No one knows if she's a victim or a predator. We don't blame Adrian for shooting that knife guy, but should we let him harm this woman?

"Let's stop here for the night," Adrian says.

We've been walking at a much slower pace since picking up the woman, plus we've had to split our rations with her. And listen to her constant sobbing for the last 24 hours. We're all pleased to stop, but we're also wondering what happens next.

We've stopped at a nail salon, choosing to skip the tents and sleep in the booths instead. There are some rooms in the back for supplies and a little office too. Adrian leads the weeping woman back there and then shuts the door and secures a chair under the doorknob.

When he glances up and sees me watching, I don't look away. "Will you feed her tonight?" I ask.

He takes a deep breath. "We can't keep wasting food on her."

"She's a human, it isn't a waste," Julius says sharply. He's behind me, watching us both like he's caught us doing something wrong.

I completely ignore him. After days of tromping around with Delilah like I don't exist, I wouldn't care if he walked in on me making out with Adrian. Of course, I wouldn't do that. I'm just saying.

"We still don't know if she's friendly or not. She could try to kill us if we aren't careful," Adrian explains.

"Well, we won't know if she's friendly by locking her up." Julie folds his arms over his chest.

"I am not eating with that woman." Delilah joins the conversation with a frown. "Her buddy tried to kill us."

He only held us at knifepoint and tried to take some medicine, but I see Delilah's point. She was the one who had to deal with him up close, though he hadn't touched her at all. Adrian hadn't given him the chance, and I don't blame him for that. But it's clear Julie does. He's spoken up about keeping the woman tied and led around like this since we first placed the ropes around her wrists. But what else are we supposed to do? Until she stops crying and talks to us, we have no idea who she is or what she's after. She could have helped that knife guy slit those peoples' throats. She could have tried to hurt us if Adrian hadn't fired. But she'd heard the gunshot and had tried to run. And got caught.

"I'll try to talk to her," Adrian suggests.

Julius shakes his head. "You killed her friend. I doubt she'll open up to you."

I shock everyone by speaking up. "I'll talk to her."

Adrian, Julius, and Delilah all stare at me.

"I haven't hurt her. And I'm a woman. Women talk to other women more easily."

Adrian nods, but Julius shakes his head. "You shouldn't be alone with her. I'll go with you."

I don't want to do this with Julius, but I won't let my emotions get to me. Not when this has nothing to do with *us*.

I slowly nod, but I don't get to respond because Adrian steps closer and hands me his gun. "Take this."

I stare at it. "Adrian—"

"I am not letting you in there with that woman without a weapon."

Julius reaches forward and takes the gun. "I'll hold on to it."

It's clear from the flat line Adrian's brows have formed that he doesn't like this, but he agrees with a tense nod anyway. "I don't think you should be in there, Julius," he grumbles. "You did tackle her and drag her back."

"But she's heard me speak up in her defense about the ropes. She knows I'll be kind to her." Julius smiles.

Adrian rolls his eyes.

He turns to me. "You've got fifteen minutes. I'll come get you for dinner."

"Okay," I say. "Fifteen minutes."

After Adrian leaves, Julie and I stand there in an awkward silence. We haven't spoken much since that conversation we had before leaving the house. And then he started getting close to Delilah again. Connor is still somewhere in the mix, so it's not like he's *with* Delilah now, but still. It hurts to see him moving on so quickly, like I never mattered.

"Are you ready?" Julius asks.

I look up at him and he quickly glances away. His shyness makes me angry. "You don't have to come with me." I hold out my hand. "I can do this on my own."

Julius grips the gun tighter. "No way am I letting you in there with her alone."

"I don't need you to protect me."

That seems to hurt him. Julius's jaw tics, and he takes a deep breath. "I'll always try to protect you, Mya. No matter how much you hate me."

Now he's playing victim, like my anger is unjustified.

"I don't hate you," I correct him. "I don't know what I feel."

"Neither do I."

The confession makes me falter. It hurts and stings and threatens to summon a wave of bitterness, but I swallow my emotions.

"I don't want to talk about this right now."

"We said we'd talk at Orly Center," he reminds me.

I nod, turning down the hall of the nail salon. "Well, we haven't gotten there yet."

I move the chair from the doorknob, and then push open the office door and find the woman sitting on her butt in the farthest corner of the room. She's still got her hands tied together with rope, but she doesn't look uncomfortable. She doesn't look like she feels anything at all—except misery.

Her eyes land flatly on Julius and me, taking us in with a single, judgmental tick. Then she looks away and sniffles, uses both her hands to wipe her tears and takes a big breath. Her shoulders shake as she quietly weeps. I stand there and watch for an extra moment, then I step into the room.

"You must have loved him," I say to the woman. "The man from the elementary school."

She looks up at me, and her mouth twists into an ugly frown.

"I'm sorry he's gone," I say.

"Liar." The word is almost hard to discern from her hoarse voice. She's done nothing but cry for an entire day, I'm not surprised her throat is a little sore. "You didn't know Garret," she croaks out.

I nod. So his name was Garret.

"I'm not sorry Garret is dead. He was trying to hurt my friends. But I'm sorry for your sadness."

She just glares at me, but after a moment, her shoulders drop, and she goes back to sniffling in silence.

"What's your name?" Julie asks, inching closer.

The woman whips her head in his direction and crawls back against the file cabinet for safety. The action makes Julius freeze and throw his hands up in defense.

"We're not here to hurt you," he says. Then, to add emphasis, he removes Adrian's gun from his waistband and sets it on the floor between us. "See? We're not armed anymore. You can trust us."

I don't think that was a smart move, but I keep my mouth shut because it seems to work. The woman visibly relaxes and even scoots closer to us. She looks back and forth between us and then says, "What do you want with me? Why'd you take me?"

81

"Honestly, we just didn't want our friend to shoot you," Julius confesses.

"Like he shot Garret?"

"Don't forget Garret killed people," I remind her.

She looks away. "We aren't bad people, okay? We're just trying to survive, like everyone else."

"By slitting the throats of innocent people?" I challenge.

"It's better than getting shot down." She looks like she wants to spit at me. "Or starving. Or getting taken by them soldiers out there."

Julius and I exchange glances. "You've seen soldiers?" Julie asks.

"Not in a while," the woman says. "I think this whole city has been evacuated for some time—long enough for other folks to go through it. Every building Garret and I been to was already picked clean when we got there. That's why we set up in the elementary school."

"So you could rob people instead of loot," I say.

She just rolls her eyes. "This world changes you, okay? Like I said, we were just trying to survive."

"And where did that get you?"

She leans forward with a snarl. "Tell me you wouldn't do whatever it takes to stay alive, princess! Tell me you ain't never done nothin' wrong to protect the people you love!"

I pause, thinking of how I burned down the supply garage at the university so I could rescue Julius. I set fire to the last bit of food and water the entire campus had, and then I packed up and left with my own supplies. Jupiter had scolded me for that, saying I'd doomed the people we left behind. But I kept the guilt away by reminding myself that I'd done what I had to do. I'd rescued Julius and that was all that mattered.

I glance at him now, wondering how we let so much come between us. There had been a time where I'd willingly doomed a campus full of people for him, and now I can hardly look him in the eye. Now, I don't know if the love we have for each other is real or not.

I swallow, shocked by the burning I feel in the backs of my eyes. I cannot let my emotions get the better of me now.

I clear my throat and lower myself to sit on the floor across from the woman. Julius mimics me. "I think we've all done horrible things out here," I admit.

"So, what gives you the right to judge me and Garret?" the woman hisses.

"We're not judging you. We just want answers."

"Answers about what?"

I take a deep breath. "When's the last time you saw any soldiers?"

"Weeks ago."

"What uniforms were they wearing?"

"I didn't get a good look. I was busy *running for my life.*"

I nod, but Julius asks the next question. "How many did you see?"

"What does any of this have to do with Garret?" She throws her tied hands into the air. "None of this will bring him back!"

"No, but it could help keep all of us alive," I say.

"I hope you all die."

Julius shakes his head. "We're just trying to be nice, okay? We want to survive just like you."

"Trying to be nice?" She holds up her hands, glaring at the ropes that bind her. "Yeah right."

"I stopped my own friend from shooting you," Julius reminds the woman, but his words don't seem to sink in.

"You played hero *after* you let him shoot my husband. I don't care what happens to any of you."

"Do you care what happens to *you*?" I ask slowly. "Garret asked us for medicine. Was it for you?"

She doesn't speak.

"We do have medicine. We could share it with you, or we could keep you tied up in this room."

"Are you threatening me?" she asks, and in her hoarse voice, the words sound like a threat on their own.

Julius uses my hesitation to take over. He motions to the gun still sitting between us. "I told you, we're not here to hurt you, remember?"

"But you hurt Garret." The woman seems to break at the memory, her face wrinkling and tears flowing down her cheeks all over again.

This feels hopeless. She can barely speak more than a few sentences without getting angry or tearful. Her emotions are all over the place, and she either doesn't have information on the soldiers and their whereabouts or she's deliberately withholding it from us. At this point, I can't really tell.

"Just go away," the woman sobs, wiping her eyes. "I don't want to talk."

"We just want to ask you—"

"My husband is dead!" she shouts, making us both jump. "Because you killed him!"

"He was threatening us," I say calmly.

"Garret was all I had!" she wails. "It was just *us*!"

I watch her weep and I start to feel a little bad. Garret had threatened us, but he'd been severely outnumbered. Maybe we could've solved the problem without shooting him. But how were we to know it'd only been Garret and his wife? Connor hadn't swept the building; for all we knew, there could have been any number of people hiding in the school, waiting to ambush us. It's not our fault it was only this sad woman left. And those bodies too. I can't forget about the people Garret and this woman killed before us. And who knows how many others?

I shake away my nerves and try to focus again. "Listen, I'm sorry—"

She spits in my face.

It happens so suddenly, I don't even realize what's hit me until the rancid smell of rotten teeth fills my nose. Her saliva is all over my face, a glob of it runs down from the middle of my forehead and threatens to get in my eyes. My hands fly up to frantically wipe it away as I shriek in shock and disgust.

Julius reaches for me. "Mya!"

I feel his hand on my shoulder, but he suddenly stiffens, and his grip grows firm enough to make me look up. When I clear the spit from my eyes, I blink away the stinging pain to see the woman holding the gun.

Julius holds his hands up. "Listen—"

"No," she says flatly.

"You won't leave this building alive if you shoot us," I tell her. "Our friends will—"

"They'll what?" she snaps. "Storm in here and kill me? Just like they killed Garret?"

"Your husband was a jerk, alright?" Julius raises his voice, growing angry under the stress of the situation. "He held us at knifepoint and then..." he shakes his head, undoubtedly thinking of how Delilah had been forced to bend over in front of him. Garret stood there with his knife keeping us at bay while he'd watched and openly groped himself. He'd been so caught up; he never saw Adrian pull the gun. His own perversion got him killed. And now this woman has the nerve to get angry about it. As if she and Garret hadn't hurt others before us.

"Garret wasn't a saint," Julius says hotly. "So don't act like we killed this great guy."

The woman shakes her head, sucking in a painful breath. Her hand shakes around the gun, trembling with her emotions. I can't tell if she's angry or sad, but it's clear she isn't thinking straight. Tears streak her face and her breaths come out in sharp, stabbing pants, like it hurts for her to breathe.

"He wasn't the greatest," she says in a hiccup, "but he was my husband. And now he's gone. Now I have no one."

"Please," Julie says, "don't do—"

His words are cut off by a gunshot. Blood sprays my face as I scream, and scramble backwards. The woman's body slumps toward me with a bloody hole in her face. It's the sight of a nightmare that almost makes me wet myself. I run into Julius trying to get away, fueled by fear and adrenaline.

The door behind us flies open and Adrian runs inside, eyes wild with fear, but then he sees the lifeless woman and relief visibly weighs him down. His shoulders relax and the wrinkles in his forehead smooth out.

"What happened?" he breathes, slowly entering the room.

Julius and I both look down at the woman's body. "Sh-She shot herself," I say.

"Under the chin," Julius adds.

"And how exactly did she get the gun?" Adrian walks toward me, eyes roving over me, taking in the spray of blood that stains my green sweater.

Julius hesitates. "I-I left the gun on the floor, and she grabbed it."

"You did what?" Adrian whirls around, but he cuts himself off when he notices the others have gathered in the doorway to see the commotion.

Delilah gasps at the bloody scene, covering her mouth in horror. Connor immediately grabs her and starts pulling her away. That leaves Jupiter and Bunny to stare through wide eyes as they wonder what the heck happened. We're all wondering the same thing. Everything happened so fast. Everything ended so quickly.

One moment, the woman was alive and yelling. Then she wasn't. She was dead. Gone. Just like Garret.

I hug myself as I suddenly start to feel chilly. "Can we talk about this somewhere else?" I ask, disrupting the glaring contest going on between Julius and Adrian. They both seem to notice me for the first time and nod together.

"There's nothing to discuss," Julie says. He reaches for the gun and passes it back to Adrian. "It's all over now."

10

Mya

Adrian says we're less than a day from Orly Center. Finally. We've been walking for two days now to get to a place that's an hour away in a car. How could we take so long to travel such a short distance? Well ... we haven't been travelling that much.

Adrian is paranoid. Ever since the elementary school, he takes Connor with him and scouts ahead for miles before walking all the way back to gather everyone and set out together. Now, we double check the perimeter every time we stop. We swap places to keep watch while we work. We're constantly looking back, glancing over our shoulders, keeping our eyes peeled for any danger.

I don't know what Adrian saw on his journey before our group got together but it left him overprotective of everyone and that elementary school drama has only made things worse. We can't move without him insisting we follow the *Safety*

Protocol he put into place. But that protocol takes forever just for us to get moving. We're dragging our feet and wasting food. We're not throwing out our jerky, but we'd eat less if we didn't take two extra days of travel to get anywhere. I could be with my father by now if Adrian wasn't so fearful.

Or maybe I'm blaming him because it's easier to do that than to blame myself.

We could have had some answers if Julius and I hadn't screwed up that interrogation. Instead of gathering information on soldiers or city evacuations, we let the woman scream at us and then shoot herself. None of us has talked about it since, except to tell everyone that we learned absolutely nothing from the woman. Since then, we've simply packed our things and kept moving. Like it never happened.

To my shock, moving on has been relatively easy to do. That woman was right, this world does change you. In good ways and bad ways. I'm tough enough to watch a woman kill herself and keep going, but I'm not tough enough to get over my own stupid emotions. Instead of being consumed by all the tragic things I've experienced, I've been keeping myself sane by stewing over what's going on between me and Julius. That's a much simpler issue, but it hurts all the same.

Julius and I still aren't speaking, and the pain of his sudden absence in my life is almost overwhelming. I've never been friends with Bunny or Connor. And Jupiter is too far into her slump to talk to anyone. I have no one right now, and for the first time, it hurts. I feel as isolated as I was back at the university when everyone turned their backs on me. My own Christian friends had betrayed me, but Jupe and I made it out regardless. I want to talk to her about all this, but I don't know where to begin.

How much does she know about what's been going on? That conversation I overheard at the gas station made it seem like Adrian and Delilah knew *everything* and that makes my skin crawl. I feel like they've stripped me naked and there's nothing I can use to cover myself anymore. My love life is not casual gossip, it's an intimate part of my life that's deeply affected me. To them, it's just a conversation to pass time while I poop in the background.

I sigh as I walk behind Delilah now. She's strolling beside Julius, right in front of me. At first, Delilah had kept her distance, but since that bathroom discussion where she and Adrian agreed something had *obviously* happened between us, she's been by Julie's side more and more—and then his heroic efforts to comfort her after Garret pointed his knife at us all pretty much sealed the deal. Even Connor has noticed their connection; when I glance over my shoulder, I see him staring straight ahead, searing Delilah's blonde ponytail with his hot glare.

He had to know this would eventually happen. It's no secret Delilah changes men like she changes clothes, and Julius has always been her favorite. But still… that doesn't mean watching it happen in front of everyone is fun for him. It isn't any more fun for me either. Julius was my *boyfriend*. We'd confessed to loving each other and had almost had sex—he would've been my very first experience and I would've touched the moon with joy just because it would've been *him*.

Julius Caesar, my best friend and secret crush since childhood, would have taken my virginity—a part of me I could never give to anyone else in the world. I'd *wanted* him to have it, like my own little gift to him. But I'd wanted to give him that gift the right way, the *righteous* way.

He couldn't wait.

And now… He's smiling at Delilah as she bumps him with her shoulder and then winks her pretty blue eye at him.

I force myself to look away and glance up to see Jupiter watching me. I offer a shy wave. She waits an uncomfortably long time to wave back, and even then, it's weak and her smile is obviously forced.

I jog a few steps to walk beside her. "Hey."

"Hey," she says flatly.

"How are you feeling?"

She shrugs.

"I'm glad we're moving forward. Once we get to Orly Center, we can put all this behind us. You know?"

She shrugs again.

Sheesh… I know Jupe has been in a slump lately, but her unresponsiveness almost feels personal.

I try to make conversation one more time. "I think we could all use a fresh start. So much has been going on."

"Yes," she finally speaks. "And the same people are always at the center of the drama."

I squint at her. Okay, that was definitely personal.

"Well, I'm glad we're all trying to get along again," I say slowly.

"Sure. Now that your boyfriends aren't feuding anymore."

Seriously? My *boyfriends*?? Like, *plural*??

I frown. "Jupiter—"

"You ran around here with two guys drooling after you, Mya." She shakes her head. "And you call yourself a Christian."

"Since when does being a Christian prevent people from being attracted to me?" I snap. "It isn't my fault two guys happened to like me."

"It's your fault for getting involved with them both."

"What does any of this have to do with—"

"I ignored whatever was going on with you, Caesar, and Adrian, but that woman killed herself, Mya."

I recoil from her, stunned by the accusation. "Jupe, that had nothing to do with my love life."

"No, but..." she shakes her head. "Why was that stupid gun even in the room? Because Adrian wanted *you* to have some sort of protection. Do you think he would've given that gun to Caesar if he'd gone in with Connor or me?"

I bite the inside of my cheek, unsure how to answer. Would Adrian have cared enough about Jupiter or Connor to pass Julius his gun? Maybe Jupiter has a point. Maybe that woman wouldn't have had the chance to shoot herself if Adrian hadn't cared so much about me.

But that isn't fair... How does being loved by someone make it my fault that a disturbed woman took her own life? That places so much blame on my shoulders. Blame I don't think I can handle.

"Jupiter, you're not being fair," I say.

She looks at me for a long time, and then sighs. "Maybe not. But ... That woman died and then everyone moved on like it was nothing. Everyone went back to the same stupid drama as if her life meant nothing."

I know what she's saying. I really do. But I also understand why we all did it. I don't want to think about that woman's lifeless body in that room. I don't want to see her face with that gaping hole in her head again. I don't want to relive that moment, feel her warm blood spray across my face, and listen to her body hit the floor with a solid *thump*. I just want to forget it. And it's easy to forget by focusing on Julius, and being angry at Delilah, and wondering how Adrian feels about all this. It's pathetic to care more about our personal drama, but this drama is keeping me sane.

I look at Jupiter, hoping to somehow make her understand. "Everyone copes differently. Some of us mourn the dead—"

"And some of us bury our troubles with boys we have no business being involved with." She shakes her head and turns away, picking up the pace so I can't keep up with her anymore.

I don't want to. I'd rather walk alone than have my own friend treat me this way and blame me for everything. But then, who else can I walk beside? Adrian is busy reading the map and leading everyone. Connor is glaring at Delilah. Bunny is drooling over Delilah. And Julius is by her side. I can hear them chatting ahead of me, Delilah tosses her head back and lets out girlish giggles as Julie speaks. He doesn't even look back at me.

This isn't fair. Jupiter blames me without even knowing that I'd tried to do the Christian thing and honor God in my relationship with Julius. But what did that get me? It pushed Julius into the arms of another woman. And now I'm alone and hurt while he's flirting and happy.

God... I whisper in my soul. It's the only word I can think of, and it brings tears to my eyes. Like a dam has broken, my prayer flows from my heart as freely as my tears streak my cheeks. *I'm so hurt. I tried to do the right thing. I honored You, and it pushed away the one person I loved. Where are You! I lost the love of my life for You! Aren't You supposed to show up and make this sacrifice worth it?*

I wipe my eyes with the back of my hand, hoping no one can hear me softly sniffling.

Where are You? I ask again, and I hear His response as clearly as I hear Delilah giggling ahead of me.

I am with you.

Where? I almost gasp, sucking in a huge glob of snot before it shoots out my nose. *How are You here when I feel so much pain? Why don't You make it go away?*

Patience.

Patience? I hate the sound of that word, but I immediately understand what God is saying. Sometimes He does wash away the pain, wipe away every tear. But sometimes He lets us feel everything. Every part of our lives serves a purpose, even the pain we feel. Unfortunately, some of us learn better from pain. We never forget the pain. It's what reminds us of what could happen. Of what we don't want to experience again.

God is here. He's crying right beside me because He loves me, and He hates the pain I'm in. But I'm learning from this pain. I'm understanding what happens when I take over and trust my foolish heart instead of trusting God's ultimate wisdom. He knows what's best for me in every part of my life—including my *love* life. So maybe I should step back and let Him point me to the right man, instead of trying to force the man *I* chose to be something he is not. Something he could never be.

I glance up to watch Julius walking beside Delilah, smiling at her, laughing like he hasn't a care in this broken world.

Was I really so wrong about him? I ask the Lord. *Jesus, will he never change? Not even for You?*

God repeats Himself.... **Patience.**

Patience? Patience that Julius will change? That he'll truly give his life to Christ and learn to wait for God? To wait for *me?*

I shake my head. I won't let that word give me hope. I can't have hope right now, the disappointment might shatter me. So instead of thinking of Julius, I decide I'm going to have patience with myself. I'm going to learn to trust God and wait on Him. I'm not going to focus on Julius anymore, or Delilah, or even Adrian. I'm going to focus on the Lord because He would never hurt me or betray me.

Give me strength, I pray inside, and even though I don't want to have it, I pray for patience too. *Teach me patience. Teach me to not grow weary in welldoing.* I say the last part of my prayer aloud, quietly finishing the scripture in my heart. "For at the proper time, we will reap a harvest if we do not give up." That's Galatians 6:9, a scripture I should've been praying from the start, instead of feeling sorry for myself.

I chose righteousness and it cost me something I loved. But how many heroes of the Bible did the same? How many Christians every day make that sort of sacrifice?

Being a Christian is about making sacrifices. It's a *lifestyle* of sacrifice. If Jesus could freely give His life for me, then I can freely give all things for Him. Even the things and the people I love because if I truly believe in Galatians 6:9, then I'm not really giving up anything, am I? I'm handing my pain *and* my peace to God and He's giving me something better in return. I just have to wait. I have to have patience. And trust that Jesus is working for my good.

We finally rest once the sun grows hazy. This will be our final day in the Arizona desert, in fact, we can all see Orly Center about two miles ahead of us, tucked into the middle of the entertainment plaza. There's also a Cheesecake Factory, a bowling alley, a Karty Mart grocery center, and about three

95

dozen department stores packed into the three-story megamall shopping center that sits like a palace in the parking lot.

I almost salivate at all the things we could loot and find in those buildings. We might even be able to set up there and camp out for days—for *weeks* if we find the right supplies. The mall is enclosed, it's got doors and locks. That makes it defensible and secure.

"But also makes it one big target," Adrian says when Connor brings up all the things I've been mulling over since we set up our meager camp.

We stopped while the sun was still up, so Adrian let us use the camp burner for exactly ten minutes to heat two large cans of Asian style chicken soup before he started pressing us about someone seeing the smoke. I tilt my cup of soup and gulp down the warm gingery broth before sticking my fingers inside and scooping the thick buckwheat noodles into my mouth. They taste like mushy salt, and I absolutely love it. My stomach growls as I swallow, whining for more.

"You think we're the only ones who've thought about moving into the mall?" Adrian questions Connor. "Orly Center was used as a refugee camp. *Tons* of people were there, and tons probably came through to loot just like us. We'll never be safe there."

Connor frowns into his soup. "I'm just saying."

"*If* we set up camp," Adrian explains, "we should keep our distance like we are now and go into the plaza to loot only when necessary. *Staying* there would make us sitting ducks for other scavengers or soldiers."

"The refugee camp may still be there," Delilah interjects. "We may get there and not have to fight anymore."

Connor nods, pleased that she took his side, but his gaze doesn't linger on her for long because she's sitting beside Julius who casually leans closer to her when he speaks up too.

"It's worth thinking about. What if Orly Center is empty? What if the refugee camp is gone and the place hasn't been torn apart? Could we set up camp and stay there for a little while if that's the case?"

"I think we can do anything if we put our minds to it." Delilah beams at Julius and he smiles down at her until he looks up and catches me watching them.

He drops his gaze and shifts away from Delilah, a guilty look on his face. I stare into my empty cup of soup.

"If Orly is empty," Adrian continues, "I'd be willing to talk about setting up camp, but we can't stay forever. We still have to find our families."

"*I'd be willing to talk*." Connor rolls his eyes and sits up straight, clenching his cup of soup. "You say that like you're in charge—"

"I am in charge," Adrian corrects him. "I have been this whole time."

"Only because you've got that gun."

The camp falls silent, all eyes on Adrian. He slowly nods and then reaches into his waistband to pull out the pistol. My eyes widen as he holds it up for all of us to see and then sets it on the ground, in the middle of our little circle. Jupiter and Bunny shift uncomfortably, but Julius leans forward like he wants to snatch it and run. Delilah doesn't move.

Connor stares at the gun. "What point are you trying to make here, Adrian?"

"I'm not holding anyone hostage here," he replies. "So, let's take a vote."

97

"You wanna vote on Orly Center with a gun sitting in the middle of the group?" Connor tosses his soup cup to the dirt and shakes his head. "That's a silent threat if I've ever seen one."

"I want to vote on who gets to be in charge." Adrian looks at all of us, completely ignoring Connor's aggression. "You don't want me as the leader anymore, fine, then pick a new one. You can even take the gun."

Everyone stares at the pistol again until Delilah says, "I think Caesar should be our new leader."

"Of course you do," Connor grunts, then he calls her a nasty name under his breath—a name that rhymes with *doe*, and Delilah sucks her teeth.

"What'd you just say?" she snaps.

"Guys, it's just a vote," Julius interrupts. "Let's not make it personal."

"Fine. My vote is for Adrian," Connor announces, totally making it personal.

We all roll our eyes because we know he only voted for Adrian because Delilah voted for Julius, and no one here would ever vote for *him*. At least I wouldn't. Someone who whines about not being in charge isn't fit to be in charge.

"So, it's between me and Julius." Adrian stands. "Any other nominees?"

No one speaks up.

"So let's finish the vote then."

"I vote for Caesar," Bunny says with a loyal nod toward his friend. Julius nods back and then glances at me, but I look away. It isn't my turn to vote yet.

Jupiter clears her throat. "My vote is for Adrian. He's been a good leader so far, considering he's the only one here who hasn't found himself in the middle of some childish drama."

My cheeks burn at her words.

"Mya..."

Adrian's voice snaps my head up to look at him. Everyone is staring at me. Waiting.

"You're the last vote," Adrian says.

"And we're tied," Julie adds.

I audibly gulp. "Tied?"

"Two for me and two for Julius." Adrian sets his hands on his hips. "You're the tiebreaker."

Guys, it's just a vote. Let's not make it personal... Julie's words ring in my ears and I squeeze my eyes shut to tune them out because I know he's the last person who will follow that advice. Everything is personal for him, especially when it comes to me or Adrian.

This isn't the first time I've been forced to pick sides, and it's never ended well for whoever I didn't side with. That's because my vote has never been about the bigger issue, it's always boiled down to the person right in front of me. I'm not picking a new leader; I'm picking the boy I like most. That's the way Julie will see it and I'll never be able to change his mind.

But Adrian would understand...

I believe him when he says he isn't holding anyone hostage. If I choose Julius, Adrian won't hold it against me. I've chosen Julius over him before. For months. I fell in love with Julius. I wanted to make love to Julius. And Adrian knew this, yet he still asked me to run off with him. Again.

If I pick Adrian as our leader, Julius will never speak to me again. Not without many tears and much pleading and a huge fight. But if I pick Julius, Adrian will understand. He'll eventually forgive me, and I'll try my best to make it up to him for the pain I'm always causing.

I sigh as I stare at the gun on the ground. I'm about to fire a bullet I can never take back.

This isn't an easy decision. Even if I just think about these two as people and not men I've kissed and fallen for. Adrian really is a great leader. He's focused on keeping us all safe and finding our families. He leads like a soldier—a general. But Julius; people naturally gravitate to him. He's enigmatic and he's been a leader before. People love him and follow him without much question. Julius leads like a cherished king.

I wouldn't mind serving a king. Submitting to his leadership. His overwhelming authority. But… voting for Julius wouldn't just place a king on this broken throne. It would make Delilah his queen. And I cannot vote for that.

"I pick Adrian," I say softly, still staring at the gun.

"You what?" Julius's voice is a hiss. "Is that how it is, Mya? Seriously?"

I jerk my head up to glare at him, and our eyes meet like a strike of lightning. The bolt of rage between us sets fire to our emotions, burning away everything except the red-hot pain. We're hurting each other. Clawing at each other until there's nothing left. It's the only way we know how to heal, because we were the only ones who knew how to keep each other together. It's no surprise we're tearing each other apart now.

My hot gaze slides over to Delilah sitting right beside Julie. Then I look back at him. My words come out like acid, burning my tongue. "That's how it is."

Adrian stoops to retrieve his gun, stealing my attention. The temperature seems to cool about ten degrees now that I'm not focused on Julius and his awful attitude.

"I guess that settles things. Let's sleep for the night and start again at sunrise." Adrian turns to the sleeping bag behind him. "I'll take the second shift; anyone want to volunteer for the first watch?"

"I'll take it," Delilah says with a raised hand.

Julius's voice is dark when he says, "I'll join you."

I freeze.

I *know* what he's doing. I know why he volunteered to join her. Neither of them plans to keep watch, just like Delilah and Connor never kept watch while I prepared breakfast in the basement each morning.

I look at Julius, at my best friend, at the man I've prayed for and prayed with. The man I thought I could give my precious gift to, and I shake my head in anger. I have no words to say. No response to offer to his petty vengeance. Sex is what he's always wanted anyway. It was the crack between us—as he put it. A problem we couldn't solve.

Well ... now he's going to get exactly what he wants, and I say this with full honesty... I hope it's worth it.

11

Mya

Orly Center is HUGE. It's a two-story building with a movie theater and an arcade inside, but the entire first floor is full of empty rooms for people to rent for parties and other big events like weddings and banquets. I probably wouldn't want to have my wedding with an arcade thumping over my head on the second floor, but I imagine the prices were reasonable and the fancy fresh new building probably pulled a lot of hungry buyers.

Adrian and Connor approach the building first while Julius and Bunny sweep from the west. Delilah will hold point in the back and whistle if she sees anything behind us while Jupiter and I keep the middle moving. We march as one and maintain a steady pace, each of us breathing hard as we rush the side entrance.

Adrian's back hits the wall with a thud and he glances back at all of us, but his gaze lands on Julius. Despite their differences, they manage to communicate effectively and quickly. Julius gives Adrian a firm nod and then both of them look at Delilah who nods confirmation that the rear is clear.

I've never seen such impressive flow and coordination but we're dealing with four guys who've trained together for years and Delilah, a sorority princess who undoubtedly partied hard with them on weekends and cheered for their games at every home meet. She's known them almost as long as I have. She's shared intimate moments with these guys—and I don't mean beneath the sheets. Yes, we all know Delilah has a reputation, but I'm talking about the fact that she was actually friends with these guys before I enrolled. Even outside of sorority or fraternity parties, I'm sure Delilah saw them around campus. She might have even had classes with some of them.

The power went out within my very first week of college. I never got to have any classes whatsoever, let alone make any real friends. But Delilah has. She's in her junior year, just like Julie—only one year below Adrian and Connor, and one year above Bunny. Her college memories are completely tangled up with theirs, even if all of them aren't pretty.

This is the connection they all have, I realize, watching Adrian nod back at Delilah and then yank open the door. They're all close enough to speak without using words, to know what each person wants or expects. I don't have that. And neither does Jupiter. That's why we were left in the middle like sheep, herded to safety without actually doing any work. *Maybe that's why Julius chose her over me.* Delilah knows what he wants, and she's ready to give it to him. She *has* given it to him before. And she did again last night.

I try not to let this bring me down as I rush inside behind my team. There are bigger things to focus on right now. Like how abandoned Orly Center looks from inside. It doesn't hold that fresh new feeling that it should. The walls aren't sparkly or clean, the arcade upstairs isn't lit up or bursting with the sounds of coins and tokens and screaming children.

The banquet halls on the first floor are all lined with cots for individuals or tents, I guess for families or couples. But they're all empty. The floor is littered with clothes and papers, shoes missing their matching pair, torn blankets, and ... blood.

As we silently pass through the second empty hall, I stare at the ripped clothing and the mattresses on the cots. They've got holes in them, exposing the cottony inside like a carcass spilling puffs of fabric.

Holes...

I stoop beside one of the beds and poke my finger into a hole. There are at least a dozen dotting the bed, and the floor, and the torn clothes I see by my foot. I pick up a t-shirt and hold it out in front of myself to examine it. Little holes the size of my pointer finger have been sprayed across the fabric.

"What is this?" I whisper. When I glance up, I notice Adrian's stern face as he stares at a holey cot too. The answer takes my breath away. It's right there in Adrian's waistband.

"Gunfire," he says darkly.

"What happened here?" Delilah walks through a row of cots with her jaw slack and her eyes wide, like she can't believe what she's seeing. None of us can.

"The center was attacked," Adrian answers, since no one else wants to say it aloud. But now that it's out in the open, the rest of us come to our senses and Connor speaks up in anger.

"We should have known this would have happened!" His voice is loud enough to fill the room, it echoes off the walls like raging thunder.

"How were we supposed to know that?" Adrian fires back. "We all agreed to come here because we all agreed it was the best plan of action."

"There were no people around!" Connor counters. "Think about it! No soldiers from the National Guard, no tables set up, no other survivors anywhere in sight! Did we really believe we would walk in and find our families?" He turns a circle in the room, stopping to kick over a bloody cot. "They're all dead. This is proof of that."

"I don't think so," I say softly.

Connor's eyes land on me with laser focus. "You can't be serious. Look around you!"

"I'm not going to give up hope just because things didn't turn out the way we wanted."

He wrinkles his nose. "I forgot you're a brainwashed idiot."

"Excuse me—"

Before I can finish my sentence, Connor is shoved to the side. He trips over an empty bucket and stumbles to the floor. When he looks up, his face shifts from anger to fear as he sees Adrian looming over him.

"Don't ever call her that again," Adrian warns.

"Just because you like her—"

"This isn't about that," he cuts him off and steps even closer, so Connor has to lean back and scoot away from him. "Just because her beliefs are different from yours doesn't give you the right to insult her. Disagreement is not a free pass for disrespect."

Connor swallows but doesn't speak.

Adrian steps over him and looks around at all of us, his gaze lingers on me for a moment, but then he's back to his normal self, handling business.

"This isn't the outcome we expected. But that doesn't mean all hope is lost," he says.

"But what happened?" Delilah insists. There are tears running down her face now, and I can't help but feel sorry for her. I feel sorry for *everyone* here, even Connor. In a way, it does feel like all hope is lost. But I have to live by the beliefs Connor just criticized. I have to trust that God is still on the throne and that He'll work things out for my good.

Please let my father be okay, I pray inside. *If he was truly here, help me find proof, Jesus. And lead me to him.*

"It looks like the center was attacked by enemy forces." Adrian stares at the mess all around us as he speaks, eyes scanning the bullet holes and the dried streaks of blood. "This was definitely a refugee camp of some sort; the cots and tents make that clear."

"And the bullet holes make it clear that soldiers ran this place over." Connor sits on the floor with his head in his hands. I could question why he's so upset, considering he isn't from Arizona, so he knows his family isn't involved in this at all—but maybe that's why he's upset. If we can't find our own families when we're this close, what hope does he have of ever finding his own from across the country?

"The good thing here is that there was a camp," Adrian says.

"How is that good?" Delilah asks.

"Because if the National Guard managed to set up one, then there's got to be another."

"Another where?" I question.

"That's what we're going to find out." Adrian kneels and picks up a crumpled sheet of paper, he smooths out the wrinkles and squints to read it. "This is a printed lunch schedule for the camp."

"That's useful," Connor grumbles.

"It's information. Which means there's bound to be more lying around here." Adrian nods like he's just made a decision. "Collect all the papers you can. We'll sift through everything. Take our time."

"This is pointless." Connor shakes his head. "There are bullet holes everywhere. And blood."

"But no bodies," Adrian says firmly. "We haven't found a single body in this building so far, and I didn't see a giant grave in the parking lot. So where do you think the bodies went?"

"There aren't any bodies," Delilah breathes.

Adrian nods. "I think this camp was attacked, but the people made it out alive." He glances down and rubs the tip of his sneaker against a bloodstain. "Injured, but alive."

"This might have been a refugee camp," Julius adds, "but it was set up and run by the National Guard. That means they would have had weapons of their own. They would have fought back."

"Maybe the camp was already empty, and this blood belongs to soldiers from both sides," Adrian continues.

"You're both grasping at straws," Connor says angrily.

"The point is that we don't know what happened." Adrian picks up another sheet of paper. "So, let's do everything we can to find out."

I nod, suddenly filled with hope. My friends are right. There's no way to tell exactly what happened here, or who won this altercation, but that doesn't mean we should give up. If this place was overrun, I want to know who was here when it happened and where they might have gone once it was over.

My father could have been here. The only way to know for certain is to find some sort of intel from the papers scattered everywhere.

Glancing around, that seems like an impossibility. There are discarded papers and belongings all over the place. Rooms full of abandoned sleeping bags, open suitcases, and scattered clothing. This center is the scene of a great escape, an exodus just as harried and desperate as our own when we finally left the campus behind. Like the Israelites, we'd run for our lives with people chasing our heels, and God had been the only One to protect us on our journey. We'd found our own Promised Land in my basement; a place of refuge with powdered milk and jarred honey. A place prepared by a dedicated man of God who had followed the Lord's instruction to prepare a way for the future without even knowing why. Without even knowing that he wouldn't get to use the supplies himself. In a way, my father was like our very own modern-day Moses, who hadn't made it to his Promised Land either.

Against all odds, *we* made it, but our journey isn't over.

Adrian, Delilah, and Connor start sorting through the papers and belongings in the open foyer of Orly Center, but I decide to start my search near the entrance. Connor made a very valid point earlier; if people had currently been here, there would have been some sort of welcome table or help desk for new guests to register and sign in. I've volunteered at enough homeless shelters and Christian centers to know that. So, my first goal is to find the sign-in desk.

As I thought, it's right at the entrance, a dust-covered table standing on just three legs. The tablecloth is torn and hanging halfway to the floor; the words, **YOU ARE SAFE HERE** are printed on the front ... and littered with bullet holes. The only good thing here is the little American flag I see printed on the tablecloth. That means this place really was set up by the National Guard, not by enemy forces.

I walk over to the welcome table and rifle through the crumpled, stained papers I can find. Most of them are covered in dust, debris, and even blood, but I'm able to make out a meal schedule, a chore rotation sign-up, and a list of new members who'd joined before this place was abandoned. The date on the sign-up sheet is sometime in November, I can't make out the exact day but that's enough to give me an idea of what day it is now, or at least the month.

I already knew it was wintertime because of the constant chill outside. We're in Arizona, so it isn't *freezing*, but I'm thankful for my sweatshirt and I can't help but shiver at night when it's nifty out. Still, as I backtrack through the last few months, I'm shocked by how much time has passed.

I left for college at the very end of August. The power went out by the end of that first week. I stayed on campus for about six weeks after that before spending a week on the road and finally settling down at home for another three months. A rough estimate would place us somewhere in January. Which means we're almost two months late. This place was attacked and abandoned while I was sitting at home safe, dreaming of Julius.

I sigh and drop the paper, but before despair can settle in, I catch a glimpse of the corner of a wrinkled page still clipped to a board on the table. Once I tug it loose, my jaw drops open. It's another chore rotation schedule, but this one has names listed on the schedule for the day. There are cooks assigned to the kitchen, tutors assigned to their makeshift library, even someone named Dr. Kendra Matthews who took counseling sessions in the library. But what truly catches my attention is the name assigned to the boiler room.

Boiler Room Attendees: 2 Scheduled for afternoon checkup

Amanda Kite 12pm

Dr. Joshua Br—

The rest of the page is stained with blood. But I know that name, it's Dr. Joshua *Brown*. My father. Yes, that's an incredibly common name, but who else could it be? My dad was an engineer, the only *Christian* scientist I've ever known. He was paranoid and kooky and very overprotective of me, but he was also a genius with two PhDs and the intelligence to build his own generator from scratch. His paranoia and ingenuity left us with a fully stocked basement while the rest of the world who'd mocked him starved or dried out from dehydration.

If my father was rounded up and sent to live here to escape the war raging around us, he would have volunteered his services. My father was not an idle man. He hated sitting still— I know he would have signed up for work, and what better work for a man with two degrees in engineering and physics?

With that paper in my hand, I sprint through Orly Center in search of the boiler room. I ignore Connor's blank stare as I shove past him in the hall, I don't look twice when I run past Jupiter, and I only hesitate when I see Adrian staring as I scan the sign posted on the wall near a stairwell in the back. The sign has been shot up, but I can make out the directions to the right room.

I end up in a small closet behind the kitchen—it isn't really a boiler room, it's more like storage space with two massive generators, piping for water, and a collection of battery powered flashlights. There's even a dead radio on the floor—

I know it's dead because it's been completely taken apart, like someone was in the middle of trying to get it to work.

I don't know what I expect to find here, but I start searching anyway, mindlessly yanking open the metal lockers on the walls, searching through the toolbox beside the dead radio, and squeezing between the massive water tanks to find dead bugs and cobwebs swaying in the far corner of the room.

This place is dead.

I ball the paper in my hand and squeeze until my hand goes numb. I'm so close to finding my father. This is the clue I need. But it isn't enough. I need more. *Something*. Anything.

"Mya?"

I glance up to see Julius pushing the door open. Sunlight from the hall pours in behind him, splashing across the entrance and illuminating the sheet of paper taped to the wall beside him.

I gasp and run over to him, eyes darting across the page.

There it is.

Weekly Boiler Schedule
Sunday: No maintenance
Monday: Amanda Kite
Tuesday: Amanda Kite
Wednesday: No Maintenance
Thursday: Dr. Joshua Brown

I don't even read the rest of the scheduled maintenance— I don't care about it. I see my father's name printed in bold black letters and my eyes fill with tears.

Julius, who is thoroughly confused by now, steps forward in time to catch me as I crumple to my knees. I can't even *breathe* as sobs wrack my body.

111

"What's wrong!" Julie says sharply, glancing around for danger.

"He was here!" I shriek. "My father was here!" I point to the list on the wall and Julius snaps his head in that direction. I watch as his eyes widen, and his jaw goes slack. He knows the chance is slim that it's truly him, but he believes it is. I can see it in his eyes, hope burning like a flame. Julius believes that Dr. Joshua Brown on the maintenance schedule is my father.

It has to be him.

My hysterical crying draws everyone's attention after a few minutes. Julius has to explain what we've found because I'm still too shaken up to even speak. I can hardly see past my tears as Delilah gasps at the news and then runs to find more papers and evidence. She's from Wakedon too; if my father was evacuated to Orly then there's a high chance her family was too.

"This is the proof we've needed," Julius says, helping me to my feet. "Now we just need to find out who else was possibly here and where everyone went after the place was attacked."

"Since this camp was run by the National Guard, there were likely strict protocols in place in case of an invasion," Adrian says, leaning against the doorpost like an angry shadow. His voice is dark and serious as he speaks, but I know he isn't mad at us, he's just an uptight person. "That means we might be able to find procedures and directions on where to go written down somewhere, the same way there's always directions and emergency exits all over the place on cruise ships and at amusement parks."

I nod, trying to get it together.

"I think I might have found what you guys are looking for," Connor says from the hallway.

We all turn to find him wearing a somber expression and I feel my shoulders slump. Whatever he's found can't be good.

12

Caesar

I keep my arm around Mya's shoulders as we follow Connor down the hall. I'm surprised she's let me touch her at all, considering we haven't even made eye contact today. But I don't protest her proximity. Despite our distance lately, Mya is still my best friend. She needs me right now, more than ever. That's why our connection has always been so strong; no matter how far we drift from each other, Mya and I always find our way back. We're meant for each other.

Connor leads us to a hallway full of doors that are all open. The rooms inside are dark—**black**—and once he steps into one of them, I realize why.

They've been scorched.

One by one, every room in this hall was set on fire from the inside. Soot lines the doorways, like they burned with the doors shut. Scorch marks stain the outside frames of a few rooms, like the fires threatened to escape but ultimately died inside due to lack of oxygen.

The rest of the group who's followed along quickly comes to the same conclusions. Bunny steps forward and says, "What the heck…"

"Why?" I hear Mya say beside me.

"Because these rooms were offices." Adrian walks into the center of the tar black room and glances around, after a moment, he kicks a charred black square of wood that I barely recognize as a desk. It whines in protest and threatens to collapse from that kick. I watch as black dust puffs into the air, and I cough.

"I bet these rooms belonged to the soldiers who ran this place," Adrian explains. "Which means there would have been documents here. Information on what the US military was doing and what they planned to do next."

"There might have been information on the location of other refugee camps and military headquarters as well," I add.

Adrian nods at me, but his next statement is cut off as Connor steps forward and produces a burnt piece of paper from his pocket. "I found this in one of the rooms."

Adrian's nostrils flare as he reads it. "Expected supply drop by the tenth of November…" Adrian's voice trails off as he tries to read around the soot stains and scorch marks on the singed paper. He's only able to make out a few sentences here and there, and none of it is particularly useful until he gets to the end. His eyes flick up from the letter. "This is signed by the order of the Twelfth Brigade of the US Army encampment forces."

"What does that mean?" I say.

"The letter I found on the tent back home was signed by the order of the Fifth Brigade," he answers. "That means there's more than one shelter or military camp. And they were communicating."

"Not just communicating," Connor inserts, "they were coordinating. Arranging supply drops."

Mya pulls away from me to step forward, a serious look on her face. "The last registration of new refugees had a date in November on it."

"Could it be that enemy forces found out about the supply drop and attacked Orly Center?" Bunny suggests.

That would make the most sense. This is war and it's being fought in a place where the power was cut out, limiting the distribution of supplies to survivors. Our enemies need food and water as much as we do, it seems like they were willing to shoot down a refugee shelter to get it.

Adrian saw enemy soldiers with his own eyes when he and Connor first made the trip to Wakedon. If the grid going down around the entire state wasn't evidence enough, then the soldiers were certainly proof that America has been attacked. It seems like some sort of war is going on and we've been living on the edges of the battlefield. Just outside the war zone, two steps behind the action.

Cross North University was an isolated campus; large enough to sustain itself with gardens and greenhouses and campus bakeries, the school was hours away from the nearest city. It was its *own* city. That's why we never received any sort of military aid when the power first went down. We were too far away to matter to the National Guard. Or maybe we *did* matter and help simply couldn't get there in time.

Either way, we were isolated from both the help and the danger too. That kept us alive, but also severely out of the loop. By the time we made it off campus, the nearest cities had already been evacuated and the warring had moved on. We still don't know who our country is fighting right now. But it's clear we're fighting *someone*. And they're fighting dirty.

"These people here were helpless," I say angrily. "They shot them down for their food and water."

"We don't know if the people were shot down," Mya corrects me sharply. "We only know they were shot *at*. They could have made it out alive."

I glance down at the paper gripped tightly in her hand. She needs this to be true. Her father's life depends on it. Despite her desperation, I believe there's some truth to that theory. Considering the lack of bodies and even the scorched rooms. When the enemy attacked, this place had enough time to torch all their papers and offices. That means they could have had enough time to fully evacuate all the refugees as well. I can only hope.

"Whatever happened," Connor says, looking around the charred room, "all the information on where everyone could have gone next is burned to a crisp now."

"That's okay." Adrian quickly tries to resuscitate the dying hope in our hearts. "Now we know for certain that other camps do exist. We've just got to find them."

"How?" Bunny asks.

"By looking," Adrian answers. "We can search every major stadium in the nearest cities."

"That would mean Phoenix is up next," I say, almost excitedly. I'm from Phoenix. I could find my foster mother there—and Adrian's family too. He knows this, which is why he gives me a small nod before continuing.

"Phoenix is next. Who knows what we'll find there? Maybe everyone met up at the shelters over there."

"Or maybe the enemy soldiers tracked them down too and killed everyone there." Connor folds his arms.

"Why are you so—"

A sharp whistle cuts Adrian off. We all stare in silence, listening for the signal.

"Was that Delilah?" I ask.

Connor nods and peeks out the burned door. "Yeah. She may have found something."

"Or someone." Adrian marches to the door but stops to look back at all of us. "Stay close and stay safe. Don't try to be a hero out there."

"Jesus," Connor rolls his eyes, "what do you think she's found out there?"

Adrian's glare is hot enough to burn. "I don't know." He pulls that pistol out of his waistband and turns away, signaling for us to follow.

Single file, we march out the room, but when it's Mya's turn to exit, I grab her by the wrist. I just need to say this before we leave, because I'm not sure I'll get another chance. Or maybe I will. Maybe we're all overreacting to Delilah's whistle, and she's waiting for us in the lobby with a case of water that she found. Maybe we'll all go to bed fully hydrated for once.

Either way, I just need to do this now.

"Mya, wait," I whisper, glancing ahead to make sure Connor, Bunny, and Adrian have kept walking. When the door shuts behind them, I start talking again, quickly, in case they notice we aren't following and come back to retrieve us. "About last night—"

She presses her lips together and looks away, clutching that paper to her chest. "You don't have to explain yourself. We're not together anymore."

That hurts more than it should.

"So, I don't care who you sleep with."

"But I didn't sleep with anyone," I say.

She looks up at me, disbelief and hope written all over her face. She isn't sure if she believes me, but she wants to.

"You stayed up with Delilah," she whispers.

"I know."

"Just the two of you."

"I know. And nothing happened."

She blinks. I should feel offended by how shocked she is, but I can't blame her. Delilah isn't the only one with a reputation, and it's time I owned up to mine. Yes, Lilah is a loose girl. She's a whore—but so am I. Isn't it interesting that words like whore, slut, or hoe are only used on *women*? Even if you looked them up in a dictionary, they would describe a wayward *female*. Not a male.

Why is that?

Why isn't there a word for a *man* who sleeps around?

Because a man who sleeps around hasn't done anything wrong. His behavior is praised and even welcomed. So, there isn't a demeaning word for a loose man, because a loose man is just a man.

But Mya's standard applies to women *and* men. That's because her standard is **God's** standard, and He's made it clear; sex outside of marriage is a sin whether you're a man or a woman. He doesn't think it's cute for a man to have any more sexual experience than a woman. He doesn't cherish the virginity of a lady any more than He cherishes the virginity of a man.

We do. Because we're imperfect humans who love to blend our manmade ideals with the Word of God. But what happens when we mix arbitrary rules with sacred Scripture? We get a hot mess.

We get generations of women being ridiculed, mocked, and even *killed* for performing the very same acts men have been doing with no punishment or consequence since the beginning of time. It even happened in the Bible. When those men dragged that woman out to be stoned, it was because she had been caught in the act of adultery. But she hadn't been alone. Yet only the woman had been dragged out.

Thank God for Jesus is what Mya used to say whenever she retold that story to me. If Jesus hadn't been there, that woman would have been stoned—*murdered*—while the man she'd committed her sin with would have walked away. But Jesus forgave her. He stood up for her. He rescued her. Like a true Savior.

Mya turns to face me fully, her eyes darting between me and the open door. I bet she'd rather make a run for it than deal with this conversation right now. I don't blame her.

"Why did you volunteer to stay up with Delilah, then?" she asks me.

I gulp, not wanting to tell the truth, but I've made it this far. Might as well own up to my own foolishness. "I did want to sleep with her," I admit, hating the pained look on Mya's face. "But then ..."

"Then?"

"Then I realized it wasn't worth it."

I'm being honest. I had a fair chance with Delilah, and I tossed it away of my own free will. We'd started off making out almost immediately. Lilah isn't a fool, she knew why I'd volunteered to stay up with her during the first watch, so when Connor and the others finally went to their sleeping bags, we practically attacked each other. For a moment, I couldn't even get Delilah to move. She wanted to strip down and do it *right there* at the campfire where we'd just eaten our food.

Miraculously, I convinced her to walk a few yards away so we could at least have some privacy. She was down to just her panties, clawing at the zipper of my jeans, when I finally came to my senses.

I didn't want to do it.

The kissing had been amazing, but with each piece of clothing we'd removed, the sensation seemed to dull. By the time she got my zipper down, I felt like vomiting, and it showed.

Delilah had stared at my pants, shocked to see a limp noodle where there should have been a solid rock. Aha. We were both shocked, but I knew why. And as I scooted away from her, I tried to offer some vague excuse, but she saw right through it.

With tears in her eyes, Delilah covered her bare breasts in embarrassment and said, "You really love her. Don't you, Caesar?"

"I do," I'd sheepishly replied.

She had choked on a sob, and for the first time, I thought she looked really pretty. Until that moment, Delilah had been hot. She'd been *so* sexy to me. But I never saw her as *pretty* until I saw her as a human being. A girl with emotions and thoughts

121

and opinions. Not some sorority chick who was banging my friend. Delilah was a person. And I'd hurt her.

"You didn't have to use me to sort out your feelings for her," she'd said, wiping her bitter tears.

I nodded. "I'm so sorry, Lilah."

That was the last thing I said to her that night. I'd wanted to run to Mya and weep—bellow out a teary apology for all my stupidity and beg her to forgive me. I'd had the chance to enjoy all the sex I'd ever wanted with a hot, willing woman. And I'd tossed it away. Because I finally understood what Mya meant when she'd said our relationship wasn't built on sex. It was a connection so much stronger. So much deeper. Sex was just a bonus. But you can't appreciate the bonus if you never enjoy the initial prize.

That prize was the relationship—the years of development and time together with Mya. I saw her as a person before I saw her as something to fulfill my desires. Honestly, she'd fulfilled them before I even knew what they were.

I hadn't realized how lonely I was until Mya made me feel loved. Hadn't realized how desperate I was until Mya gave me all her attention. Hadn't known how pathetic I felt inside until Mya loved me for myself—not for my title as captain or for my popularity. She was my prize, but I'd skipped over that because I'd only been looking at the bonus. And now I'm sorry. And I'm praying she'll forgive me.

"Mya," I say, "I was a fool. I was a complete idiot. But I've learned from my mistake. I want to do things right." I pause. "I want to do things *righteously*."

Her eyes grow wide as she stares at me. "What are you saying?" she whispers.

"I'm saying I'm in love with you. And I'm willing to do whatever it takes to keep you in my life. If that means waiting for sex, then so be it. If God can give you strength to wait, then He can give me strength too." I hold out my hand. "Let's wait together, okay?"

Mya blinks at my hand as she speaks. "I've been thinking about all the drama going on lately. I've thought about you. About Delilah. About Connor." She hesitates. "I've even thought about Adrian."

I swallow thickly, still holding out my hand, waiting for her to take it.

"I've prayed to God to remove my complicated feelings. To keep me focused on Him so I won't be distracted by two boys who weren't good for me."

I swallow again. This is really starting to sound like a gentle rejection, but I keep my hand there. Ready for her to take it.

Mya looks up at me, tears in her eyes. "I've prayed to God for a partner. I've prayed to God to help me desire the right man. A righteous man. And I think ... I think I finally know where my heart belongs."

"Where does it belong?" I whisper, shocked by how much my voice shakes. It's nearly trembling, and no wonder, this is the scariest thing I've ever done. I don't know what I'll do without Mya. If she rejects me... I may drift away.

"You know where it belongs," she whispers back. And then she looks down at my hand again and she finally uncurls her fingers, releasing her grip on that crumpled paper.

"Mya..." I say softly—and it's the *last* thing I say before gunfire rips through the halls.

13

Mya

There's no time to react. One moment, I'm staring into Julie's eyes, the next, he's tackling me to the floor as I scream in terror.

I'm not angry at Julius. As I fall, I recognize the distinct popping sounds of gunfire and I know our worst nightmare has begun. We've been found. Soldiers are here.

Maybe not soldiers. Maybe it's more drifters like the people who shot Connor on the highway, but it's someone who isn't friendly. Someone who made Adrian shoot back.

I'm not familiar with weapons, but I've played enough video games to know the difference between an automatic rifle spitting a hundred bullets per second and a handgun firing rounds as quickly as the shooter can pull the trigger. Someone is shooting at us, and Adrian is firing back. But he doesn't have endless bullets.

"We've got to help!" I shout over the noise, shoving Julius off me.

He looks bewildered as I scramble away and run toward the door, but as soon as I get there, it's knocked inward, and I have to jump to avoid being whacked by it.

Connor stands in the doorway, breathing heavily. "There you are!" he snaps. "We thought you guys were taken."

"We got held up," Julius explains, shoving himself to his feet. I feel bad for abandoning him so easily, so I walk over and help him up, he takes my hand and then stands there awkwardly wiping dirt and soot from his jeans.

"Sorry," I mumble to him.

"What's going on?" he says to Connor.

"I don't know. We didn't make it very far after we heard that whistle. Halfway down the hall, we heard voices in the lobby."

"Voices?" I repeat, then I duck as gunfire pops off somewhere in the distance.

Connor and Julius are both crouching now, faces pinched in anxiety. "There's at least ten of them," Connor says.

"Armed?" I ask.

He bunches his shoulders. "I didn't see them. Just heard the voices. Adrian wanted us to split up and try to circle around the building to meet the others out front, but then we realized you two weren't with us. I came back while he and Bunny went ahead. Now there's gunfire going off."

"Which means they bumped into the men who owned the voices you heard," Julius says angrily.

"What should we do now?" Connor peeks out the door and then glances back at us when neither of us answers.

Julius is the one they voted to take over when Connor spoke up against Adrian, but now that a decision must be made, he's sitting here like a deer in headlights. This isn't like him. Julius is enigmatic, inspiring, sometimes he feels otherworldly. But maybe I was seeing him from the perspective of a girl with a crush. A best friend who admired him. Not as a woman whose life is on the line.

For the first time, I begin to wonder if maybe I've been wrong about Julius. Maybe he isn't a great leader like his namesake.

I take a deep breath. "We should continue Adrian's plan. Find a way outside and circle back to the front. He would want us to keep going, and it wouldn't be bad to avoid the guys with guns anyway."

Connor nods like he agrees, but Julius frowns. "Someone should help Adrian."

He has a point.

Before I can think of a new plan, Julius finally decides to become a good leader and volunteers himself for the job. "I'll find Adrian."

"Wait—" I say, but he keeps speaking right over me.

"Connor, get Mya out of here. I'll meet you both out front. If I'm not there in twenty minutes, head back to our campsite from last night. No matter what."

Connor, who is clearly more committed to Julius than to me, nods vigorously and grabs me by the shoulder. "Let's go, Mya. I'll lead the way."

Sheesh, both of these guys were just scratching their heads like confused little monkeys. Now that the job involves protecting a small woman, they've leapt into action and completely overlooked anything *I* might have to say about it.

126

When men think they're protecting someone, they work like there's a fire burning behind them.

I'll be honest, I'm not entirely upset about this. But I don't completely *like* it either.

Adrian is out there fighting strangers with powerful weapons. And now Julius is running out there to help him with *no* weapon. Meanwhile, Connor and I are heading out to hide in the parking lot for twenty minutes.

I feel so helpless right now.

I watch in misery as Julie leaves us, walking in the opposite direction, fearlessly rushing toward the danger. My heart begins to ache. I didn't get to tell him that I'd made up my mind. I didn't get to tell him that I'd finally chosen someone to love. And now I'm not sure I ever will again. But I have to hold on to hope. I have to believe that this isn't the end. *Patience*, I remind myself of God's single instruction for me.

"Mya," Connor says, tugging me by the elbow.

I let him pull me away, moving down the hallway in the opposite direction. We pass charred and burnt rooms in silence, ignoring the bullets that fire behind us. I can hear the voices Connor mentioned earlier, the sounds of grunting and yelling, but everything is muffled and distorted from the weapon fire.

"We need to find an exit!" Connor says, ducking and turning a corner. We've managed to loop around the building, going toward the front entrance again, but that's where the voices are coming from. I still can't make out any specific words, but I can tell the voices are a mix of men and women. They sound older, serious, professional.

"Let's cut through one of these rooms." I tap Connor on the shoulder, and he hesitates but agrees. The room we pick is a small banquet hall that was divided into smaller rooms by hanging sheets from the ceiling. One section is the tiny library I saw printed on the schedules earlier, it consists of two shelves and overturned crates for chairs, another section looks like a children's play area.

Connor and I walk quickly, never slowing our pace, not even when we hear the door open behind us and the voices grow louder. That's when Connor grabs me and yanks me behind a curtain. This area looks like it might have been for sleeping since there are three cots lined up and pillows all over the floor. I try not to stare at the bullet holes as I move past them, but Connor stops abruptly.

I walk into his backside and remind myself not to grunt aloud. The soldiers are in the room with us. We can't make a noise—apparently, we can't move so easily either. Connor is staring up at the ceiling with a hard look on his face. It takes me a moment to realize he's looking at the curtain dividing up the room.

It's swaying because we were walking so close to it.

"See that?" a muffled voice says somewhere in the distance. "I told you I saw someone go in here."

Another voice replies, "That could be the wind."

"Bravo Team already reported gunfire. Someone is here."

The other voice sighs. "You check it out, then. I'm moving forward with the others."

We stand in silence, listening to the sound of the soldier's retreating steps, but it's hard to tell who's walking toward us and who is leaving. Not that it matters much—we've got to move regardless.

Connor taps me and makes a motion with his hands flattened. I know what he's saying. Crawl. Quickly and quietly.

I get down on my hands and knees and follow him toward the nearest door. Crawling for your life is not an easy task, but we manage to move swiftly and keep the noise to a minimum. Occasionally, I can hear that lone soldier cursing as he marches through the room. By the time we make it to the door, he's resorted to snatching down the sheets that hang around him. Each time one is torn from the hooks in the ceiling, my heartrate jumps up a notch. I'm practically sweating when Connor finally presses a firm hand to the door.

I hold my breath, praying it doesn't squeak, but then the door is pulled open from the other side and Adrian appears. He's wearing a shocked expression, but his surprise doesn't make him lose focus. When Connor presses a finger to his lips, signaling him to keep quiet, he simply nods and lowers to his knees, eyes glancing through the room.

Connor points to the hallway, but Adrian shakes his head.

My stomach churns in anxious agony. Adrian is running from someone too, and he came here seeking safety. But how? He's supposed to be on the other side of the map. He's supposed to be with Julius right now.

So ... Where is my best friend?

I swallow and wince at the sudden dryness in my throat. That other soldier left. Was he going to track down Julie? What about the others? Have Delilah and Bunny or Jupiter been caught? What is going on??

"Found you!"

Pain explodes in the back of my head before I register the soldier's voice. He's grabbed me by the hair and is lifting me from the ground, dragging me away. Now that we've been caught, I don't bother trying to be quiet. The scream I let out rips through the room like a whip, even Connor winces before pouncing to his feet and throwing himself at the man.

I jerk my head backwards to alleviate the pain of my braids being tugged. I feel the back of my skull connect with my perpetrator's face and the satisfying *crunch* I hear almost makes up for the pain of headbutting him.

His grip on me loosens and I bring my foot down on his toe—he's wearing boots, so I don't cause any damage, but I do pin his foot in place, so he careens backwards when Connor full-body tackles him.

Adrian raises his gun, but the door opens behind him at the same time, and I shout, "Behind!" It's the only word I can get out, but it's enough to make Adrian shift to the side so the soldier who walks in swinging a bat, misses him by a hair.

A bat. I get a good look at the soldiers, both are armed, but not with guns. One has a bat and the other has a metal pipe. How strange. Maybe they aren't soldiers? But their clothes are matching; dark cargo pants and a dark shirt. They're even wearing gloves and combat boots. The attire doesn't scream US Army, but it certainly gives an air of coordination higher than your average vagabonds. I don't know who we're dealing with right now, but that doesn't matter. First, we've got to survive. We can figure everything else out later.

The man with the bat lifts it to take another swing, but Adrian lifts the gun again. He doesn't fire, just yells for them to hold it right there. I want him to shoot these guys, but maybe Adrian wants to ask questions or maybe he doesn't want to kill anyone. I don't know. But the guys don't listen anyway.

The bat guy drops his weapon and charges Adrian. He fires a shot, but it misses by a mile, going into the door behind his attacker. He gets tackled to the ground, but Adrian's a big guy.

He takes the hit with a grunt and easily rolls the man so he's on top. Except there's another man, and now he's swinging that metal pipe … at me.

I shift with a scream and hop out of the way. The wind whooshes by me and sends a shiver down my spine. One hit from that pipe and I'm done for.

"I don't want to hurt you," the man says.

I seriously doubt that, so instead of offering pointless banter in the middle of a life-or-death fight, I lunge at him. He clearly was not expecting me to do that because he takes a step back and swings at the same time, but the swing is wide and weak. I take the hit to my ribs, grunting as I tuck his pipe under my arm and roll with the swing to soften the blow.

I pivot and ram him hard with my other shoulder. He coughs as the wind is knocked out of him, dropping the pipe and losing his footing. I shove him once more and he trips backwards, away from me. Now I've got the pipe, and he's standing there blinking at me in stupefied shock.

We did a lot more than hang laundry and pout while we lived in my basement for the last three months. We trained. We ran laps through the neighborhood. We took turns practicing defensive moves on each other. All of it was Adrian's idea, paranoid after getting shot at on the road. We all complained about his rigorous schedule, but he promised us the training would come in handy, no matter how amateur it was. I wish I could tell him how right he was, but this pipe is reward enough. There's no time to brag.

The man runs at me, and I swing, but he's ready for the attack. He catches the pipe as easily as I caught his attack, and we both roll to the ground as he tries to wrestle it away from me. I grunt and twist and turn, holding on with all my might—

only the sound of a gunshot stops me. It stops us *both* with a jolt as I jerk my head in the direction it came from.

Adrian stands over the guy who'd had the bat, breathing heavily, gun in hand.

"You little—" The pipe guy shoves me away and I drop the pipe in shock, then he grabs me by the throat and holds the pipe up like he's going to bash my skull in.

I wheeze for air.

"Drop the gun!" he shouts at Adrian.

The command is loud enough to get Adrian's attention, and the guy still wrestling with Connor. Panting, they both glance our way, studying the situation. Just like the pipe guy, the soldier takes advantage of the disruption and gets Connor in a headlock.

Now we're both being held hostage.

Adrian glances back and forth. He looks perfectly calm, but the grip on his gun leaves his knuckles white and raw.

"Can't shoot us both, white boy," the pipe guy says, and I have no idea if he called Adrian white because he's albino—or because he's actually a white guy.

He isn't fazed by the insult. Adrian's too busy weighing his options. He can't make a choice. But he has to. If he shoots Connor's attacker, I'll get my brains bashed in. But if he shoots my attacker, Connor will have his neck broken.

"Adrian…" I say slowly. The pipe guy's grip on my throat tightens, but I cough through it. "It's okay," I whisper.

He shakes his head. It isn't okay at all. Not for any of us. We all know who he's going to choose. That's why I close my eyes as he lifts his gun—because I don't want to see the look on Connor's face as his head is twisted at an odd angle. He gets his neck snapped. And he dies screaming, shouting Adrian's name, and wondering why he chose a woman over his friend. A girl over his own teammate.

I know why. And Adrian knows why. And it'll haunt us both for the rest of our lives.

14

Adrian

Mya screams. The sound is piercing—almost frightening—and I'm not sure if it's from the shock of having a bullet fly past your *face* and lodge into the skull of the man holding you hostage, or if it's from the pain of watching your friend die. And knowing it could have just as easily been you.

I had a choice, but we all knew which choice I'd make. In my defense, I honestly thought I could save them both. I thought I could shoot the guy holding Mya and then quickly pivot to shoot the one holding Connor—and I did do that, but I overestimated myself. Or maybe I underestimated my enemy. I thought it took more time, more pressure, more *effort* to break someone's neck. I thought I could shoot Mya's guy and still have time to turn and save Connor. But I was wrong. Connor's head was already locked in the guy's arms before I ever fired. All he had to do was twist.

The moment I raised my gun in Mya's direction, Connor's attacker jerked his head in the wrong direction. By the time I turned to shoot him, Connor was already dead, neck twisted, mouth frowning. *Frowning.* He died angry, knowing I could have saved him and that I'd chosen not to.

I shot the guy who broke his neck, his body hit the floor right beside Connor's. But it was too late. The damage was already done. And then Mya screamed. She's crawling across the floor now, blood from her perpetrator smeared across the back of her shirt. Her voice is warbled and high pitched, letting go of these miserable whiny noises. It's painful to hear, worse to watch as she drags Connor into her lap and weeps.

She wasn't even his friend. But she's crying like they were lovers. It reminds me of the time I found her outside her dorm, desperately trying to help Jupiter save that kid who'd fallen from the roof. He'd broken his back and his neck. He was done for, but Mya had tried to save him anyway. She'd cried and screamed for someone to help. To do something. But she and Jupiter were the only ones to step forward.

Eventually, I'd come forward to. And I'd used a bat to put the kid out of his misery. It seems that's all I'm ever able to do. Kill and move on. While Mya cries in the background. Is this what this world has become? Is this how it's going to be from now on? Running for our lives. Shooting at people. Fighting just to see tomorrow.

I can't do this. I can't live like this.

I feel my heart rate picking up and my head begins to pound. *No—not here, not now.* I take a deep breath, stumbling to the side as my vision blurs. **Fear** grabs me by the ankles and claws its way up my legs, up my torso, stabbing me in the heart.

I can't *breathe*. I'm sweating, trembling so badly I drop the gun and bend over, hands on my knees.

"Adrian!" Mya is by my side now, her grief over Connor momentarily forgotten.

I feel her hands on my body, pulling me close to her. I let her lower me to the floor and I sit still while she strokes my face with her hands, asking me if I'm all right. My sweaty bangs stick to my forehead and Mya wipes them away, looking down at me with nothing but concern on her face.

I don't deserve her attention, but it's the only thing that gets me through this panic attack. *Get it together*, I tell myself, exhaling hard.

"It's okay," Mya whispers. "You did your best."

She thinks I'm freaking out over Connor, which technically, I am. But it's so much deeper than that. I can't control these attacks, and they've been happening more and more often. I don't really know what triggers them, but I've got to get them under control. I can't let myself fall apart, because when I'm *not* in control, nothing happens. We sit here in misery, weeping and wondering what we should do next. My friends need me. Mya needs me.

"I-I'm not mad at you," Mya tells me, "God isn't mad at you."

I almost chuckle. Through all of that, I hadn't thought about God in the least. Not for a second. I wonder now, as my breaths come out in strangled pants, if I had asked for His help—for His divine intervention—would He have given it? Could God have saved all three of us? I'm sure Mya was praying the entire time. And Connor is still dead.

Where were You? I pray inside.

"God, please help us," Mya gasps and clings to me, praying hard and fast. "Please, Jesus. I don't know what to do!"

I feel awful now. Here I am, reduced to *this* while my friends are still missing, and Mya is panicking right here in front of me.

Get it together.

I grit my teeth and force myself to take slow breaths, in and out. My nostrils flare as I gulp, hiccupping for air. Spittle flies from my mouth, and I grunt, exhaling hard. Mya keeps praying.

"We need Your help! We need something, God!"

Why won't You answer? My prayers inside are just as desperate, but I don't say them aloud. I don't say anything. I just focus on the gun I dropped, just a foot away from me, and I muster the strength to reach forward and grab it. Then I concentrate on my legs, telling them to move. I focus on my breathing, counting to ten until I feel like I can open my mouth without screaming.

"Adrian," Mya says beside me.

I wave her off. "I'm fine."

"But—"

"We need to find the others." My voice is raspy and strained, but Mya doesn't argue, doesn't insist I take a rest or talk about what just happened. She looks at me with sorrow tugging at the corners of her downturned mouth, and she simply nods.

"Okay."

I pull the last of my bullets from my pocket and reload my gun, then I wipe the sweat from my brow. "Stay close and stay quiet."

Mya nods again, and without a word, she follows me from the room and into the halls.

I'm honestly shocked the gunfire didn't draw any extra attention, but maybe the rest of those men are busy with our friends. When I heard Delilah's whistle, I quickly led the group back to the lobby where we ran right into an entire team of soldiers. I counted ten of them. Each one armed but only two with guns.

As soon as I saw them, I pulled the trigger and took one down. The rest scattered and started spraying bullets in every direction, which meant they hadn't seen me. That was good; they had no idea how many of us there were or if we were armed. But when I gave the order for us to move forward, Connor told me Mya and Julius were missing. That was when we split up.

We were down to nine enemies, but it was more important to keep everyone together than to fight. So I sent Connor back while I pushed ahead and tried to find Delilah and the others.

I never found them.

The soldiers didn't let up on their gunfire, fearfully spraying bullets wherever they heard movement. I was forced to turn back and cut through another hallway, hoping to find someone along the way. But I only found soldiers who'd broken off from the main group. I took another one down, and then ducked into the room where I found Mya and Connor. No Julius in sight.

Now, we're here.

Thus far... I shot one right away. Then I took a second down before finding Mya. Finally, I killed all three soldiers in that room with her and Connor. That's five total. Which means there's only five left. We officially outnumber them. But none of the soldiers I shot had guns, so we have the man count, but they have the weapons.

I press my lips together hard as I peek around a corner, holding up my hand to signal Mya to hold still. I can hear her breathing behind me, letting go of staggering, quick, little breaths, like she's trying not to exhaust herself or breathe too loudly.

I hear voices just around the corner, but I can't pinpoint how many. Right now, it sounds like at least three. But I recognize one of them.

"Where are the others?" a hard voice says.

"There aren't any more."

That voice. It … It's Julius.

Mya realizes this at the same time as me, and practically crawls over me to get a better look, but I grab her by the waist and physically lift her up to keep her from sprinting around the corner. I don't blame her haste, we just lost Connor, no one wants to lose another friend. But we also don't want to act without thinking. I need to know what exactly is going on before we burst from our hiding spot.

But Mya isn't having it, she writhes and wriggles in my arms until I almost give up and decide to let her go, but I hold tight, letting her exhaust herself. I'm *this* close to bashing her in the head with the butt of my gun just to knock her out. But, mercifully, she stops and goes limp in my arms with an angry, teary eyed huff. She twists just enough to look me in the eye, muscles straining in my grasp. I can see the hatred rolling off her as clearly as I see the tears running down both her cheeks. She hates me for this. And whatever happens next, she will blame me for it. But I'd rather have her alive and hating me than dead and wishing I'd stopped her.

I'm leaning against the wall with Mya held in my arms, her back is to my front and her feet dangle helplessly in the air.

She's five feet tall and starving, little more than the weight of a child, so I can hold her like this all day. I adjust my grip and squat a little so she's resting on my lap, then I take my chances and inch toward the end of the hall, craning my neck to get a peek around the wall.

Julius is on his knees in the middle of the open lobby, four people stand around him; two with guns, two with knives. I swallow and pray they don't hear me gulp.

"Where are the others?" A tall woman asks, she's holding an assault rifle with two hands, glaring down at Julius as she waits for an answer. Like the soldiers from before, she's wearing dark cargo pants and a matching shirt with combat boots and a bandana tied around the lower half of her face, but nothing else about her looks like she's from the military. I don't recognize her clothing, so she must be some sort of foreign force. But from where? Whose side is she fighting for?

Clearly not ours. Julius looks like he's been in a fight. His shirt is disheveled and torn, and he's bleeding from his nose. They must have subdued him and now they want to know who else is here. These people shot at us, killed Connor, and would have murdered Mya and me too if I hadn't pulled the trigger quickly enough. I can't take the risk of exposing myself. Not yet.

"You're telling me you're here all alone?" the woman says, doubt lacing her voice.

Julius only nods.

He's protecting us.

"That isn't possible. When we arrived, someone fired at us. But you don't have a gun," the woman explains. "So, there's at least one person here with you. Where is he?"

Julius slowly lifts his head—and he looks right at me. I know he sees me from the way his eyes widen, but that's his only reaction. He plays it cool and drops his gaze to the floor as he takes a deep breath. "There was a guy. If you can't find him it's because you killed him, or he got himself out of here."

"Would your friend really abandon you?" the woman questions.

Julius looks up again, and I know his words are for me. "It's what I'd want him to do."

Move, I tell myself. Julius is telling me to get out of here. But I can't. He's *right there* and I have a *gun*—I can do something. I *should* do something. But what? They have assault rifles; versus my handgun, the winner would be obvious.

What can I do? *What can I do?*

Mya shifts against me again, trying to pull out of my grasp. I hold on to her, but only to keep myself centered, rooted. I feel like I'm slipping away, even though it's Julius who's being held at gunpoint. He's perfectly calm, every part of him is in control. Yet, I'm losing my mind.

How many people will slip away from me?

My family. My friends. Now even my own rival. Everyone is leaving—*God, GOD! HELP!*

The only response I hear is the pounding of boots, it shatters the madness threatening to swallow me whole. My eyes pop open and I glance back around the corner to see a soldier running toward the group. That's the fifth guy. They're all there now, which means the rest of the building is safe for us to travel. This is it. Our chance to get away. But Mya would never let me leave without Julius. I can feel her thrashing against me now and it's all I can do to keep her there in place. I hold her tight, arms wrapped around her in a bear hug, and I

141

sit there and watch this play out like my own personal punishment.

I can't save Julius, but I can do everything in my power to remember this. To learn everything I can so when the time comes, I can track these people down, and I can get Julius back.

The jogging soldier calls out, "I found a body!"

The woman with the rifle snaps her head up. "One of ours?"

"Three of ours," he replies. "And one of theirs."

He's talking about Connor and those other guys.

"Some sort of fight happened," the jogger continues. "They're all dead."

Julius opens his mouth, but no sound comes out. I can see his eyes blinking rapidly—he's panicking, realizing one of us is dead.

"Looks like you were telling the truth," the woman says, though she sounds disappointed. "We did kill your boy."

"He went down swinging," says the jogger. "Took out three of ours."

The woman's eyes narrow. "By himself?"

The jogger shakes his head. "Our guys were shot."

She nods. "Where's the gun?"

Right here. In my waistband. I'm itching to snatch it out and fire, but if I do that, I'll get mowed down by two assault rifles, and then everyone will be dead.

"Couldn't find it," the jogger says. "Maybe it was lost in the chaos."

"Or maybe someone else has it," she says, looking around.

One of the other soldiers sucks his teeth. "Keoni, we don't have time for this. We weren't even supposed to stop here— and now half of us are dead!"

142

Keoni, the female soldier, whirls around and glares at the man. "What are you trying to say?" she snaps.

"I'm saying we should get out of here. We've lost enough."

The rest of the group shifts uncomfortably, unsure if they're allowed to agree or not.

The woman sighs. Hangs her head. "Fine. Let's take him and go."

"Take him?" The jogger looks confused.

"You know the rules," Keoni says, swinging her rifle over her shoulder. She unclips a radio from her hip and speaks into it. "Enrique, pull around front."

In response, one of the other guys steps forward to grab Julius who immediately begins to struggle.

Mya starts to fight too, shoving against me and writhing in my arms. I lose her for a second, and she stumbles right into the middle of the hall where those people can see her. But Julius is still fighting like a mad man, so they're all distracted by him. The woman is holding her rifle and yelling orders, two guys try to subdue Julius while another aims his rifle but clearly isn't sure if he should shoot or not. The last guy runs over with a black bag and tries to cram it over Julius's head, but he shoves and kicks and screams.

And then he stops.

He's staring across the lobby at Mya who is watching with tears streaking down her face. Then his face disappears beneath that black bag and the other guys are dragging him away. At the same time, I yank Mya back around the corner by the collar of her shirt. She doesn't fight me. In fact, she collapses against me and sobs like a baby, screaming into my chest. The only sound louder than her wails is Julius's voice. He's shouting over everything, a message for us all.

"I WON' FORGET THIS PLACE! ORLY CENTER IS WHERE I'LL GO!"

I know what he's saying. If he gets the chance to escape, he'll meet us here. But that's only *if...*

Julius shouts until his voice cracks, and then he starts again, fumbling and fighting the entire time. I hold on to Mya as she weeps, pressing her face into my chest to cover the sound of her crying. If Julius weren't so loud, we'd have been caught twice already. But his fighting and his shouting saved us. He's still screaming now, until that woman gets angry and yells, "Someone make him hush up!" And then there's a thud and, finally, silence.

15

Mya

I can't breathe. Julius is gone—he's *gone*. As I stare across the now empty lobby, I hear the sound of a vehicle driving away and it breaks me. They're taking him. They're taking him!

I don't realize I'm screaming until I see Adrian's face appear in my narrowed vision. His handsome features block out everything; I stare at his nose as he speaks, trying to stay focused, listening to each individual word.

"It'll be okay … Listen … Find him."

I only pick up bits and pieces of his words. My hearing goes in and out with my heartbeat, like my mind can't choose what to focus on, the panic or the pain. Both of them are overwhelming, but I snap out of my daze when I see a figure emerge from behind a destroyed desk ahead of us.

Adrian notices my attention and turns to see what I'm staring at. It's a person. Bunny.

"You're okay," Adrian says, momentarily forgetting about me.

Bunny nods solemnly. "We're all okay." His voice sounds raspy, like he's dangerously close to breaking down. Just like me. "Delilah! Jupiter!" he calls, and the two ladies slowly crawl out of their hiding places.

Adrian looks relieved, but I feel infuriated.

"You were all here!" I shout, jabbing an accusatory finger at them all. "You were there, and you watched him get taken! None of you tried to help!"

"What could we have done?" Bunny sounds so miserable, I almost feel bad for him. But I'm hurt too. I lost my best friend, the one guy I'd known since childhood, the only constant figure in my life. My mother left. My father is gone. Julius was all I had. And now he's gone too.

Why? The question shreds me from the inside, and the pain bleeds from my mouth in a gut-wrenching **scream**. I break. Shrieking, bellowing out terrible sobs as my strength and my mind leaves me. My hands slap the dirty tiles of the lobby floor when I fall to my knees, deranged and in so much pain that I cannot even think.

I feel Adrian by my side, but I can't tell if he's talking to me, if he's telling me to calm down, if he's rubbing my back, trying to let me know it'll be okay. All I can do is cry. Scream. And pound my fists on the floor. My throat goes raw, and I choke on my tears, ribs aching from the exertion. I'm vaguely aware of someone else nearby, and I try to push myself to my feet, but I slip.

That's when I see the blood. My fingers are bloody, the nails broken and bent backwards into sharp, jagged edges. I've bruised my hands, clawing at the tiled floor in anguish. I've torn the flesh of my palms, banging my fists on the gritty ground. I've chipped every nail on every finger. I'm a mess. And I don't care—I *can't* care. The only thought in my mind is that Julius was here … and now he is not.

"They took him…" the words are poison leaking from my mouth, acidic on my tongue. The truth burns worse than the tears and summons another storm of violent grief.

I curl into fetal position and sob until I see only darkness.

— * —

When I open my eyes again, I'm no longer in the Orly Center lobby. I'm on a carpeted floor with a blanket of some sort pulled over my body. Slowly, I sit up and blink away the crust in my eyes. I feel the salty residue of my tears crumble down my cheeks, and I exhale slowly, trying to figure out where I'm at. When I reach up to wipe my face, I pause and stare at the bandages on my fingers.

That's right… I'd nearly lost my mind after watching Julie get taken. But there's no time to focus on that. From my position, I can see a circle of people in the distance, they're all standing together and staring at something in the middle of the group. A large lump covered by a sheet.

I try to speak, but my throat is so dry I just end up coughing. The sound catches the attention of one of the figures in the distance. I recognize it as Adrian right away, his white hair makes him stand out so much.

He jogs over to me and squats so we're eye level. "You're awake," he says.

147

I nod.

"I have some water in my pack. Are you thirsty?"

I nod again, feeling very much like a child.

Adrian doesn't seem to mind, he turns, and I notice his bag in a pile with a bunch of others. That's what makes me glance around and study the room. It looks familiar.

"Where?" That's all I can get out before my dry throat closes and I lapse into a coughing fit again.

Adrian passes me a bottle. "They wanted to see Connor one last time."

Oh... We're in the room where he was killed. Those figures standing in a circle are our friends ... and that lump in the middle is Connor's body, covered by a sheet.

I gulp down the water just to buy myself some time. I don't want to say anything because if I open my mouth, I'm not sure if words or sobs will come out. So I drink until Adrian reaches for the bottle.

"Take slow sips," he says calmly.

I nod and let him take the bottle, watching sadly as he recaps it and puts it away.

"You told the others?" I ask.

He knows what I'm talking about and simply tucks his chin in reply. "After you passed out, we had a long talk. Delilah told me how she heard a truck pull up and then heard footsteps. She only had time to whistle before running to hide. When the shooting started, she ran and bumped into Bunny—who'd gotten separated from me—and then they found Jupiter together. They managed to find Julius, but then they were cornered by the soldiers. Julius exposed himself to give them time to hide. We walked into the middle of the showdown."

I press my lips together. "Oh."

"When I told them what we'd been up to, they asked to see Connor's body." Adrian runs his hand through his hair. "I carried you here in case... I mean—" he sighs. "You should join us if you want to say goodbye."

Adrian helps me to my feet, and we make our way to the small circle in the distance. Each of them looks at me but no one makes eye contact. Bunny stares at my thickly bandaged hands, Jupiter glances at my unruly hair, Delilah offers a weak smile to my forehead and quickly drops her gaze to Connor's covered body.

"We've already said something." Adrian nudges me. "If you have any special words."

I lick my lips, trying hard not to lose myself to the tears I feel pricking the backs of my eyes. "Um... I'm so sorry. I wish things could be different. But ... we'll find Julius for you. We'll bring him back—"

Jupiter sucks her teeth, and I immediately fall silent, blinking in confusion. Her face is pinched in anger, emotions barely contained within the lines of her wrinkled forehead. When she opens her mouth, her voice is cold and dead.

"Connor is *dead* and you're making this about Caesar."

I blink. "Th-They were friends."

"And now they're not because of you."

"Excuse me?"

"Why do you think any of this happened?"

"You cannot be serious."

Here she goes again with the blame game.

I place my hand on my chest. "You're blaming me for all of this?"

Jupiter's voice becomes a growl. "Ever since we left campus, you have been at the center of every problem in our group."

"J-Jupe…" I have no idea what to say. Jupiter is my closest friend from school, the only friend I made, considering I was only there for a few days before the power went out. She was my roommate, a pink-haired princess who stood out as much as I did for my goth clothes. We were a match made in Heaven. And now she's blaming me for the hell we've been through.

This isn't the first time she's turned her back on me. Back at campus, she remained silent when our dorm parents told me I'd been involved in too much drama. They thought I wasn't being a good Christian because I'd been friends with Julius, and he'd stirred up trouble with the sorority and his own fraternity brothers. I'd had nothing to do with that, but just being associated with Julie had marred my reputation around the Hope House dorm.

It seems the same thing has happened here. Except Jupiter is the one pointing her finger, not my uptight dorm parents. But that doesn't matter because, like before, no one sticks up for me. Except Adrian.

"Jupiter, how can you blame Mya for this? Connor wasn't killed because of her."

Except he was… Adrian had a choice and he'd chosen me. I know that. Adrian knows that. Connor knew that. But our friends have no idea. That's why they stare between us with shocked looks on their faces. Bunny and Delilah have no idea what to say or who to side with, but that doesn't stop Jupiter from spewing more hatred.

"She might not have pulled the trigger, but it's all the same," Jupe hisses. "Did you fight for Connor as hard as you would have fought for Mya?"

Adrian's wide-eyed stare slowly narrows into a hard glare. His voice is a solid grunt, firm, unmoving, like this last word will be the end of the discussion. "Yes."

"*Liar,*" Jupiter spits. "We all know you're in love with Mya. You probably let Connor die—"

"That's enough!" I snap.

"It's the truth!" Jupiter snaps back. "I'm so tired of all the drama we have to live through because of you. As if surviving an apocalypse isn't hard enough."

"What drama?" I say stupidly, as if I don't know.

Jupiter chuckles. "Adrian is in love with you. Caesar is in love with you. But Delilah loves Caesar, and since he was obsessed with *you*, she decided to bang Connor as a distraction."

Delilah shifts uncomfortably.

"Do you know what kind of atmosphere that built for everyone else? Do you even care?" She scoffs. "Probably not. Just like you don't really care about Connor."

"He was my friend too," I say weakly.

"Yet, your last words to him are about *Caesar.*"

"Jupiter, that's enough," Adrian says calmly.

She shakes her head. "Look at you defending her. Why was our group even separated? Because MYA and Caesar stayed back—for what? Probably to screw," she sneers right at me, mouth wrinkling into a puckered frown. "Some Christian you are."

"How dare you," I whisper.

"You think I don't know about you two sneaking off? I'm not stupid. I know you and Caesar did far more than any Christian couple should have."

"What I do in my relationship is none of your business."

She shakes her head. "But it became my business because your relationship took over the house, Mya. You, Adrian, Caesar, Delilah, Connor—*all* of you were tied up in some stupid drama where *you* were at the very center. All day. Every day." She motions to Connor's lifeless body in the middle of our little circle. "Now look where it's gotten us. One of us is dead and another is missing."

"You are so far out of line," I say. "This place was attacked by enemy soldiers—that had nothing to do with *drama*. And the last I heard, Julius exposed himself to the soldiers so you and the others could hide." I take a step forward, getting right into her face. "That means Julius is gone because of *you*."

Jupiter glares at me, but as I look into her eyes, I don't see hatred anymore. I don't even see anger. I see pain. Raw pain with nowhere to go, nowhere to hide. So instead of letting it sink into her heart, she's spewing it at me.

Pain ... something we're all feeling too much of right now. But it does make me wonder if maybe Jupiter cared more for Connor than anyone else ever knew. If maybe, she blames me for something else that she isn't saying.

Delilah loves Julius, but since Julius loves me, she used Connor to get over the pain of rejection. And maybe Connor was too distracted by Delilah to notice the gaze of a quiet pink-haired Christian girl. Maybe if I had let Julius go, he would've dated Delilah. And Connor would have been free for Jupiter to love. And then... Maybe those two would have been together when the soldiers arrived. Maybe I would have been

152

by Adrian's side, and Julie would've been with Delilah, and Jupiter and Connor would've been together. Safe. Alive.

But that isn't how things went down. All that is just wishful thinking, desperate speculation. An 'if only' that never happened. This is the reality we are facing, and we've got to deal with it. No matter how painful it is.

I feel sorry for Jupiter. But I never get to tell her this, the next second, Adrian pulls me out of her face and steps between us.

"That's enough," he says calmly. "Let's say our goodbyes to Connor and move on. It's all we can do."

Bunny clears his throat. "Maybe this is the time we should discuss splitting up."

"Are you serious?" Adrian questions.

"I'd love to split up," Jupiter mutters.

"That's your pain talking," Adrian replies. "We need each other right now. All of us."

"Adrian is right," Delilah agrees. "You heard what Caesar said. This is where he'll come back to."

"That's only if he gets away," Bunny replies. "What if he doesn't escape? What if they kill him?"

"They won't," I snap.

Bunny glances at the floor. "So, what should we do? Stay here and hope Caesar miraculously appears? What if more soldiers come? And..." he looks at Connor's covered body. "I don't *want* to stay here anymore."

Adrian sighs slowly. "It isn't safe to stay here. But we owe it to Julius to wait a few days at least. Maybe he will get a miracle chance to escape. Maybe not." He looks at me, a sheepish expression taking over his normally hardened features. When he speaks, he drops his gaze. "Let's stay for two

153

days. Spend that time looting and collecting information on where we should go next. Then we'll move out, with or without Julius."

The others nod agreement. I don't move, but that doesn't matter. I've clearly been outvoted. In two days, we are leaving whether I want to or not.

16

Caesar

I'm moving—well, not *me*, I'm sitting in a vehicle and *it's* moving. Taking me somewhere. A place I have never been and likely will never leave. They got me. They've taken me. I belong to them now.

The truth awakens a slow panic. It starts in my gut, churning, making me nauseous, and then it travels to my chest, burning, and settles in my mind. Flashes of Mya's tearful face pop into my head like two-second nightmares. The look on her face as she realized this was the end hurts as much as the ropes that keep my hands tied behind my back now. They're knotted so tightly; I can barely feel my fingers anymore. But nothing hurts more than the truth, the fact that I'm here and my friends are back there.

I see Mya's awful, fearful expression again, and I squeeze my eyes shut to block out the memories. There's no point in doing that; with this bag over my head, it's so dark I can't tell if my eyes are open or shut.

The slow panic returns.

I'm hyperventilating now, sucking in gasps so deep, I get a mouthful of the tattered bag over my head and exhale a scream. Pain erupts in my side, sending me toppling over in a heap. Someone kicked me, the realization hits me with another jolt of pain as I'm kicked again—*no*—as I'm *stomped* by a heavy boot. I grit my teeth, curling up on the floor of the truck as the foot comes down once more. It stomps the wind out of me.

"Shut up, kid!" a dark voice barks.

My teeth snap shut, cutting off the cries of pain I'd been wailing. I hadn't even known I was screaming. That's what this awful black silence does to you. It drives you mad. The unknown. The mystery. I'm swimming in murky waters, and in the absence of truth, they've filled my mind with lies and fear and assumptions that are only dark and frightening.

"W-Where are you taking me?" I whimper pathetically. "Please…"

No one answers.

I sniffle, unsure if its blood or snot dripping from my nose. "Please…"

"Someone make him shut up," that dark voice says.

I feel him raising his boot again and I tense, trying to protect myself from the blow, but a feminine voice speaks up.

"That's enough. He's scared, leave him alone."

There had been a woman leading the group, they'd called her name at Orly Center, but I can't remember it now. Still, I try to reach out to her since she's the only one showing any sympathy right now.

"Lady," I say cautiously.

156

Someone snickers nearby, mocking me. "*Lady*..."

"What is it, kid?" the woman responds.

"We aren't supposed to talk to him," that dark voice barks again.

The woman ignores him. "What is it, kid?" she repeats.

"Can you untie me?"

There's a short pause. "You're a fighter. We don't trust fighters."

I *almost* understand her sentiment. I broke someone's nose back at Orly Center and kicked another guy in the nuts— probably that angry barking dude who stomped on me. Vengeance and all that. Plus, my famous last words which I'd screamed at the top of my lungs.

I WON' FORGET THIS PLACE! ORLY CENTER IS WHERE I'LL GO!

I have to get away from these people. Find an escape. That is my only goal from this point forward. So I get it; these people don't trust me, which is probably a good call. I won't make any promises to sit still if they do untie me.

I shift uncomfortably, tugging on the ties keeping my wrists bound. There are ropes tied around my ankles too, so I'm lying helplessly on my side as I plead my case.

"I ... I won't fight," I whisper behind the dark bag.

I hear someone sigh and then footsteps shuffle toward me. There were five people left in Orly Center, plus the driver who stayed in the vehicle. I never saw the vehicle, but I know this group was originally ten strong, that means this is large enough to hold nearly a dozen passengers. We must be in some sort of truck or van—maybe a military Humvee. From the hollow sounds of the footsteps approaching me, I'd say there's no carpeting inside, and clearly there is walking space. Plus, my face is pressed against a cool *metal* floor. Definitely a van, then? Like those giant white serial killer vans from horror movies. The ones they snatch women and children into.

I gulp, trying not to think about that right now, and then my dark worries vanish when I feel something shove me onto my belly. I scream and thrash, but a heavy boot comes down on the center of my back. The pain pins me in place, and I stiffen.

"Wait!" I shout, panicking.

"Calm down," the woman says, then I feel the ties around my wrists loosen a bit and I sigh as blood rushes back into my fingers.

"There you go," the lady says.

The boot is finally removed from my back, and I realize I can breathe again. I'm still tied up, but the ropes aren't cutting off my circulation anymore. Progress, I suppose.

"Thanks," I breathe.

No one replies for a while, until I hear that dark snappy voice again. "You shouldn't have done that, Keoni."

That was her name.

Keoni sounds perfectly calm, almost … sympathetic? "His fingers were purple, Claudius."

Claudius… I commit his name to memory, and vow to kick him in the nuts again. I don't know if I'll ever get the chance to do that, but that's my second goal now. Well, maybe my first. Kick Claudius in the nuts and *then* escape. For now, all I can do is hope. Hope and pray as I lie here at the mercy of the ruthless soldiers who held me at gunpoint.

I feel so pathetic, I could gag, but this is my lot. If I hadn't given myself up, we'd *all* be here in ropes with bags over our heads. That's a reality I simply couldn't live with. I surrendered so my friends could be safe. So Mya could be safe. And I was blessed enough to see her before getting taken away.

That ... That was a gift from God. It sounds weird to call it that, considering I was kidnapped and all that. But at this point, I'm so desperate and nearly broken, I have to look on the bright side. Because if I don't focus on the blessings, I'm only left with the darkness. And that will swallow me whole. How could it not? Right now, it seems like there's so much darkness. More darkness than light.

Where are You, God? I pray inside. I'd tried to do the right thing. I had decided that waiting was worth it. I was turning my life around, and now *this*. Why didn't I get taken when I was rolling around with Delilah? Or trying to convince Mya to abandon her faith and sleep with me? Why was I taken right after trying to do the *right* thing for once?

Sometimes I feel like Christianity doesn't make sense. The closer you get to God; the more darkness comes after you. Why? I thought it was supposed to get easier after you surrender to the Lord, but the fighting has only gotten worse. The *world* has gotten worse.

Where are You? The question burns me, almost makes me angry. *I was kidnapped!* Yes, Mya is safe, but one of my friends isn't even here anymore. I haven't forgotten that tidbit of information. One of Keoni's soldiers said they found a body in a room somewhere.

Whose body...

It wasn't Adrian's or Mya's. I know because I saw them— and I'd been with Delilah, Bunny, and Jupiter right before the soldiers found us. I told them to hide and revealed myself to give them more time to get away. That only leaves Connor...

But … Maybe I'm wrong. Maybe Delilah and the others didn't get far enough away. Maybe they bumped into more trouble somewhere else.

I slowly exhale, smelling my own sour breath as it fills the bag over my head. I stink. Everybody stinks, but I stink of sweat and fear and growing rage.

Why did You let my friend die… I expect the question to leave me bitter and infuriated, but the anger cracks me open inside. Instead of being angry at God, I feel hurt. *Don't focus on the darkness*, I tell myself, but it's useless. I've already let the darkness in. Here comes the pain, the sorrow, the worry, the fear.

Everything was fine. Everyone was safe. Mya had found clues to her father's whereabouts; and she'd been so happy to hear that I'd decided to wait with her. She was going to give me another chance. I know it. I can see her reaching for my hand in that room, I can see the hesitant, fearful smile on her face. As if she hadn't been sure if she could trust me yet. I was willing to wait as long as it took to prove to her that I loved her. That she was worth the wait. And that God would give us both the strength to make it through this.

But our happiness was cut short. Disrupted by a whistle that changed everything. And now, here I am. Writhing on the floor of a van as I battle my own sorrows. *I'm hurt…* I tell God. *I don't want to be here… I'm hurt, God…* So deeply hurt that I cannot form any more words in this desperate prayer.

So I don't pray. I just lie there and weep, pretending the silent soldiers aren't listening.

17

Mya

I stare into my bowl of canned chili. It's cold and unappetizing, like all our food lately. Adrian won't let us light a fire unless we absolutely need it, since hot food is a luxury not a necessity—as he put it—we've been enjoying our rations straight out the can. Like true survivalists.

I'm miserable. We're all miserable. Connor's death and Julie's kidnapping has brought out the worst in all of us. Jupiter went from drowning in silent depression to snapping at everyone over everything. Delilah walks around with red-rimmed eyes and doesn't make eye contact with anyone. Bunny only speaks to Adrian, and lately their exchanges have been strained, like they're one word away from screaming at each other.

This is bad. But I don't know how to make it better. I can barely grieve over the loss of Julius because everyone thinks I'm making the whole situation about myself. So I have to keep my pain inside, all because Delilah had a crush. It isn't my fault Julius didn't like her back. It isn't my fault Adrian developed feelings for me too. It isn't my fault Delilah used Connor to get over Julius. These things just happened. Simple college drama, nothing more. But nobody else sees it that way.

Even Adrian has been distant, but in his defense, I can't tell if he's avoiding me or just trying to stay focused on keeping the group alive and together. That isn't an easy task.

It's been two days since the big event, and we've found no other clues about my father or any other family members. Adrian's best suggestion is to simply check all the major stadiums and large buildings in the nearby cities until we find another shelter. It's a shot in the dark, but what else are we supposed to do? Those soldiers showing up proved that no place is safe. If we want to find our families or get Julius back, we've got to keep moving.

We all know this, but we're severely lacking motivation right now. No motivation means no morale. No morale means no peace, no unity, no long-term survival.

I glance around the circle of people I once called my friends, each of us is frowning, staring blankly at our food, or even crying. There are literal tears running down Delilah's face, dripping into her cup of chili. She doesn't seem to notice, not even when a dribble of snot folds over the curve of her upper lip. I try not to grimace as I watch her.

After a few agonizing moments, Bunny tears off a strip of fabric from the sleeve of his shirt and passes it to Delilah. I'm not sure if he's being kind or just grossed out like the rest of us. Lilah doesn't reach for the fabric, so Bunny huffs and drops it into her lap. It lands on her cup of chili.

Jupiter sucks her teeth. "Seriously, Bunny?"

He bunches his shoulders. "What do you want me to do? Wipe her face for her? She's a grown woman."

"She's a *hurt* woman." Jupiter glares at me. "She needs help right now."

"We're *all* hurt," Bunny snaps. "You don't see me drooling and dripping snot everywhere. What's next? Should I wipe her butt when she wets her pants—*again?*" He says the last part loudly and harshly, like we don't remember Delilah waking up shrieking about soldiers last night. She'd had a nightmare about Connor's death—which she didn't even witness—and woke up screaming. Jupiter and Adrian had to hold her down until it passed, she wet herself and then lapsed into a sobbing fit which kept us all up for the rest of the night.

Adrian had to change his shirt since he'd been holding her down when she peed. Jupiter used the last of our wet wipes to clean Delilah up like a 20-year-old baby. She undressed her right there in the middle of the room and wiped her down, whispering that she'd be okay. Delilah had only stared blankly ahead.

To my shock, no one seemed to react beyond a silent glance in Lilah's direction, not even Bunny seemed interested, despite finally having a chance to see Lilah fully naked again. It seems his burning desire toward her has somehow extinguished over the last two days. Now, it's like he can't stand the sight of her. But how else are you supposed to feel when the girl you like is wetting herself over another man right in front of you?

Bunny raises his voice as he adds to the argument, "She's a mess. I've never seen someone fall apart like this—over someone who called her a *whore* behind her back."

The sad part is, I'm not sure if he's talking about Connor or Julius. I'm sure they both had nasty things to say about Delilah when she wasn't in the room. To be honest, we all did. But it hurts to hear it said so plainly, especially with Lilah literally weeping right next to Bunny.

I wince as his words echo around the large Orly Center foyer.

We're still here. Camping out near the entrance doors. After two days of endless searching, Adrian finally told us we would leave tomorrow morning. I don't want to abandon the one place Julius said he would return to, but Orly Center feels like one big tomb now, filled with death and sorrow.

Jupiter takes the strip of fabric and gently wipes Lilah's tears, then her nose. "Blow," she whispers, and Delilah blows into the makeshift handkerchief.

Bunny grumbles and shifts away, glowering into his chili. "This is ridiculous."

"What's ridiculous is how callous you've gotten," Jupiter scolds.

"I'm not being callous. I'm being practical. Delilah is useless now. We should leave her."

"How dare you…" Jupiter stands, but she doesn't move, just glares down at Bunny who hasn't even bothered to turn and face her. "Is that really how you feel?" she goes on. "As soon as someone starts to fall behind, you want to give up and leave them?"

"I'm just saying," Bunny grumbles. "We can't afford to take care of a vegetable right now."

"We're not leaving her," I say softly. Jupiter snaps her searing gaze toward me, but I ignore her, staring at my cold food as I continue, "Adrian said we're staying together."

"*Adrian* said…" Bunny grips his can of chili. "Thanks to what *Adrian* said, we're eating cold food now."

"Have you forgotten how those soldiers found us?" I challenge. "You heard what they said before they took Julius away. They weren't planning on stopping here, so what made them change their minds?" I shake my cold can of chili. "They saw our fire the night before. The fire we used to heat our chicken soup."

This is all speculation, but we had a pretty big fight about the no-fire or flashlight rule the day after Julius was taken. Obviously, we all wanted to heat our food, but Adrian had insisted we skip the flames until we leave this place. When we pressed him on the decision, he explained his theory, saying the soldiers found us because we'd lit a fire in the surrounding area the night before. They likely saw the smoke and figured whoever lit it had moved on to Orly Center during the day. And they'd been right.

It's speculation, like it said. This could all be entirely wrong. But it could also be completely true. Either way, Adrian made himself clear; no more fires until we're far away from Orly Center. As our elected group leader, no one challenged him on that, not even now when he's marching the perimeter and we're all alone with the few matches we've got left. We could light a fire and put it out before he gets back, but we all know there's a frighteningly real chance that Adrian's theory is correct. After losing Connor and Julius, we're not willing to take that chance.

Bunny knows this, which is why I won't let him hold this against Adrian now. Besides, cold food is the least of our worries.

"We have bigger problems than cold food," I say, glancing down at my half-eaten can. "Let's do our best to get along and put our differences aside."

Bunny drops his can and stands. "Of course you want to put our differences aside when everyone hates you and blames you for everything." He walks away before I can respond, kicking aside his can of chili. It topples over and splatters, spilling red tomato sauce and kidney beans on the tile floor. I stare at the stains, hoping no one sees my cheeks and ears burning.

Bunny's footsteps fill the foyer, sounding more like claps of thunder as he stomps away in anger. This place is so empty of life yet completely full of all its hardships and frustrations. We need to leave before it consumes us all. It's already gotten Delilah who can barely speak or control her own bladder anymore. It's changed Jupiter into an angry, bitter enemy. And now it's set its sights on Bunny, turning a charming, sweet young man into this grumbling fox who skulks away after every disagreement.

Bunny's platinum blonde hair and shining blue eyes had been so pretty when I'd first met him. Like his nickname suggests, he'd been cute and full of life, though rather small for a guy in his twenties. If he weren't on the track team, I would've guessed that he was a model. He wasn't handsome, he was beautiful. *Picturesque*, like a living doll with a smile that could make a grown man blush. I've seen just as many men as I've seen women staring at Bunny. Even his own frat brothers had made jokes, calling him the babe of the house, saying he was prettier than half the sorority girls. But now ... he does nothing but scowl and complain and kick over cans of food.

I sigh, wondering how much I've changed since everything went down.

Something beside me shifts, and I realize Jupiter is still standing, staring after Bunny who's on the other side of the room now. She nibbles her lip in thought.

"I meant what I said," I say gently, hoping my words don't start an argument. "We should put our differences aside."

For a second, I think Jupiter might agree with me. She holds her gaze on Bunny, still nibbling her bottom lip like she's contemplating my suggestion. But then she closes her eyes, takes a deep breath, and looks down at me. Her eyes are dead, void of all emotion.

"Someone died, Mya. That's not something we can just put aside."

She blamed me for the death of that woman from the elementary school, I shouldn't be surprised she's doing it again. But I am—because she sounds ridiculous.

"I didn't pull the trigger myself. Connor was killed by a soldier. Julius was taken by a soldier. How can you seriously blame me for that?"

Jupiter shakes her head. "You don't get it."

"I do." I look away, unsure if I should bring this up, but I'm out of options. This is the last card I can play, and I'm not playing it to hurt her, I'm just trying to reach her. To relate to her. "I know you had feelings for Connor—"

Someone gasps, and I look up in shock to find Delilah glaring at me. For the first time since Julie's kidnapping, she looks more alive than dead. But the fire in her eyes is aimed at me and it makes me swallow, glancing back and forth between the two girls. Girls who had previously never spoken to each other before, but now—because of me—they've suddenly formed an alliance.

"Look," I say slowly, "Connor was a nice guy. I can see why you fell for him, Jupiter."

Jupiter lets out a noise that isn't quite a chuckle or a scoff, it's the literal sound of disgust. Like she might have even gagged. "Are you serious right now? Do you honestly believe every problem in everyone's life boils down to some boy they had a crush on?"

I blink at her. "You've been so upset—"

"I'm upset because someone *died!* Not because I wanted to be his girlfriend!"

Delilah shakes her head at me, and I can see the bricks falling into place, building a wall between myself and them. I'm on the other side, slowly getting boxed out, and there's nothing I can do about it.

"How could you twist this into some stupid love triangle again?" Delilah says angrily.

"That's not what I—"

"Connor had real feelings for me!" Her voice is sharp and loud, loud enough that I see Bunny look up from across the room. He's staring at us now, unsure if he should mosey back over or steer clear of the drama. Delilah wobbles to her feet and stands beside Jupiter to glare down at me too. I suddenly feel so small. So pathetic. I hate the way my eyes begin to burn with tears, and I reflexively drop my head to keep anyone from seeing.

Don't cry. Don't cry. Don't cry.

"You think every boy who paid me any attention was only after one thing," Delilah hisses. "You think every guy in my life was some leftover chump from a love triangle with you at

168

the center." I hear her take a step closer. "Connor's feelings were *real*, and they had nothing to do with you."

"I never said they did!" I snap, jerking my head up. I don't care if they see me crying, I'm tired of being the good little Christian girl. Sitting here and taking their insults without ever responding.

It's okay to stand up for yourself, I tell myself. *Meekness is not weakness.*

I think of Jesus who drove merchants out of his Father's house with a handmade whip. I think of Paul who debated Jewish leaders for hours over the truth in the resurrection of Christ. I think of Queen Esther who broke the law and threw away her husband's authority to carry out God's will and stand up for God's people. I am God's child, and I can stand up for myself too.

I clench my can of chili, squeezing so tightly, I feel it begin to fold inward. "I am not placing myself at the center of all this," I say firmly. "I'm trying to tell you guys that I'm not the reason any of this happened, but you're all so consumed with your own pain that you won't hear me out!"

"There's nothing to hear!" Jupiter yells. "Connor got killed because he went back to save you—and why had you fallen behind? Because you were in a room alone with Julius." She folds her arms. "You are the one I blame."

"Then why don't you blame Julius too?" I say. "Connor came back for *both* of us."

"Three people were left behind, and only one is still here now." Delilah looks like she could spit at me. "I think that makes it clear who's to blame."

My eyes slide over to Delilah, and I feel a cold anger wash over me. The door to my emotions flies open and they pour out, coming to life in my hateful words. "No matter what feelings Connor had," I say coldly, "you're only angry because of Julius. A boy who never thought twice about you."

Delilah's eyes widen, then sharpen as the insult begins to sting. "He slept with me the night before we entered Orly Center. You know that, right?"

I shake my head. Julie and I had discussed that night—that's why we'd fallen behind. Because he'd confessed that he'd wanted to sleep with Delilah, but he'd found the strength to say no. And he'd wanted God to give him the strength to wait for me. To wait for marriage with *me*. He had finally rejected Delilah and all of his distractions. I won't let her twist the truth as a weak attempt to hurt me.

"Julius left you there that night," I say darkly. "He left you and came to me. Like he's always—"

I don't get to finish my sentence. Delilah's hand is a quick blur, and there's no time to react. She slaps me across my face so hard, my head whips to the side and my neck cracks with the sudden motion. I cry out, more in surprise than pain, and drop my can of chili to the floor.

Slowly, I reach up and touch my cheek. It stings, making me blink rapidly as tears fill my eyes. She hit me. She hit me in the face.

I glance up. Delilah looks hot with anger, but Jupiter has the decency to look shocked. No one had expected that, not even Bunny who's standing now, staring across the foyer through wide, bewildered eyes.

"You think you're so much better than me." Delilah points at me. "You think your boring little Christian life makes you a princess and makes me a whore, but you're just like me."

I clench my jaw, still too shocked to speak.

"How many men have you slept with *up here?*" Delilah taps the side of her head, and I feel myself shrivel up inside.

She's completely right. Sexual sin can live in your thoughts, in your mind, in your daydreams, in your heart, just as much as it lives in your physical life. You can commit adultery without ever taking your clothes off, Jesus said as much when He declared, *anyone who looks at a woman lustfully has already committed adultery with her in his heart.* Delilah has a bad reputation because we all know what she's done. Some of us have witnessed it. But how many would shake their heads at me if they could crack open my skull and peer into my darkest thoughts?

Delilah laughs, it's high-pitched and lilting, like a witch's cackle. "You think about Julius exactly the same way I do, don't you? And Adrian too."

I squeeze my eyes shut.

"I bet you fantasize about them both. At the same time. I bet you practice your moans at night as you touch yourself."

"That's enough!"

My eyes pop open to see Jupiter standing between me and Delilah. She's glaring at Lilah now, issuing a silent warning. Whatever that warning is, it makes her yield to my pink-haired friend.

Without a word, Delilah returns to her seat and flops down with a huff. Jupiter glances down at me and then walks away. She offers no apology. She doesn't even speak again. She just sits down and grabs her cup of chili. I reach for my own and eat my cold food in silence.

18

Caesar

We've been riding for days. The only time anyone acknowledges my existence is when I make too much noise, and someone kicks me in response. We've stopped a few times; I think I've counted two stops a day. Which means we've been driving for at least two and a half days.

I have never had my bag removed.

Each time we stop, someone yanks me to my feet and shoves me out the van. After they untie the ropes on my legs, I walk slowly because I tripped during the first stop and nearly twisted my ankle. Typically, one of the soldiers will take me to a spot and let me use the bathroom, then they'll give me food and water. Twice a day, that's it. And the bag never comes off. Shamefully, neither do the ropes on my wrists. This means, when I use the bathroom, someone yanks down my jeans and underwear and lets me pee. When I'm done, I do a little hop to shake off excess urine, and some lovely unnamed soldier yanks my jeans back up and zips me up nicely.

I stopped feeling embarrassed for myself a long time ago, but I have enough dignity not to pop a squat and push out a turd. Whoever is in charge of bathroom breaks is *not* gentle. My junk is *sore* from being crammed back into my own pants.

As a man, I totally understand the anger one might feel with being handed the task of yanking down a prisoner's pants and watching him pee. It's a miracle they don't make me wet myself, so I seriously doubt anyone would be willing to wipe my butt if I ever tried to poop out here. That means I'm probably constipated. But I'd rather suffer a hard poo than have a grown man bend me over and wipe my rear while I'm tied up and blinded.

That's just not happening.

Eating is a lot less embarrassing. One of the soldiers simply slides food under my hood and I'm hand-fed something like stale bread and hard salami each day. Afterward, the mystery solider snakes a straw under the bag and I enjoy a few precious sips of water.

Annnnnd it's back in the van after that.

They're feeding me and going through the awkward trouble of yanking down my pants just to let me pee. I'm fully convinced these people aren't going to kill me, but I don't feel secure enough to believe I'm out of danger yet. No one speaks to me. They give me the bare minimum of food and water even though I hear them munching on snacks all the time while we drive. And they aren't afraid to smack me around whenever I get on their nerves.

These people are keeping me alive, but I'm not sure what for or for how long. I want to ask, but I just *know* Claudius is waiting for another chance to stomp on me. At this point, I've been kicked so many times I'm sure there's a boot print over my ribs.

Suddenly, the van begins to slow, and I feel my muscles reflexively tense up. We made our first stop about two hours ago. We haven't been driving long enough to stop again. Maybe they're switching drivers? The thought swells in my head like a balloon inflated by hope, but it bursts when I hear Claudius's dark voice rasp, "Finally." The word comes out like a groan, and I imagine him stretching—something I would love to do myself. But instead of unfurling and feeling my joints pop, I'm grabbed roughly by the collar of my shirt and dragged out of the van.

I hit the ground hard and, despite the darkness of the bag over my head, I see stars burst into my vision. It's only made worse when the bag is snatched off my head entirely and my eyes are assaulted by afternoon sunlight. It burns, summoning painful tears and making my nose sting like I've got horrible allergies. I haven't had a breath of fresh air in days. I almost feel nauseous as I gasp and blink around, trying to clear my blurry vision.

"Give him some space." I hear Keoni's voice and jerk my head in the direction it came from. "I'm right here," she says warmly. I feel something tug on my wrists and relief floods through my hands as the ropes are cut away and I'm set free.

My open palms are the first thing I see clearly once the burning tears finally run down my cheeks. I'm not crying from any sort of emotion, it's honestly the dust and the sun that hurts like crap but as I glance around, I realize no one really cares so I don't bother wiping my tears. I just stare at my hands, then at Keoni. I see Claudius a few feet to the side, a bored look on his face. He blinks away like he'd rather be anywhere else than here.

That's when I realize where *here* is.

I'm at a camp. A bustling, thriving refugee camp. Like what Orly Center was supposed to be—except better. There are people everywhere, and they don't look hungry or half-dead or filled with fear. There are men carrying baskets of laundry and women pushing carts of fresh vegetables. I even see children laughing and dashing in and out of the rows of tents set up like little houses along the dirt road.

There's a log cabin with a cross out front; it looks like a church but as a woman in a white coat walks out the front and waves goodbye to a child with a cast, I think it might be a little hospital. Or maybe both. There's another log cabin with a line of children sprinting out the front door and into the arms of smiling adults—a school. There are little shacks toward the further end of the road with people holding up various goods like merchants from a village. It's a sight I can't really comprehend. I don't know if my tired mind is playing tricks on me or if any of this is real.

"What... What is this?" I whisper.

"Welcome to Eternus." Keoni waves her hand as if to introduce me to this little paradise.

"Eternus?" I frown.

"Yes, the Latin word for—"

"Eternity," I cut her off, noting her raised eyebrow. "I'm quite familiar with Latin," I mutter. Somehow, I doubt this is the time to tell her my name is Julius Caesar and because of that, I've maintained a deep interest in my namesake as well as Roman history and the Latin tongue he would have spoken during his lifetime. Instead, I just say, "I studied it in school."

"How old are you?" Keoni points to the building I suspect is a school. "We're accepting teenagers for the high school classes now. There's only one teacher so most kids have class every other day, but I think we've finally got enough older kids to give the high schoolers a session by themselves. Instead of mixing them in with the elementary students."

"Um…" I don't know what to say. I'm partially surprised by how young this woman thinks I might be, but also completely shocked that we're standing here talking about school classes after she just killed one of my friends, kidnapped me, and dragged me out to Eternus—whatever the heck that even is!

Keoni must see the frustration on my face because she holds her hands up and says calmly, "Take it easy. You're safe here, buddy. This isn't a prison."

"I'm trying to figure out what the heck it is," I grind out, trying to keep myself from panicking. "You kidnapped me. You killed one of my friends—"

"*One* of them." Keoni glances down for a moment. "I knew there were more of you."

"And you knew you were taking me to a safe place." I squeeze my eyes shut, wiping my hands down my face in anger. "Why? Why didn't you say you were friendly?"

My friends would have come out of hiding. We'd all be here together if they had said they weren't there to hurt us! But instead, I'm here with a school and a church and a hospital and my friends are searching for scraps in abandoned buildings.

I double over and set my hands on my knees, taking deep breaths. Fresh tears burn my eyes—this time, they're emotional tears. Tears of pain and anger and bitter frustration. All I can see is Mya's panicked face, and it makes me want to scream. I

176

left her. I left her behind and ended up here, safe and sound. Only God knows where she's at right now, and she's probably worried sick over me.

"God…" I whisper, not caring who hears. "God *help* me."

"Kid," Keoni's voice is gentle. She squats beside me, and I focus on the shin-guards on her legs. "I'm sorry we left your friends behind."

"*Why?*" I grate out, sniffing back a glob of snot.

"Because we weren't sure we could trust you. When we arrived, you guys opened fire before we could introduce ourselves."

Adrian. Adrian and his trigger-happy, paranoid mind. Shoot first, ask questions later. That's what he did at the elementary school and that's probably what he told himself at Orly Center, thinking he was so brave and such a great leader in that moment. He damned us all. And got Connor killed. That decision immediately turned us into hostiles and made Keoni wary of our intentions. That means she took me as a hostage and willingly left the others because she wasn't sure if Adrian would murder them along the way.

If I didn't hate the guy before, I definitely feel a passionate anger burning toward Adrian now. But I don't focus on that, instead I stare at Keoni's kneepads and force myself to stay right here. Search for answers. Gather information.

"Where is Eternus?" I ask, standing upright. I wipe my nose with the back of my sleeve and look Keoni in the eye; most of her men have dispersed by now but Claudius still lingers nearby, watching us from the corner of his eye. I ignore him as I rattle off questions to his superior. "How long has this camp been around? Are you taking in survivors from anywhere?"

Keoni raises her hands to slow me down. Once I've fallen silent, she turns to leave and waves over her shoulder with a wink, "Walk with me, kid. I'll explain everything as I show you around."

19

Caesar

Eternus was established exactly two weeks after the grid went down. It was originally a Christian summer youth campsite, but when the National Guard showed up with wounded soldiers, the camp's pastor agreed to give them the soccer field and half the log cabins to use as their HQ. But that was only on the condition that they send soldiers out to find the parents of all the children who were now stranded at the camp. With the power out, their parents had no way to get to them in a timely manner, especially since the camp was hours away from the nearest city.

That turned the camp into a refugee center and established an official search-and-rescue team within the military. Keoni is in charge of that team, that's why her men were out near Orly Center. They'd already searched nearby buildings and were heading home when they decided to stop there on a whim.

"Eternus Camp was off grid before the power ever went out," Keoni explains as she points to the Eternus Chaple. It's the largest building in the camp, a big wooden church with a cross and a steeple. The whole place looks like something from an old western movie. Very old, very dated, but clearly filled with love. No one at Eternus is frowning or crying. Everyone here looks perfectly fine, like they've no clue what's happening in the world around them.

"These people didn't even know what'd happened when the Guard arrived. And for a little while, they didn't believe what the first wave of soldiers told them." Keoni looks back at me, and I gulp, afraid to ask. Apparently, I don't need to. She reads me like a book and her voice comes out in a sympathetic whisper. "You don't know either, do you?"

I shake my head, running my hand over my dark hair again. For some reason, I can't look Keoni in the eye. I don't want to see that sorry look she's wearing. Because that means things are worse than I thought. That means there's a lot to be sorry for.

"I've been living in hiding or on the run since everything went down. I have no clue how the world turned to crap like this."

Keoni sighs. "Do you want to know?"

Question of the year.

I slowly nod.

"The United States of America was attacked."

I let go of a held breath, and then I suck in a gasp at her next words.

"And so was Canada, Mexico, and parts of South America. At the same time."

My eyes widen. "How?"

"EMP bombs set off simultaneously."

"By *who*?" I think of the foreign soldiers Adrian and Connor bumped into. "They set off the bombs and invaded at the same time, didn't they?"

Keoni presses her lips together as she nods, like she hates the taste of her next words. "The attack was devastating. Giving us little time to properly respond because we didn't know who the enemy was."

"Do you know now?"

"The rest of the world."

I blink at her.

"Before the attack, the United Nations had been under intense pressure due to the war in Ukraine, China's attack on Taiwan, and the attacks launched against Israel from the Middle East." She shakes her head. "All of us were living on a knife's edge, waiting to be cut."

"World War Three had already begun," I say. "We just hadn't realized it yet."

"That's right." Keoni sighs. "At first, we assumed the attack was a Chinese-Russian joint effort. But the enemy soldiers we captured in combat were from Great Britain— wearing French uniforms and speaking Urdu. A Pakistani language."

I shake my head. "What the heck?"

"Behind our backs, the United Nations had already dissolved, deciding it was easier to wash their hands of all the drama rather than try to find the right side to pick in any of the brewing conflicts. That left the world in a free-for-all."

"Century-old alliances vanished," I whisper.

"Meaning, anyone could attack anyone."

"And so they did." I glance around at all the men and women passing me by, some in strange uniforms like Keoni's. Dark cargo pants and a matching shirt, handmade weapons, very few guns. "So, what happened to the US?"

Keoni stands back to model her uniform, showing off the fancy patch on her right shoulder. "We are now the United Americas. Since we were all attacked first and at the same time, our nations decided to stick together."

That would explain the strange military uniforms, the mysterious *5ᵗʰ Brigade* from that letter Adrian found, and the various accents from Keoni's soldiers that I couldn't pin down. The US doesn't really exist anymore, not as it used to.

Keoni senses my understanding and smiles. She'd finally removed the bandana that'd covered the lower half of her face all this time, so now I can see she's got perfectly straight teeth and full lips that match well with her dark brown skin and short mohawk.

"There's a lot to work out with what this country has become. But we *are* working on it." She turns and points to Claudius who's been stalking behind us like a wolf all this time. "Claudius is Canadian; I met up with him when my battalion was reassigned to this HQ." She points to another man. "That's Enrique, our driver. He's from Mexico and he wasn't even in the military originally."

Enrique shrugs and twists his cap in his hands, like he's nervous. "I volunteered in exchange for my family to be allowed to stay here in Eternus."

"We're proud to have him. His mother designed the patch which we'll use on our new flag soon."

I raise my eyebrows as I stare at it. The patch is the traditional thirteen stars from the colonial flag of the USA, but

182

there's a Canadian maple leaf in the center and the background color is red, white, and green from the Mexican flag. It looks nice. Different, but nice.

"That's incredible," I say quietly. "So much has happened..."

Keoni pats my arm. "Don't be upset. It might be a lot to take in, but you're safe now. That's all you really need to understand."

Yeah ... I'm safe. But what about my friends?

I take a deep breath, glancing between Keoni and nervous Enrique. "So, you guys accept volunteers in this new military force?"

"Yes..." Keoni nods slowly.

"If I volunteer, will I be on your squad? The Search-and-Rescue team?"

She inhales and then lets it out slowly, motioning for me to follow her again. We walk past large tents with the flaps pinned back to reveal families inside. There's a road with log cabins in the distance, but there are also those big military vans like the one I arrived in. I guess that area is for the new army.

I see teams of people wheeling barrels full of water and food, entering an open shack to begin cooking for the entire camp. There's already a line of people waiting outside and I'm not sure if they're volunteer cooks or hungry refugees. My stomach growls as I watch a large, muscular woman light a huge firepit and heave a massive cauldron over it to begin making stew of some sort. I've only eaten once today, and it wasn't much.

"Here," Keoni's voice snaps me to attention. We're standing in front of a small shack with a table set up. Two people sit with clipboards and welcoming smiles. "This is our welcoming table," she says, nodding to the man and woman.

They both smile at me. "Is this a new arrival?" the woman says.

"Picked him up a few days ago, on our last run," Keoni says.

I resist the urge to tell the smiling lady how they killed my friend and left the rest of us behind. "Can I sign up for the military here?" I say instead.

The smiling man and woman both shoot glances at Keoni who shuffles her weight from one foot to the other. "Eternus is always looking for new soldiers. The war won't end without them. But we also need help in other areas, kid."

"I want to join the Search-and-Rescue squad," I tell her, hating how desperate I sound. Even Enrique looks away, squeezing his cap like its wet laundry. Behind us, Claudius simply crosses his muscular arms and glances off, bored. I hate Claudius.

"Please let me join," I say.

"I know you want to find your friends." Keoni pats my arm. "But you've only just gotten here—"

"And each day that passes puts more distance between us," I cut her off. "You can't seriously expect me to sit here and do nothing while my friends rot out there."

"Don't forget they killed five of our men." Claudius steps forward, his voice the rumble of an angry bear. He looks like a bear, well over six feet tall with a thick mane of wavy locks surrounding his bearded face. He's older, I can tell from the lines around his mouth and eyes, but the tattoos stretched across his muscular arms are warning enough not to mess with this guy. He's a walking tank and I know he's itching to fire all

184

his missiles at me. Just like he did in the van when I was tied up and blinded. But I'm not anymore. If he puts his hands on me again—

Keoni steps forward enough to block my view of her scowling guard dog. I look down at her and realize how short she is. She reminds me of Mya, but more womanly. More authoritative. Mya could never be a soldier like this. She'd be one of the women I saw handling the vegetables, or maybe working this welcoming table.

But she isn't here, I tell myself. She's lost somewhere. Gone. Maybe for good.

I've got to find her.

"I'm sorry about your soldiers," I tell Keoni. "But I still need to find my friends."

She nods. "I know that. But there's order here at Eternus. There are rules you've got to follow. We can't just rush out to find people at every request we get."

My shoulders fall, but Keoni keeps talking, trying to make the best of this situation.

"Let's get you registered first, okay? Sign in with these campers, they'll get you set up with a new United Americas ID and see if we can get you into a tent for tonight."

"And what happens tomorrow?" I say.

Keoni extends her hand for me to shake. "Tomorrow, we talk about what sort of work you can do."

I stare at her hand for a moment, letting her words swim through my mind. She didn't give me a sure promise that I could join the Search-and-Rescue team, but it's better than nothing. If I follow their rules, they'll eventually hear me out. Best to get along with them, for now at least.

I shake Keoni's hand. "Alright. I'll see you tomorrow, then."

"First thing in the morning."

I watch her walk away, ignoring Claudius's hateful eyes and Enrique's nervous wave. Once they're gone, I turn back to the welcoming table and offer a sheepish smile. "What now?"

The woman grabs her clipboard and picks up a sharpened pencil. She smiles up at me like all is well. Like we're not living through World War III and establishing an entirely new country which will remap the entire globe as we know it. My home country won't exist anymore. Once I sign up at this stupid booth, I'll be a member of a new nation. But that nation's got an army, they've got a team dedicated to finding survivors and taking them to a safe area. I can't join that team until I become a citizen of this nation. So I don't care about the past anymore, I'm only focused on finding my friends. On finding the woman I fell in love with. And it starts here.

"What's your name, son?" the woman says. "And how old are you? If you can remember."

I'm actually not sure how old I am right now.

"What month is it?" I ask slowly.

Her smile widens. "Today is January 27th."

Sheesh, my birthday passed, and I had no idea. "My name is Julius Caesar, and I'm 21 years old." I watch the disbelief cross her face, it's the same look I get whenever I introduce myself to someone new. They never believe this is my real name; I can't imagine what this lady thinks since I don't have any proof to show her I'm not making this up.

I shrug. "Yes, that's my real name. I promise I'm not lying."

She laughs. "Honestly, I've had people claim to be Adolf Hitler and Atila the Hun. Julius Caesar sounds nice, in comparison."

"I can't prove that's my real name. I was adopted anyway, so it's not like I've got paperwork."

"No one has much paperwork," she tells me with a shrug. "We can take your word for it, or if you have friends and family here, they may be able to verify for you." She says that last part quite slowly, regretting her words a little too late.

"I don't have anyone here," I say, trying not to get angry at her. "My friends were all left behind."

She picks up her clipboard. "You'd be surprised how many families have been reunited here. Maybe some of your folks are already here. Is Caesar their last name too?"

I shake my head and then pause. "Uh... Can you check for Dr. Joshua Brown? He would've come from Wakedon, and probably registered as an engineer of some sort. Maybe even a professor. He's also a strong Christian, so maybe he volunteers at the church here."

"Is he your adoptive father?"

"No." I look at my shoes so I don't have to see her questioning eyes, wondering why I'm asking about some random man instead of my own parents. But Dr. Brown is like a father to me. I have a foster mom but finding him is just as important. And also... I don't want to ask about my mother. I don't want to hear the words, 'I'm sorry,' from this lady's mouth. Because that would mean she isn't here or that she's dead. And I don't know if I can handle that news.

"He's a family friend," I explain.

The woman nods and scans her clipboard. She flips a few pages and then smiles. "Congratulations, Julius Caesar. We do have someone here by that name."

20

Adrian

Bunny is oddly quiet. We aren't the best of friends, but we've been sitting side by side for the last hour and he's said less than six words to me. Normally, I wouldn't complain about this, but the silence feels deliberate—like he doesn't want to talk to me. I just can't figure out why not.

I glance sideways at Bunny, noting the blonde fuzz on his jaw. It looks weird on him. He's always been smooth like a child, not a single facial hair in sight. I figured he couldn't grow a beard, the thought of him shaving had honestly never crossed my mind all this time, but it's not like I regularly stared at Bunny's jawline anyway.

I face forward before he catches me looking. We're sitting in the living room of an old log cabin. It's the first house we've seen for miles, but no one is complaining, even though this place looks like a shack straight out of a horror movie. The floorboards are gone, leaving the inside of the house with nothing but packed dirt to walk on. There's a sofa infested with rats, a tiny kitchenette with a single counter and a fridge that's older than me. The power is out, so the fridge is full of moldy food, which has been keeping the rats alive. Lastly, there's a single bedroom down the hall but it's boarded up. None of us has tried to pry the wood loose to get inside. Our plan is to stay the night sleeping in the living room altogether and then get the heck out of here first thing in the morning.

There's a well on the property, so the girls refilled our bottles and then took buckets of water out to the lean-to to have a shower. We were worried about drinking the water since it'd been poisoned back at the university. It'd killed a kid and lit the match which sparked the fierce battle for supplies throughout the entire campus. But wells don't run through the public water supply; so, unless enemy soldiers found this house and personally poisoned it, we figured it would be okay to drink. Just to be sure, Bunny and I decided to boil it before filling our bottles.

I glance down at the burner just as steam begins to rise from the pot like a hot, wet cloud. Little bubbles follow and a rolling boil takes over the pot.

"How long should we boil it?" Bunny asks beside me.

That's the first time he's spoken in almost forty-five minutes. I contemplate pointing this out before I reply, "Just a few minutes. Then we'll start heating the food."

"When do we get to shower?"

"After dinner, I guess."

Bunny sighs and shifts so he's staring out the grimy living room window. It's smeared with dead bugs and crusted with some mysterious yellow liquid, but even I can make out the naked girls in the lean-to across the overgrown grassy yard.

Their figures are blurry and distorted from the muck on the glass, but I know Bunny's staring at them as they clean themselves.

Delilah is the tallest figure with her long blond hair flipped over as she pours a bucket of water through it. Jupiter's pink hair is hard to miss, she's squatting and scrubbing her arms like she hates them. Mya is the last figure, nothing more than a brown blur wringing out a cloth over a bucket. She stands and starts to wash her legs with the cloth, moving up toward her knees, then her thighs.

I watch for an extra second before looking back down at the pot.

"Pick a can for dinner," I grunt, roughly nudging Bunny.

He snaps to attention and grabs his backpack. We have more supplies now since we lost two people; I'm thankful for the food but the extra cans and such only remind me of everything that's happened. Just to keep my mind distracted, I focus on shutting off the boiling water and swapping the heavy pot with one of the empty ones in Connor's old bag while Bunny sorts out which flavor of soup he wants to eat.

"This one," he says, holding up two big cans of Italian wedding soup.

I pass him the can opener. "At least it's got meatballs in it."

"I can't believe we got stuck with dinner duty." Bunny carefully peels back the lid on one can and passes it to me while he works on the other.

I pour the soup into the fresh pot. "The girls can clean up while we shower."

"You think Delilah will want to shower with me?" Bunny snorts, but I don't laugh.

"Don't talk about her that way."

191

He blinks as I take the second can. "Seriously? You know how she is."

"I know she's mourning Connor."

"And Julius." He sighs as I click on the burner. "The girls were all screaming about him the other day."

I raise an eyebrow. "I don't remember any screaming."

For a second, Bunny doesn't speak, and I'm reminded of the tense silence we'd sat through earlier. Now that I think about it, *everyone* has been quiet lately, and I'm starting to understand why.

I look at Bunny. "What happened?"

He swallows. "Just, like, a girl fight. You know? Chicks being chicks."

I blink. "I have no idea what that means, Benson."

He winces, like his real name is a cuss word.

"What happened between all the girls?"

"They got into a fight while you were scouting the perimeter back at Orly Center." He bunches his shoulders. "It was nothing."

"If it was nothing, then why did I have to press you about it?"

He palms the back of his neck. "Because ..."

"Bunny!"

"Because the fight got physical!" he says quickly.

"Physical?" I don't understand what he means right away because the thought is so far from my mind. How could any of the girls get angry enough to hit each other? They're all friends. Or at least, I thought they got along better than the guys did. I can't stand Bunny, Connor is okay but had no time for anyone except Delilah, and my interactions with Julius were two wrong words away from a screaming match.

192

My gaze lands on Bunny again and he withers under my glare, shrinking back like I might start pummeling him. I will if he doesn't finish this story.

"What happened, Benson?"

He gulps. "Delilah—she slapped Mya."

When something jerks my arm, I realize I'm standing. In that split second, I've launched to my feet and started moving toward the front door, but Bunny lunged forward and grabbed me.

"Wait!" he pleads. "What are you going to do?"

"I…" I pause. I hadn't thought about what I was going to do. I hadn't even realized I'd *moved*. But I feel an awful, burning anger building inside of me now and I can't ignore it. Delilah slapped Mya. They'd fought over Julius. What the heck happened while I was out on scouting duty? And this was *days* ago.

I turn on Bunny. "Why didn't you say anything? Delilah slapped Mya and you just let it happen."

He lets go of my arm and folds his own. "I didn't say anything because I'm not Mya's guardian or her *boyfriend*." He says that last word with a little more emphasis than necessary. I know what he's getting at, but I don't let it bother me. Everyone knows how I feel about Mya. It isn't a secret.

"Look…" Bunny motions toward the window where the girls are walking back toward the house. They're fully clothed now, awkwardly carrying buckets and towels and washcloths. There's no evidence of the slap fight on their faces or in their behavior except the stony silence between them. It's the same silence I felt with Bunny. The sort of silence you get from people who don't want to talk but are forced to be around each other.

"They're all getting along now," Bunny says, still watching the girls.

"That's not the point."

I turn and march across the room to the pile of clothes and supplies I know belong to Delilah. I snatch up her backpack and start cramming things inside. My intention is to pack all her crap and then send her off, but as I shove one of her dirty shirts into the bag, something falls out and hits the floor in a clatter.

It's loud and heavy, leaving an imprint on the dirt-packed floor. It takes me a second of bewildered staring to figure out what I'm even looking at, and then it hits me. Hard.

I stoop and grab the item, feeling the cool metal in my hand. I'm still holding it when the girls open the front door.

"We're back," Jupiter mumbles. "What's for dinner?"

Mya slowly crosses the room in silence, but I hear Delilah's gasp and I turn to confront her, holding up the item as I speak. "Dinner will have to wait."

All eyes are on me now, but Delilah's pretty orbs are focused on the object in my hand. I shake it as I glare at her. "You want to explain this?"

"Is that..." Bunny squints.

Mya steps forward, eyebrows furrowed. "It's a radio."

Delilah is bright red now, but I can't tell if she's filled with anger, embarrassment, or fear. She should only feel the last one.

"What is this!" I bark, squeezing the little hand-radio. I throw it at her feet when she still doesn't speak. The action startles everyone, but Lilah remains silent, so I step forward and grab her by her damp shirt. "Start talking or I will *beat* the answers out of you."

"Adrian!" It's Mya's voice, sharp and hard, forcing me to come to my senses.

I let go of Delilah's shirt collar and Mya quickly stands between us, protecting the girl who slapped her. How very Christian of her, but this is not the time. Getting a palm to the face is the least of our worries right now.

"You took that, didn't you?" I point at Delilah, over Mya's shoulder.

She still doesn't speak, so Mya turns to look at her, voice coming out calmly. Almost pleadingly. "Delilah, we can't understand what's going on until you explain it. Please..."

She swallows. "I found it on one of the bodies of the soldiers from Orly Center."

I knew it. That female soldier had spoken into a radio just before they took off with Julius. The soldiers who'd chased me and Connor months ago had one as well. I'd heard it through the walls of the door as I hid from them. That radio is what God used to save my life.

The grid went down months ago, but with all these radios and the generators we saw in Orly Center, it's clear someone somewhere has power or maybe military forces have been able to restore it to some locations. Whatever the case, that doesn't explain why Delilah took one.

"*Why?*" I grind out, feeling so angry I could scream. "Do you know what this means? Radios can be *tracked*. Whether it's a two-way radio using GPS or a radio connected through a station, if there is a receiver, a radio's signal can be traced." I point to the radio on the dirt floor. "That means, so long as we have this thing, those soldiers who killed Connor can find us and kill us too!"

The room gasps because now everyone finally gets it. Now, I don't seem like an angry, overreacting jerk. Even Mya stiffens and blinks in shock at Delilah. She looks sullen, unable to hold eye contact with anyone. Her long hair is wet and stringy now, revealing dark roots in her middle part. It takes every ounce of strength I have not to reach forward and snatch her by that pretty hair.

"I'm going to ask you one last time," I growl. "Why?"

Delilah looks at me, jerking her chin up in defiance. Like she's had enough of this. "Because the people on the other end of that radio didn't just kill Connor. They took Caesar. If we hold on to that radio, maybe they can track us down. But that just means—"

"Just means what?" I snap. "It means we can nicely ask them to please give Julius back?"

"Maybe they'll be willing to talk."

"Do you think they'll want to talk before or after we apologize for killing half their squad!" My voice is nothing short of a bark, words coming out in thunderous bellows. "You've put us all in danger, Lilah! All so you can chase after some guy who thought nothing of you."

For a long moment, Delilah doesn't speak. She just stares at me, eyes full of hatred. When her jaw finally unscrews, her voice is the hiss of a snake. "*You* killed half their team, Adrian. If anyone put us in danger—if anyone put a target on our backs—it was you."

"I killed them to protect us."

"That's your side of the story."

My hand flashes out—Mya steps forward at the same time, but I'm much bigger, stronger, and faster than her. Delilah's slender pale neck is in my grasp before either of them can draw their next breath.

I squeeze.

"You weren't there... You didn't see what happened. They ... They made me *choose*..." I glance around at the panicked faces surrounding me, but I don't see *them*. I only see the fear they feel. It matches my own. That same black fear that finds me at the worst moments. It sets my heart racing; it breaks sweat out on my body. It squeezes my own throat closed, so I'm gasping for air as much as Delilah is.

Please... Not now...

I shut my eyes, panting, sucking for breaths that won't come. I feel every nerve in my body come alive, and it suddenly feels like I'm on fire. My own clothes are razors dragging across my skin with every movement. My eyes burn. My throat is sealed shut. I can't breathe—I can't *breathe*.

"Adrian!"

Someone shoves me hard and my eyes pop open as I trip sideways. I lose my grasp on *something* and I realize, a second later, that I was still holding Delilah by the throat. She drops to her knees right beside me, clutching her neck and taking deep, gulps of air. Her face is tomato red. Her lips are the lightest shade of blue.

She looks at me, tears streaming down her face, but it's Mya who speaks. "I think that's enough for now."

I wipe my hands through my sweaty hair. "No."

Everyone blinks at me.

"Delilah put us all in danger. She stole a radio without telling us. She slapped Mya. And now she's causing division in our group."

"What are you saying?" Mya asks slowly.

"I'm saying maybe it is time for us to part ways."

The room falls into a tense quiet, like a balloon full of nerves, anger, and uncertainty.

Delilah pops it. "Fine. I'm happy to leave." Her voice is raspy like a smoker's, but she clears her throat and gets to her feet like she's perfectly fine. We all watch in an uncomfortable silence as she crams the rest of her things into her backpack, grabs three water bottles and marches back across the room. She only stops to retrieve that stupid radio and then pauses at the front door, holding the knob. "It's been fun. Safe travels."

No one speaks, and no one tries to stop her.

21

Caesar

I've been here for about five days now. I haven't seen Keoni much since the first day, but I also haven't had the time to really look for her. I'm just going to assume she's a busy soldier out on another search and rescue mission. Honestly, I've been just as busy as her.

The nice camp lady hadn't been lying. Dr. Brown is here—yes—*that* Dr. Brown. My jaw nearly hit the floor when I saw his happy, smiling face again for the first time. He's a bit thinner and his hair is shorter now, even the beard is gone. But I'm sure I look different too. I thought Dr. Brown might not recognize me from weight loss, tanning, my hair getting longer, and being covered in dirt. But he gasped when he saw me, and the next second I was crushed in a hug.

We both cried, clinging to each other like a real father and son. I cried because I'd missed him. Because I couldn't believe he was really here. And because I felt miserable that I'd experienced this reunion without Mya.

She should be here now. All my friends should be here— should be safe. But they're still out there. I can't stop thinking about it, but all the work around Eternus helps to keep my mind busy.

After meeting Dr. Brown again, the welcome desk asked me a bunch of questions and had Mya's father verify them for accuracy. I was given a little certificate which declared me as a citizen of the United Americas. Then I was assigned a chore, a tent, and handed a meal schedule.

I'm a runner. Seriously, after telling them I used to run track before my university imploded, the welcome committee couldn't sign me up fast enough. Being a runner means I'm on a team of men and women who are responsible for hauling all our supplies from the trucks back to the camp. Of course, the trucks could drive all the way up to the camp, but they've been having serious problems with looters and enemy soldiers, so the trucks drive to a secure location and hide the supplies there. The runners are given coordinates to find the stash, so it's our job to secure and transport the supply. Since there are multiple trucks and teams of looters going out every day, the job is endless. I'm so tired and embarrassingly out of shape, one of the girls on the runners' squad asked if I had really been on the track team during my first run.

"You think I'd lie about that?" I said, huffing for breath.

"Maybe not. But … the *captain*?" She had tilted her head to the side and raised one of her eyebrows when she'd asked me that. Her eyebrow had a piercing and the sunlight flickered off it for a second when I'd glanced down at her.

The captain? How sarcastic, inching toward flat out rude.

I'd rolled my eyes. "I suck now, but I promise I used to be worthy of the title."

She'd passed me a sack of potatoes. "Prove it, Cap."

That potato sack had weighed fifty pounds, but I'd done my best. Honestly, I was just happy to have potatoes.

Eternus is connected to a handful of other military headquarters. It's been tough to set up and maintain communication; war continues to rage around the world and nearly the entire nation is still without power. Major General Rico was able to transport functioning generators to the camp when the area was first established as an official HQ. Unfortunately, we don't run them often because General Rico is afraid that drifters or enemy soldiers will find us. Dr. Brown has been working on a new model for the generators that will function at the same power level but produce half the noise and require half the gas to run.

Today is my day off, so instead of moping around the camp, I'm sitting in Dr. Brown's tent as he tinkers with his new model. It's nothing but an engine with pipes and screws poking out of it but I trust the doc knows what he's doing.

"Wrench," he grunts, hovering over his creation with a frown on his face.

I pass him the wrench. "How's it going over there?"

"I haven't made any progress."

"Well, that's not the response I was expecting." He's been working on this thing for the last few hours while I've just been sitting here watching.

Dr. Brown glances up and sighs. "I don't have all the parts I need."

"What do you need? Maybe I could try to find them."

"They won't be here in camp, my boy. I'm talking about parts we'll need to travel to find."

"I could do that too."

Dr. Brown eyes me a moment and then sucks in a long breath. He looks so much older than I remember, but the look suits him. Instead of appearing as an insane Black version of Einstein, he just looks like a tired old man. A little nerdy, but harmless all the same. I like this version of him, but I do miss the kooky guy I grew up with as a kid.

"Any excuse to get out of here, right?" Dr. Brown says softly. When I don't answer, he sits on the little wooden stool beside me. His tent is nice and spacious with a chair, a stool, a small desk for his work and a sleeping bag rolled up in the corner. There's a box full of clothes and tools beside the sleeping bag, but I don't question it.

"I need to get out there," I say firmly. "I can't stay here forever."

"I understand."

"No, you don't—"

"Mya is my daughter." Dr. Brown's voice is serious, the closest I've ever seen him to being angry at me. "I want her back just as much as you do. I *need* her back."

I can't hold his gaze. My desperation suddenly feels selfish. How could I ever convince myself that Dr. Brown doesn't understand the pain I feel? Sure, he didn't live on the run like I did, but that doesn't mean he didn't spend each day worrying for his daughter. Or worrying for me.

My mother isn't here. Dr. Brown told me after we managed to get ourselves together and wipe our tears on that first day. He'd searched for her and had even tried to make his way into Phoenix a few days after the power went out, but the city was overrun with desperate survivors already. Dr. Brown was attacked, his backpack of supplies stolen, glasses smashed, and his ribs cracked. The thugs who beat him up left him for dead on the side of the road. That's where a few soldiers found him when they began evacuating the city. They thought he was dead, but he'd groaned in pain just before passing out and woke up in Orly Center. He stayed there for about a month, nursing his broken ribs, and volunteering his skills as an engineer. But that place was attacked by enemy soldiers and the refugees were forced to evacuate here.

The journey had been long. I know because I'd taken it myself, driving for days while tied up and blinded. But Dr. Brown had made the journey on *foot*, travelling in a caravan of over 700 survivors. He said he'd prayed the entire time, unsure which he feared more: another attack, or starvation. They'd left in a hurry with few supplies and even less hope. But Major Banks had been determined. She led the largest migration of the New Americas so far and lost no refugees along the way.

"God kept us," Dr. Brown had sobbed as he told me that story. But his tears held more than the joy of survival, he was also crying over guilt.

With downcast eyes, Dr. Brown told me how guilty he'd felt for never making it to my house to see if my mother was okay. I'd reassured him that it was alright as best I could, biting my lip until I tasted blood. The old man had clearly felt bad enough, crying in his face over my foster mom wouldn't have made him feel any better. But I did want to cry. I wanted to scream and beat my fists on the ground until my knuckles were bloody.

All this work. All this travel. All this struggling to still be left with so much mystery. *When will it end?* My next thought is agonizing, but it's a frightening, pitch-black truth.

It may never end.

This could be our lives for the *rest* of our lives. Fighting an endless war, searching for supplies, risking ourselves just to gather goods from delivery trucks. Never having running water again. Never seeing my foster mother again. Never seeing Mya again.

No... I close my eyes and pinch the bridge of my nose to clear the dark worries away. I cannot think like this. If I do, I'll never recover.

Dr. Brown pats my arm, his heavy hand is warm and comforting. "Don't fret, my boy. If God could bring you here safely, then He can bring Mya here too. And your mother."

I nod glumly. "But I know I could find her if they would just let me try."

"Caesar," he pauses to let out a wet cough. Ever since he got his ribs cracked, he hasn't been breathing right. He says it's only bad on days when dust storms kick up—like today. That's why I'm off right now, we can't find the supply stash when visibility is low.

Dr. Brown clears his throat and takes three deep breaths, wiping his watery eyes with a handkerchief. "Caesar," he says again, "Do you think it was a coincidence that Major Banks stopped at Orly Center?"

Major Banks is Keoni, I guess that's her military name or whatever. She didn't use it when she'd introduced herself to me, so it always takes me an extra second to remember who Dr. Brown is referring to when he brings her up.

I shrug one shoulder. "Keoni told me she hadn't planned on stopping at Orly Center."

"Exactly. But she *did* stop. And it's because God needed her to get you."

I wish I believed that. "I didn't know Keoni was a Christan."

"I don't know what she believes, but I believe God can influence and direct the unsaved as well as the saved. He did so in the Bible."

"He did?"

"Of course." Dr. Brown gives me a flat face, like my ignorance disappoints him. "It was not a coincidence that Rahab met the Shittim spies in the Book of Joshua. God planned for that to happen. He made sure everything was aligned, and placed Rahab in the right place at the right time because He knew she would be willing to help His children.

"God knows our hearts, that means He knows who can be of use to Him and when. Rahab's heart was open to His influence at just the right time, and God was able to use that for the good of His people." Dr. Brown pats my arm again, his warmth radiating through me. "Now, if God can use a prostitute to help his people, what do you think could possibly stop Him from using a fully loaded military HQ to find my daughter?"

I sit there in silence, utterly lost for words by this simple revelation.

Dr. Brown stands and hobbles over to his generator again. "I know what it's like to feel useless. I know the frustration of sitting still while someone else does all the work. But, son, that's what it means to be a Christian. You sit back and you let God handle things. It may not be fun, but it's always better."

"Right now, it feels like I'm being forced to let *Eternus* handle things," I say with a sigh. "Getting Mya back is completely out of my hands now."

"It is," Dr. Brown agrees. "And maybe that's how God wants things to be."

"He doesn't want me to find my friends?"

"He wants you to trust that *He* will bring your friends back."

I shake my head, trying not to get angry, but I can't help it. My words come out in a snippy, clipped voice. "So, God separated us so He could show off?"

"God took you off because this is the only way you will ever learn to let go and let Him handle things." Dr. Brown looks at me with that stern expression from before, treading the edge of anger. "Some people are hardheaded. Some people are stubborn. That means the situations God uses to teach them a lesson tend to be harsher. He doesn't want us to be in pain, but He also knows some children need to touch the flame to believe it'll burn them." He sighs deeply. "Some people need to have everything stripped away before they can see that God is right beside them."

I glance at my calloused hands, staring at the new scars and the hardened skin as I mutter, "*See* God... Sometimes I don't even know if I *believe* in God."

"Maybe that's why God brought you here and not Mya. She's got strong faith. The Lord Jesus knows she won't begin to doubt Him, no matter how long she wanders in the wilderness out there. But you..." Dr. Brown nods, like he's just come to some sort of conclusion. "You have to make a decision, my boy. And God brought you here to make it."

"Why did He have to bring me *here*?" I glance around. "What's so great about Eternus?"

"Nothing in particular. But *I'm* here. Perhaps God allowed us to reconnect so I could point you back to Him. Since my daughter's influence clearly wasn't enough."

"It had been enough," I say softly, thinking of my last conversation with Mya. The conversation where I'd asked her to go steady with me again, to commit to a serious relationship so we could honor God together. As one. I never got her answer, but I know my offer had been sincere. I'd meant every word I said to her in that room.

"I had wanted to try to love God," I say aloud. "I'd wanted to try being a serious Christian because I had fallen in love with a serious Christian girl."

When Dr. Brown doesn't speak, I feel the hairs on the back of my neck rise. I hadn't meant to get so personal—so open— with him, but I figured he could read between the lines anyway. Might as well put it out in the open. I fell for his daughter. I don't think that's a bad thing, but when I look at Mya's father, I suddenly hope I'd kept my feelings a secret.

Dr. Brown shakes his head at me.

"I can't control my feelings," I try to explain. "Mya's always been that one girl by my side. I couldn't help but fall for her."

Dr. Brown stops shaking his head and frowns, momentarily confused. Then he tilts his head back and lets out a hearty laugh. He even removes his glasses and wipes them on his work apron. "My boy, I don't care that you fell for my daughter. I had expected it, to be frank. Don't know what took you so long to finally notice her."

"Oh…" I palm the back of my neck. "Now that I have noticed her, we've been split apart. Just when I decided I was ready to give the Christian life a try."

He goes back to shaking his head, more aggressively this time. "Caesar, you've got it all wrong. You *try* chocolate cream puffs. You *try* a new diet. Last week I *tried* the cook's new recipe for green bean soup." He makes a disgusted face. "God is not a food or a hobby. You don't get to test the waters with Him. You are either hot or you are cold, but those who are lukewarm will be spewed from His mouth."

I blink at him, not really knowing what to say.

Dr. Brown sighs deeply. "Now I see what God is doing. You wanted to give your life to Him because you loved Mya. But God wants you to give Him your life because you love *Him*. That's a decision that can only be made away from Mya." He nods, giving me a sympathetic look. "When you're all alone, with no pretty girl to remind you of the perks of a Christian marriage," he wiggles his eyebrows, "will you still choose to live for God?"

I look away, ashamed that he's seemingly figured out my heart's motives. I had wanted to try God, but only because that was the only way I could truly be with Mya. The only way I could have sex with Mya. That had been the end goal.

I mean… she wouldn't even *date* me unless I became a Christian, so what choice did I have except to convert? But clearly that conversion hadn't been sincere. I guess I hadn't meant it in my heart.

But now I'm here. And Dr. Brown is saying God has all these plans. But is this confusion part of His plan? If loving God for Mya isn't good enough, then why should I love Him?

208

That's a scary thought. To realize I'd only cared about God because that had been the doorway to getting into Mya's pants. But now Mya isn't here. It's just me and God, and He's waiting for me to do something. But I don't know what.

I look at Dr. Brown, shocked by the tears I feel welling in my eyes. "God hasn't been there for me," I say. My voice starts as a whisper, but I gain strength with each complaint, almost yelling by the time I'm done. "He gave me parents who threw me away. He gave me the gift of speed but then ruined my track career by allowing this chaos to happen. He took Mya from me just when we'd finally reached a good place in our relationship. He didn't protect my friends when they needed Him most." I grunt, thinking of how much they're probably suffering while I'm here cozy and safe. "How can God expect me to love Him when He hasn't given me a reason to?"

"He did give you a reason, Caesar. Over two-thousand years ago."

I start to shake my head, but Dr. Brown keeps talking.

"God gave you His Son, Jesus Christ. He sent an innocent man—a *God*—to die for humans who didn't believe in Him. And you still want more?"

"Of course I do," I mutter angrily.

"You might not have had great parents, but God gave you a foster mother who loved you and..." Dr. Brown pauses, hesitating for a second. He clears his throat. "And He placed me in your life, my boy. And I've loved you like a son from the moment I first met you."

I glance away.

"Your track career might have been taken away, but God made it possible for you to run here in Eternus. Now you're running for a reason—to deliver supplies that will keep this

209

camp afloat—instead of just running for your own glory. God gave your speed a purpose."

I blink in shock. I'd never thought of it that way.

"God didn't take Mya, He took you. And who says He hasn't been protecting your friends? I'm sorry for any loss you've faced along the way, but the Bible says trouble will come. Believing in God doesn't promise you a cushy life. It promises that God will be with you through the storm."

"This storm is too great."

"That's why He's here, Caesar. Will you allow your troubles to push you into God's arms or will you let them influence you to turn your back on Him?"

I take a deep breath. "I don't know what to do."

Dr. Brown smiles at me, it's lopsided and goofy looking, but it's the smile I grew up seeing for most of my life. The smile of the only real father I ever knew. "You make a decision, Caesar. You believe. Or you don't. Which will it be?"

22

Adrian

We're in the worst shape we've ever been in. I thought sending Delilah away would be a good thing for us, but it's clear everyone resents me now. Bunny has gone back to pretending I don't exist. Jupiter is outright hostile with me, snapping back her replies whenever I speak to her or sometimes completely ignoring me. Mya is the only one who treats me like a human, but it's obvious there's distance between us now.

Fine. I can admit sending Lilah off on her own was a bit harsh and maybe even unnecessary. At least, that's how everyone seems to feel *now*. But no one voiced their objection AT ALL when everything went down. They all stood around like wide-eyed mice, too afraid to speak up whether in agreement or not.

Since I was the only one with a voice, I used it. If anyone had a problem with what I said, they should have said it then before Delilah packed her crap and left. Instead, they kept their complaints to themselves and have now decided to take their resentment and anger out on me in the most annoyingly passive-aggressive manner I have ever seen.

I know they've never liked me being in charge in the first place. I know I barely won that vote against Julius for leadership—I'm not stupid. Connor only voted for me because Delilah voted for Julius. Mya only voted for me because Julius had been flirting with Delilah. Everything I have right now is some hand-me-down from that man. I can't stand it. I can't *stand* the fact that I was the default option for people who were momentarily angry with Julius.

The fact is, if they had all been on good terms with him, I would've been squeezed out. The same way I was squeezed out of the running for captain of the track team. Jupiter had been the only genuine vote in my lane, but with the way she's been treating me these last few days, I know how she would vote if we had another go.

It's the same cycle on repeat. Whether for the track team or for my friends. I give myself over to the group; I'm completely devoted, completely dedicated, placing them over my own self and making sure they're taken care of. And everyone still hates me. After all that I've given.

I glance over at Mya who is putting up her tent across the room. We're camping out in an old art museum just outside Phoenix. I suppose we could just lie on the floor and roll out pallets, but everyone is fed up with each other. No one wants to see each other's face for a second longer than necessary. So the tents are going up.

It's taken us much longer to get to Phoenix than we initially planned, but the long journey hasn't been entirely in vain. We've stopped at a few other centers and malls to check for refugee shelters. Of the five we found, only two were shelters and both of them had been overrun or long abandoned.

We didn't find any information about our families, but we did see papers about the 5th Brigade again and some sort of communication between American and Canadian forces. The papers were difficult to understand, considering they were ripped in half and stained. In the end, we decided to loot and move on to the next place. This museum wasn't on the list, but we were tired and didn't have the motivation to make the last push to Phoenix. Hopefully, that'll be our last stop. I'd love to find my family and let all this go.

I glance at Mya again; she's got her tent up and is dragging her backpack inside. Our relationship is nearly ruined now. She doesn't speak to me unless she has to, but I can't tell if she's avoiding me because of the Delilah drama or because of her grief over Connor and Julius. I never realized how torn up she was, but I guess I should've expected that.

The two of them weren't just childhood friends, they had clearly crossed the lines into a new territory recently. A territory I thought she'd reserved for *me*. But I had been wrong. I'd always assumed whatever had happened between them wouldn't last because I thought Julius wouldn't appreciate Mya. I thought he would be their downfall. I'm afraid I was wrong. I'm afraid what they had was *real*, and if Julius hadn't been taken, they'd still be together now. And I'd be alone.

Even miles away, Julius is still standing between us. The thought makes me angry. I'm tired of standing back and letting everything happen around me. I waited too long to check on my family and they were evacuated without me. I waited for Mya, and she chose Julius—again and *again*.

213

Now ... finally ... he isn't here. And I don't know if he ever will be again. If I don't make some sort of move, I'll lose Mya forever. But my desire for her isn't just for my own sake, it's for her too.

As much as I care for her, I can admit that Mya is weak. She is not an independent woman. She needs someone to lean on, to trust. That person had been Julius, but he'd betrayed her for Delilah and then got himself taken. There's a chance it could have been Jupiter, but she stabbed Mya in the back when she let Lilah slap her and said nothing in her defense about it.

I'm the only one left who can be there for her. And from the way she's been falling apart recently, I'd say I'm running out of time to step up. *Everyone* is running out of time. We're slowly unraveling. If we don't find our families or at least nail down solid clues on their whereabouts soon, we're going to lose our minds.

We never laid down a Plan B. We never discussed the possibility of being wrong about all this—of never finding our families. It's not like we can simply turn around and head back to Mya's house. That's a long journey with a dead end waiting for us. And it isn't safe. That's one thing those soldiers proved to us; sitting still is going to get us killed.

"Dinner." The voice is Jupiter's, I know from the dry, dead emotion in her tone.

I don't know what's up with Jupiter, but she has slowly become a bigger nuisance than Julius ever was. She has a terrible attitude now and is flat out mean to everyone except Bunny. And that's only because Bunny isn't very close to me or Mya.

I miss the days when Jupiter was silent and depressed. Now that she's started speaking up, I can't stand her.

214

For now, she's been on dinner duty, looking more like a witch at a cauldron than a lady stirring soup. She's opened three cans of mixed vegetables and added an entire pack of jerky we found at the last shelter. She didn't heat it because we're on our last canister of butane gas. We decided to only burn it for boiling water; that means cold meals from this point forward. I don't like it any more than the rest of us, but as we gather 'round for our cold food, I feel like everyone is blaming me for this.

It wouldn't be the first or only thing I've been blamed for, especially considering I did make the decision to stop using fire earlier. But that was before, when we might have been getting tailed by dangerous killer soldiers. Not that anyone understood just how much of a threat we'd faced back then. All they could focus on was their cold food and my decision. Every bad thing was my fault. It still is now.

Jupiter shoves my serving into my hand so hard, it sloshes over the rim of my cup and splashes salty juice onto my fingers. I mumble a thank-you and sit on the floor with a huff. No one speaks as we eat, but I notice Jupiter and Bunny are sitting beside each other while Mya nibbles her jerky in a chair that's placed a good five feet away.

If the other two have isolated Mya, that means I really am the only person she can trust or lean on. I just have to somehow make a move. But before I can think of anything to say, Mya stands and mumbles, "I'm gonna finish my food in my tent," then she leaves before anyone can respond.

I watch her go, carrying that pathetic cup of vegetables and salty meat. It tastes awful, but it's all we've got. We're saving the last few cans of soup for special occasions. I can't think of anything special that could happen to us out here except finding our folks, but I suppose when that happens, I'd rather split beef stew with them than veggies and jerky.

The rest of us continue our meal in silence. I contemplate excusing myself to peek into Mya's tent, but I don't want to give Jupiter and Bunny anything else to gossip about. So I force myself to sit there and slowly finish my food. Then I pack up my things and go to my own tent alone, because what would I say or do if I *did* enter Mya's tent?

In the confines of my own little room, I light a candle so I can see and then start my personal routine instead of berating myself for passing up this chance to reach out to Mya. There's no point in stressing over it. Besides, if Mya truly wanted to make a connection with me, she would reach out and do so. I've given her more than enough hints and outright confessions for her to know exactly how I feel about her.

I was supposed to ask her an important question when we made it to Orly Center, but I never did. Granted, unforeseen events did occur and interrupt everything, but now I feel like I'll never get that chance to ask her again.

Get it together, I tell myself, folding up my dirty clothes. Reaching out to a girl who already knows how I feel shouldn't be this hard. I feel myself getting angry, but instead of cramming my clothes back into my bag in a rage, I continue neatly folding and arranging them around my tent. I have a pile for shirts, pants, and even underwear. Everything is stained and wrinkled, but that's not the point. The point is to be organized and neat, to be perfectly in control at all times.

But I'm not in control. I haven't had control in a long time. My friends hate me, one of them is dead, the other is gone—even though he wasn't truly my friend. I couldn't stop it from happening. I had a gun and all I could do was watch as Julius was taken. And it's that gun that's tearing the group apart now.

Everyone hates my leadership, and they think I'm only in charge because I've got this weapon. If it weren't for my gun, no one would listen to me. They think I'm holding them hostage. They think I'm the type of guy who would threaten them just to remain in charge. But I'm not like that. I never have been. Don't they remember Memphis and how insane he was? How could they ever put us on the same page?

I stare down at my gun now, it's black shadow flickering against the walls of my tent from the dim candlelight. After a moment of hesitation, I place my finger on the trigger and imagine firing. But not at my friends, I think about firing at myself.

Is it worth it to keep going like this?

I pull my hand away and set the gun down. I still need to find my siblings. They need me. And they actually want me around. So I will live for them. Maybe finding them will give me peace. Maybe finding them will drive the nightmares and the panic attacks away. I'd had one as I'd screamed at Delilah. Right there in front of everyone. But they all thought I was just trying to kill her. No one knows I couldn't control myself— that I had no idea what was even happening right in front of me. They saw my anger and jumped to one conclusion, and now it'll be nearly impossible to change their minds about me.

I wonder if Mya thinks I tried to kill Delilah. She's the one who snapped me to my senses, shoving me away from her with a frantic shout. The look on her face had been just as panicked as everyone else's but there had been a small sense of understanding in the wrinkles of her brow. Like she knew that wasn't me. That wasn't something I would ever really do.

But she didn't say anything to me after that. Like everyone else, she walked away and left me to the silence.

I sigh and place the gun into my bag, then I turn and remove my boots, then my socks. I press each one flat and set it into the corresponding shoe, then I lift my shirt over my head, but I stop when I hear a voice outside my tent.

"Adrian?"

I freeze, halfway in and halfway out of my shirt.

"Adrian?" the voice says again, and I recognize it.

In a rush, I shove my arms back through my shirt sleeves and scramble to the flap of my tent. When I pull it back, I see Mya standing there, looking very shy and unsure of herself.

She came. She came to me.

"Come in," I say immediately.

Once inside, she stands awkwardly in the middle of my room, glancing around at everything but me.

"You've always been so neat," she says.

"That hasn't changed."

"But so much else has."

I clench my jaw.

"You never told me about the panic attacks."

So that's why she's here.

"What's there to tell?"

"You need help, Adrian." She steps forward. "You could have told us—"

I point at the tent flap. "I am not talking to *them* about my personal issues."

She nods, falling silent for a moment. And then, in a gentle voice, she says, "You could've come to me."

218

In my bitter pain, I laugh. "And when was I supposed to do that? Before or after you got your tongue out of Julius's mouth?"

"You know it's possible for us to just be friends, right?" she says quickly, hotly. "There was room in my life for both of you. But both of you wanted all or nothing with absolutely no consideration of the stress and frustration that placed on my shoulders."

"Boo-hoo, you had to pick one guy to date." I wave my hand, shocked by my own callous response, but I can't help it. Mya has always acted like the victim while breaking someone else's heart. And it's that heartbrokenness that's speaking now. An angry pain and shame that cannot face the truth that no matter how many times Mya has broken my heart, I'll come back. Desperately hoping that this will be the time she finally chooses me.

Mya looks more shocked than angry, but the anger is there. And just as quickly, it's gone. Her furrowed brows relax and the wrinkles in her forehead smooth out. The anger on her face melts into sadness, and I'm suddenly lost for words.

"You're right," she says in a guilty voice. "I had to choose one of you, but the truth is that I wanted *both* of you. And I hated having to give one of you up. But I had to." She hugs herself. "I couldn't be with both of you. And I chose Julius because we had such a strong history. But…"

"But…" I repeat, gently nudging that door between us open a little further. My hope is that she steps through and finally shuts it behind her. My hope is that she makes a decision here and now—and doesn't regret it.

"But Julie isn't here anymore," she says shakily, then she drops her gaze and stares at the toes of her socks.

I sigh. "Why did you come to my tent, Mya?"

She doesn't speak. I can see the weight of her confession pressing down on her, and I realize just how difficult this is. Because part of it isn't genuine. Yes, Mya has feelings for me, but she isn't here for those feelings. She's here because of her feelings for *Julius*.

She wants me to help her forget them.

And I'm desperate enough to do that.

"Come here," I say, stepping forward, and that's all the encouragement she needs.

When I reach for Mya, she grabs my hand and pulls me toward her. I easily wrap my arms around her waist, and she responds by standing on her tiptoes, chin tilted up, her eyes closed.

I stare down at her. In the candlelight, I see her sweaty forehead, and her lovely cheekbones, and her full lips, and her round nose. I see every part of her, and I hold her in my arms, knowing I've got every part except her heart.

"Please…" Mya whispers.

This is the closest I've ever come to having a real relationship with her. The fact that I lean down with no hesitation says a lot about us both, but I don't care.

I guess I don't need her heart.

23

Mya

I won't lie. I came to Adrian's tent knowing exactly what would happen—it's what I *wanted* to happen. Well… What I wanted was to forget. Forget the pain of losing Julius, the fear of never finding my father, the failure of waiting so long to begin searching in the first place. I needed to forget that Connor is dead and that my closest friend blames me, his recent lover hates me, and his friends only see the worst in me now.

I'm such an awful mess. And right now, I can't think beyond the pain. The anger. The guilt. All I want is to feel something else—to feel *good*. To feel wanted. To feel loved. All the things Julius made me feel.

But Julius isn't here right now.

All I have is…

I can't say his name. I don't deserve to. What I'm doing to him is worse than watching Julius get taken away. At least the people who hurt him were his enemy. But what do you call the person who breaks you when you still love them? Are they an enemy? A friend or a foe.

Honestly, I thought he would send me away when I walked into his tent. I thought he would see my tears and hate me for them. I thought he would be disgusted by how attached I am to the man he can't stand. I'm here because I need him to help me forget. I need him to take my mind off the pain.

He is a distraction. And he's accepted that.

Loving each other was the only way Julius and I knew how to get along. How to truly connect. Maybe this is the only way we can connect too. Through bitter pain, for the both of us. Pain over losing Julius, and anger by the fact that all he could ever amount to is his desperate replacement.

Why?

The question climbs into my head as he kisses me. *Why would you still accept me, knowing that I'm using you? Why would you agree to this fleeting moment?*

Maybe he needs it as badly as I do.

"Adrian…" his name falls from my mouth in a breathy whisper. He catches it with another kiss, his mouth hot and wet and covering my own with a gasp.

Here, in his arms, I feel the rest of the world melt away. The pain peels off like a sweaty sock, and all that's left is a cold sweat. Relief floods my mind as much as my body. His hands are large and grip my waist like he's angry, pulling me close until I can't tell his body from my own. He's so tall, my calves are cramping from standing on my toes, but just when I think I can't hold on, Adrian lowers us to the floor. His long fingers tug at the hem of my shirt, and I nod slowly, letting him pull it over my head. He blinks at me, his expression like steel. I can't tell what he's thinking, but I see his throat bob as he swallows and then reaches over his head to pull his own shirt off.

I pause.

I've gotten so used to seeing Adrian, his creamy albino skin, his stark white hair, his ice-chip eyes. But this is something no one can ever be fully prepared for. Slowly, I reach up to run my hand over his firm chest, and he closes his eyes. Like my touch hurts him.

The color of his ghostly skin isn't what makes me hesitate. It's all the scars.

Welts cover his chest like the zigzagging lines of a map. They're red and puckered, brutal evidence of a nightmare he's survived. I've seen them once before, through his sweaty shirt back at the university. But up close like this, they look entirely different.

I can't stop myself from staring. Against his pale skin, the red marks look as angry as the rage I know Adrian feels inside. I wonder if any of that anger is reserved for me. Anger at the woman who so cruelly uses him this way. Like a toy to be tossed away after the fun is over.

I slide my hand down Adrian's chest, feeling his heart flutter beneath my palm. He peels his eyes open when I brush the buckle of his belt. The touch is gentle, just the tips of my fingers sliding along the cool metal, but Adrian is keenly tuned to my every movement. I think he could hear my *thoughts* if I weren't breathing so loudly.

He reaches down and takes my hand in his, sliding it lower. I gasp. Touching him like this slams a weight onto my chest. The last time I was this close to a boy, I'd stopped him because I knew going any further would have broken my relationship with God.

So, what am I doing now?

I pull my hand away from Adrian. I can see the rigidness in his jeans. I know I'm the reason for it. I want to pull down his zipper and keep going. But I can't. If I couldn't do this with Julius, what gives me any right to go forward with Adrian?

My pain doesn't negate the Word of God.

Adrian leans down and kisses me, but I press a hand against his chest. "Adrian..." I say, and he leans back, a pleading look on his face.

I don't stop him when he leans down again. He kisses me until I'm breathless and I feel my own heart start to break. *What am I doing? When did I let myself fall so low?*

I turn my head to the side as Adrian kisses my neck. I squirm when his hands deftly unlink my bra and tug it away from my body. "Please..." I whisper, feeling tears burn in my eyes. "We have to—" my words become a gasp when Adrian moves.

He grips my hips and shifts so I'm on top. I blink, not really knowing what to do now.

"A-Adrian," my voice is a whisper.

"Close your eyes," he says.

"I don't understand."

In response, he stretches his long arm to the side and puts out the candle beside us with his fingers. The flame dies with a bitter hiss, filling the tent with the acrid smell of smoke. We're hushed by the darkness, squinting, trying to make out each other's inky silhouettes.

"In the dark," Adrian's raspy voice makes his chest vibrate, "I can be whoever you need me to be."

No...

I shake my head. "Don't say that." *Don't be this desperate.* "Please—"

"Think of him," Adrian says quickly. "Fantasize about him. Scream his name if you need to. Just…" he pauses, and his breath comes out in a shudder. "Please, Mya."

There's a long pause filled with nothing but heavy breathing. My breaths are staggered, like I'm holding back tears. Adrian's are long and deep, like he's already begun to shed them. I wouldn't be surprised if he was crying. We both know what my answer is going to be.

"I can't do this." I sniffle, hating myself for crying now. "I can't do this," I repeat.

Adrian sobs.

It shatters me, and the pain only doubles because, as I climb off him and feel around the floor for my bra and shirt, I realize the only person I want to wipe away my tears is the one crying with me.

We share the same pain and it's tearing us both apart. It seems that's all I'm good at, hurting the people who love me.

Adrian doesn't speak again as I gather my clothes and cross the room. When I lift the flap to the tent, I glance back over my shoulder to find him sitting up, watching me. He doesn't say anything, doesn't nod or smile—doesn't even blink. He just stares at me, and I stare back.

I'm sorry… I want to apologize. I want him to know that I'm hurting as much as he is, but the look on his face tells me that nothing I say will make this situation any better. So I don't speak my sorrowful thoughts, I just turn and walk out. And then I freeze.

Jupiter stands before me, her eyes wide and her face full of shock. Her vision snaps between my surprised face and the bundle of clothes in my hands. It doesn't take her more than a second to piece everything together. I'm standing here with my bra and my shirt pressed against my bare chest as I exit Adrian's tent in the middle of the night. Even an idiot would guess that we'd been hooking up—and he'd almost be right.

But it doesn't matter that this assumption is only *almost* right. I know from Jupiter's expression that she will never believe I walked away. That I stopped things and left before all my clothes were gone and irreversible mistakes had been made. To Jupiter, making it this far is already an irreversible mistake.

I don't disagree with her. I've shamed my body—my *temple*—and I've made an awful name for Christian women. I know God will forgive me. I know *you* won't even hold this against me forever. But what if Bunny had caught me leaving Adrian's tent? He would think I'm no different from Delilah, and I'd never be able to change his mind about that. My faith would become a joke to him. If it hasn't already.

This is why my father had always put so much stress on me as a kid. I'd hated his rules so much—no staying out late, no hanging out with friends he didn't approve of, no drinking, no smoking, no tattoos. What kind of music are you listening to? Is that a *Christian* book you're reading?

It all seemed like awful overkill, but now… Now I get it. As Jupiter's eyes narrow on me and the judgment rushes in like a storm, I understand all my father's precautions. He hadn't been trying to control me or limit my freedom, he hadn't even been trying to prevent me from making mistakes. Everyone will make mistakes, no matter what rules you put in place. So Dr. Brown had no concern about that, instead, he'd been trying to stop me from looking bad. Because it is our image that matters most.

That sounds so shallow, doesn't it? But it's the truth.

Delilah has called me a *good little Christian girl* enough times for me to roll my eyes just thinking about it. But you know what? Despite her insulting tone, that was the worst she had to say about me. That's what she saw me as—a good little Christian girl. Not a whore. Not a drunkard. Not a girl with a sailor's mouth. She saw me as a good Christian.

Now what do I look like?

That's the question my father used to ask me whenever he'd let me go out with friends. *What do you look like to them, Mya?* Because it isn't always a question of whether your behavior is sinful, sometimes it's a question of whether your behavior truly reflects all that Christ stands for. For some people, the only example of Christianity they will ever see is you. They won't step foot into a church or watch another corny Christian movie. But they will see you in class, they'll bump into you at the movies, or they might live next door.

So, when these unsaved people see you, what do you look like?

Do you have a beer in your hand? Are you wearing tight, unflattering clothing just like them? Are you standing beside them at the same concert for a singer who has never mentioned God in their music and doesn't support Christianity in any way?

When they see you, do you look like a disciple of Christ?

No. Not right now. In this moment, I look like a complete hypocrite. The guilt makes it hard for me to form words as I stare at Jupiter who still hasn't even blinked. Even if I *could* form words, I have no idea what I would say to her.

We stand here in muted surprise, neither of us able to bridge the gap between our thoughts and our mouths. Jupiter's eyes start at the clothes held in my hands, then they move higher to stare at the smooth, nut-brown skin of my bare shoulders, she finally meets my eyes again, and then, to my horror, her gaze rises once more and lands on something over my shoulder.

I turn to find Adrian emerging from the tent right behind me. He's wearing his shirt, but there's a split-second delay between him noticing Jupiter and then offering a greeting.

He hadn't been expecting her either. This thought is about five minutes late, but I finally begin to wonder *why* Jupiter is standing here at Adrian's tent, and my brows furrow in response. That seems to snap me out of my shock; I'm actually able to form words now.

"I was just leaving," I say dumbly.

Jupiter finds her tongue too. "So was I."

Now I'm back to being stupefied. All three of us blink at each other until Adrian's warm hand touches my side. It's an intimate gesture that is far too calming for me to move away from. Instead of shying away, I turn to stare at Adrian, relieved to see a serious look in his eyes instead of that pained expression he'd been wearing moments earlier.

"Go back inside," he says calmly, and then he turns away, giving me no choice but to do what he said.

I sneak behind the tent flap and start getting dressed, keeping an ear open so I can listen to their conversation. Adrian says something first.

"You came here for a reason."

Jupiter laughs, though the sound holds no joy. "So did she."

"You said you're leaving."

For a second, Jupiter doesn't speak, like she's shocked Adrian didn't respond to her comment. We both are, but my shock is quickly washed away by relief. I really didn't want to stand here in my bra and listen to Adrian explain our complicated relationship to Jupiter. Honestly, it's none of her business.

Jupe takes a big breath. "Bunny and I have decided to split ways here. We'll only take half the supplies—you can even keep the camp burner if you give us the can opener. Either way, we'll be gone by the morning." She pauses to let him digest her abrupt decision.

"Why?" Adrian asks.

"We're tired and we don't want to be part of this group anymore."

I deflate, hoping neither of them heard me sigh inside the tent.

"We're going to Phoenix right now, but I'm not from there," Jupiter continues. "Bunny isn't even from *Arizona*. So, there's no reason for us to continue travelling together except camaraderie and perhaps safety in our numbers." She pauses again, and I imagine her looking Adrian up and down. "But after recent events, I no longer feel completely safe around you. And I don't feel a strong sense of camaraderie in the group anymore either."

Basically, Jupiter hates that Adrian killed those soldiers and her and Bunny both blame him for sending Delilah away so harshly. Not to mention how much blame Jupiter has placed on *my* shoulders for everything that's happened.

Adrian's response stuns me. "Alright then," he says calmly. "Let me get the can opener for you."

He pushes the tent flap aside too quickly for me to gather myself. We're face to face before I know it. A breath of silence fills the tent for a heartbeat, and then Adrian blinks and turns to walk past me to his neatly arranged tools in the corner. I watch as he grabs the can opener and then marches right by me in silence.

"Here," he says, undoubtedly passing Jupiter the tool. "It's been nice having you around. Stay safe. And please take care of Bunny, he isn't the strong one between the two of you."

Jupiter releases a chuckle, it sounds genuine. "I'll remember that."

"I'm guessing Bunny didn't want to see me."

"You two aren't very close anyway."

"Not really." Adrian sighs. "So, this is goodbye?"

"It is. We're leaving at first light, heading to Koshen—my hometown."

"That's only a few hours from Phoenix."

"On foot, during an apocalypse? It might as well be a lifetime away."

"Take care of yourself."

"I will."

I listen to Jupiter's retreating footsteps, wondering why I didn't have the bravery to speak up and say something. But what? Goodbye? Or please stay?

I almost laugh at myself. I'd had a slim chance of convincing Jupiter to stay before, but getting caught leaving Adrian's tent with my clothes in my hands pretty much sealed the deal. She's done with me and my lukewarm Christianity. I can hardly blame her.

What do you look like to them?

A joke.

"A joke cannot change, save, or influence anyone," I mumble, but I quickly shake my head and pull my shoulders back. I don't get to feel sorry for myself when I'm the one to blame. Besides, there's no time to feel sorry. The next second, Adrian is back inside his tent, staring down at me. His eyes are pleading again, but his words are firm and serious.

"It's just us now."

I swallow, and the weight of that statement sinks into my bones. This group started seven strong—it began on a college campus—and just like that, we're down to two. Probably the worst two of the bunch. Adrian has a temper and is paranoid and clearly suffering from some sort of anxiety that he refuses to acknowledge or talk about. Meanwhile, I've earned my keep by bouncing between two boys just as quickly as Delilah had. But only one of us earned a reputation from it.

As I watch Adrian unroll his sleeping bag, I wonder what the difference between myself and my blonde rival truly is. *I didn't go all the way*, I remind myself, but does that make a difference to God who said lustful thoughts are just as sinful as the act?

It doesn't.

Stop beating yourself up. I bite down on my bottom lip and wince at the pain, I must have let out a gasp of some sort because Adrian glances at me and pauses. He's on his hands and knees, very neatly arranging his tiny pillow on his sleeping bag. When I don't speak, he goes back to fluffing the cushion.

"You're overthinking things," he says, focusing on his pillow.

"I don't know how you can be so calm about all of this."

He shrugs. "Maybe because I've experienced it before. It isn't new to me."

"Living like this isn't new?" I glance around the tent.

"I'm talking about the drama."

"Oh…"

"Friends betraying friends. Couples breaking up. Gossip, fights, backstabbing. It's all the same, just a new backdrop."

"Did you see this coming?"

He slowly blinks. "Eventually."

I have a hard time believing he's only talking about Jupiter's exit. Not about everything that happened before.

"I should get back to my tent," I say, pulling the flap back.

He nods. "Sleep well, Mya."

"You too."

24

Caesar

I've been a runner long enough to get used to the schedule, the people, and even the sort of supplies we gather and deliver. It didn't take me long because we maintain the same routes and mix them up by randomly rotating through them. It allows enough variety to prevent drifters from tracking us so easily, but just enough continuity for an observant runner to notice things.

I've noticed how much weight my running partner can carry, except when she's eaten a heavy breakfast—then she slows it down a bit. I've noticed how much time it typically takes for each runner pair to finish their routes. And I've noticed how relaxed our security team is when they know runners are returning from a delivery.

I've paid attention because I need to notice the good habits and the bad habits of our group. Good habits maintain order and keep the place running. But bad habits allow people like me to slip through the cracks.

A little while ago, Dr. Brown asked me a very important question. I didn't give him an answer because I wasn't ready to. And I'm still not ready.

Faith … It's harder than I thought. It isn't just empty words, it's a real act—a verb. There's a difference between faith and hope, and I realized that the day Dr. Brown asked me if I would believe in God. The truth is that I'd always *hoped* there was a God. I *wanted* God to be real. But I didn't truly have faith that He was. And the Bible says it's impossible to please God without faith. So, what can I do except abandon the whole thing altogether?

If I don't even have the basics down, then I'll never be good enough to serve God which means I'll never be good enough for Mya. She's the reason for all of this. So if I can't have her, then I'm not going to stick around here any longer.

Dr. Brown is safe. He's got hot food, a decent day chore assigned by Eternus staff to keep him busy, and he's living in a cozy tent behind a strong iron gate guarded by the United American soldiers. He's even secure in his faith, blissfully believing there is a God who cares and listens to his prayers, that He will bring his daughter to him one day.

Dr. Brown doesn't need me. I could hang around and pretend to believe in his God, but we both know any faith I put forward would be a false coverup for the doubt I truly feel inside.

The thing is, I don't doubt God's existence, I doubt His love for me. If He loved me, then why is it His will for me to be here in this stupid camp doing nothing? Mya is still out there. The rest of my friends are still out there. My foster mother is still out there. But God wants me to relax while they suffer.

I can't do that. I won't do that. If staying here serves as some sort of proof of my trust in God, then I'll gladly admit that I have none. Because every day that I'm here eating hot food, gathering boxes of supplies, and performing chores in this happy little camp, my friends, my family, and the love of my life wanders in the wilderness with no help at all.

I can't trust God because He hasn't helped me.

So I've got to help myself.

I've spent the last week of my running schedule studying everything, and I think I've finally got it all nailed down. My routine today is one of the longer ones which means it'll be at least five miles out, near an abandoned music hall. There's a huge parking lot and about a dozen little boutiques nearby for all the trendy, artsy folk who used to frequent this area. When I get to the music hall, I'll search each boutique for the supply drop. They never tell us the exact location just in case we get caught by someone.

Drifters and enemy soldiers have been a serious problem lately. We don't have enough weapons to properly fight them, but most drifters are just survivors like my friends; people just trying to make it out here. So they're not running around with military grade assault rifles, but the soldiers are a different story.

I've never encountered a drifter or a soldier during my few weeks here, but I've heard stories of runners being beaten, killed, or kidnapped and tortured for information. Normally, drifters want to know about supply drops, but enemy soldiers want info on Eternus.

Our only measure of defense against these guys is a hunting knife and the Rule of Flight. Most military operations function on a no-man-left-behind strategy, but Eternus can't afford to lose men *nor* supplies. That means if runners encounter lethal trouble or are separated for more than sixty minutes, Captain Hughes, leader of the runners, fully expects us to leave our partner behind and make it back to camp on our own. It sounds like a crappy rule, but when you're outnumbered and bringing knives to a gunfight, your only option in a fight or flight scenario is to flee as quickly as possible.

"Just make it home," Hughes tells us each morning before he rings the bell to open the gates to Eternus. He stands by as we all run out single file, slapping each of us on the back. It wasn't until today that I wondered if that pat would be the last one I ever got from him.

The answer is yes—because I'm not going back after this run.

My running partner is a girl named Raven, she's about my age with dark curly hair and evenly toned skin the same shade of brown as Mya's. She's extremely pretty but she's also a little crazy which I think is a result of some awful fight she had on a bad run before I got here. Apparently, her older sister is a runner too, but she's been in the infirmary for the last month, recovering from four broken ribs. Raven says she got caught by drifters and barely managed to survive a bad attack. Raven risked her life for her sister and managed to drag her back to Eternus all by herself. So, I'm her new running partner. At least until her death-defying sister gets better.

Raven's cool, when she isn't going on and on about how much faster she is than me. Or sharpening one of the knives from her collection. Or telling me about some fight she's been in which required her to use one of those knives. If you ask me, I think she's a little too excited to be a runner. But I won't have to deal with her for much longer.

She's beside me now, running at a nice even pace. If we keep this up for the next hour, we should be able to make it to the music hall by early afternoon. We'll probably stop for lunch right before we find the supply drop, then we'll pack up and head back. Easy day. Except for the part where I 'go missing' with my half of the drop.

Most of our deliveries are a few boxes of goods weighing up to 150 pounds. We divide everything up and take a slow pace back to Eternus, running with stuffed backpacks or even dragging a wagon behind us. I'm hoping today is just a backpack day, but I'll figure out a way to *go missing* with a wagon if I need to.

That's the task that takes up most of my thinking as I run beside Raven. The good thing about running is that you're so focused on making good time, keeping an even pace, and controlling your breathing, there isn't much room for conversation along the way. Raven can be a chatterbox at times, but never while we're in motion, so I get to spend the next hour and a half locked in my mind, sorting through my escape plans.

When we break, we split a gallon of water and then stuff down our lunch. Runners always get really dense meals since we need to refuel and maintain high energy throughout the day. Our food isn't the *best*, but it's more than enough to keep us from passing out during a run.

Raven and I both have a backpack stuffed with dried meat and rice balls which remind me so much of my Korean foster mom. Yeah, onigiri is a *Japanese* dish but I'd grown up as a stupid kid obsessing over all the anime I'd watch on the weekends. Almost every Saturday, I'd beg my foster mom to make me onigiri because I was too dumb to understand the differences between Korean and Japanese culture and cuisine. As a child, I simply didn't notice race the way grownups do. I just wanted to eat the foods I saw my favorite anime characters eat and my foster mom was kind enough to cook them for me, even if it meant making food outside her own culture.

Now, as I stuff the last of my third rice ball into my mouth, I swallow more than just the food. I feel a fat lump of emotion clog up my throat and I have to reach for my bottle of black tea to clear it out with three huge gulps. The tea is in a canteen and is still warm and slightly sweetened with honey. Captain Hughes says caffeine is a must and will help us on our runs, so we have to return with empty canteens, or we'll never hear the end of it.

Raven rubs a plum on her shirt to clean it before taking a huge bite. She wipes her mouth with the back of her hand. "You okay?"

"Yeah," I take another quick sip, "I'm just gonna pee and then we can leave."

Raven shrugs and takes another big bite.

I could sneak away instead of going to pee, but we've stopped at an old burger shop with only two exits. Raven is standing at the front windows, if I try to make a break for it, she'll see me running by. Plus, I want to see what sort of goods I can get from the supply drop. There'll be cans of food, jugs of water, and maybe even a few weapons. I've heard rumors that Major Banks has been pushing for better gear, I can only hope her urging has made some sort of progress.

When I get back inside, Raven is all packed, but her bag sits by the door instead of resting on her back. "My turn to pee," she says, punching my shoulder as she walks out.

I turn my back to the window to give her privacy, then I wait in silence, hoping I'm not doing the wrong thing. I don't see any other way here. I need to find Mya and my mother. I've survived once out there; I know I can do it again—especially without Adrian stupidly waving his gun around and screwing things up for everyone.

I figure I'll find my way back to Orly Center and start from there. After being on the runners' team for a few weeks, I've learned Eternus camp is just a few hours' drive from a small city named Koshen. It isn't far from Phoenix, but it took us days to get there from Orly Center because we'd been circling certain routes to throw off any drifters or enemy soldiers who might have been trying to follow us. If I'm careful, and I pace myself correctly, I'm sure I can make it back to that mall. That's where I told my friends I'd go if I ever got the chance to escape. Now I finally have that chance.

If I can't find my friends, I'll keep searching for my foster mother. If I can't find her, then I'll make it back to Eternus and start over again. I'll admit, it isn't a great plan, but it's better than sitting around doing nothing.

"Ready?" Raven pokes her head back through the door. When I nod, she grabs her backpack and slings it over her shoulder. "Let's head out."

We run for another two hours and make it to the music hall right on time. I'm soaked in sweat by then, and coughing up

239

Arizona dust, but Raven seems just fine as she swiftly moves toward the first boutique, ready to search for the drop.

We cover three different shops before we break for another meal, searching from the bottom floor all the way up to the emergency exit on the roof. No supply drops. It's obvious Raven is frustrated by the way she stuffs down her food and shoves her arms through her backpack straps. She doesn't even speak as she stomps away, just marches onward and expects me to follow.

I don't blame her for her irritation. It's hot, we're both tired, and there are still another ten shops to check, not to mention the fact that we've still got to divide up the supplies and then haul them all the way back home. Well ... I won't be going home, but still. This is taking longer than I thought it would, but that isn't a bad thing. In fact, our timing gives me the opportunity to make a suggestion.

"Why don't we split up?" I say, jogging beside Raven. We're on our way to a hair salon, hoping our delivery guys stashed the supply boxes in the cabinets or something.

Raven glances sideways. "Split up?"

"Splitting up will allow us to cover more ground in less time," I say—and it will also give me the chance to find the stash first, take what I need, and get going before Raven ever suspects a thing.

She nibbles on her bottom lip before slowing her jog to a full stop. "All right. I'll take the hair salon; you take the pet grooming shop. We meet back here in exactly one hour, no matter what you find."

I give her a thumbs-up and a wink. "Gotcha."

It takes me forty minutes to find the drop. I stumble upon it by chance, sprinting to the next shop. A flash of light reflects through the glass display of the donut shop right next door to the grooming facility I'd torn apart. At first, I think it's the muzzle of a gun—I even duck and take cover behind an empty dumpster some desperate soul has dragged from the alley into the middle of the street. But when nothing happens, I peek my head out again and realize the metallic glint of light isn't from a gun. I'm not sure what it's from until I take my chances and kick in the side door of the donut shop.

Inside, there's a pile of baking sheets, cupcake tins, and other bakery supplies near the display window. That was the reason for the metallic reflection. When I step closer, I see half a dozen boxes stored beneath all the kitchenware and it takes everything in me not to shout with joy.

Without wasting a beat, I drop to my knees and begin ripping open the first box. By now, it's been at least fifty minutes since Raven and I split up. I don't have time to go through all the supplies and pick what I want. Mercifully, the first box is filled with cans crudely labeled with permanent market and sloppy handwriting. I squint and read like a child until I find two cans of beef and barley, two cans of chicken and dumplings, and one can of tortilla fiesta soup—whatever that is.

I take a pack of jerky, a glass jar of peach preserves, and two gallons of water. I have to tie the water jugs to a rope and loop that around my waist because my pack is full already. Of course, it doesn't help that I also unboxed a flashlight, a better-quality hunting knife than the one I've got, and a first aid kit. All of that goes into my bag too, along with a clean shirt and a fresh pair of jeans which I packed before leaving.

With an anxious glance outside, I quickly exit the donut shop and shuffle down the dark alley in the opposite direction of the hair salon Raven had been searching. The jugs bounce against my thighs as I run, making me paranoid that I'm making too much noise. If Raven is somewhere nearby, she'll hear me and then I'll be caught. So instead of continuing through the echoey alleys, I dart through the backdoor of the shoe shop right beside the donut bakery and quickly make my way through the store.

The place looks like it used to be expensive, but none of that matters to me now. All I care about is finding the stairwell to the second floor so I can make my way to the roof. By the time I shove open the squeaky metal door, I'm drenched in my own sweat and panting hard. Hauling all these supplies is going to be tougher than I thought.

I got the idea from Adrian since he carried multiple bags of supplies from Wakedon almost back to campus all by himself. He'd stopped along the way to hide bags at various rest stops, but still. He'd made it look easy, but I can barely catch my breath. Now I've got no choice but to keep going, and I'm not even sure if that's possible for me right now.

I came up to the roof to get a better look at the street below. It's definitely been an hour by now, so I'm scanning the area for Raven. Or anyone else who might be nearby.

Sure enough, Raven's dark curly hair appears before the rest of her body emerges through the broken window of a tanning salon. She starts down the street in the direction of our meetup spot, and I release a heavy breath.

"Time to go," I say aloud. I even give Raven a little wave, though I know she doesn't see me standing behind her on top of a building. Knowing her, she'll wait ten minutes before worry sets in, and then she'll spend another ten minutes debating whether she should look for me, look for the stash alone, or simply abandon the delivery altogether.

She's a smart, strong young woman. Whatever she decides to do, I know she'll make it back to Eternus okay. That's the hope I hold on to as I turn to leave, except when I take my first step, my foot comes down on a discarded beer bottle and my ankle pivots awkwardly. Sharp pain needles through my foot, tingling up the back of my calf, and I gasp as I throw my weight onto my other foot to alleviate the ache.

Big mistake.

When I try to shift my weight, I end up throwing myself off balance and I begin to fall. Backwards. I can feel myself tilting over the edge of the roof, those cursed water jugs spinning and tugging me even more off balance, by my *waist*. I can't regain my footing. I'm falling off the roof of this shoe shop.

The realization steals a shout of frustration and fear from my chest, only cut off by a sudden nauseating, weightless feeling that makes my stomach flip. It's all over in a second. The ground rushes up to catch me, but my overstuffed backpack takes the grunt of the fall—except my head whips backwards upon impact and whacks the cement with a loud *slap!*

I'm engulfed in darkness before I even register the pain.

25

Adrian

We've been walking for days, but I'm used to that. I'm not bothered by the travel, or the hunger, or the dwindling supplies. I'm not bothered that our friends ditched us—or by the fact that I'm mostly to blame for them ditching us. I'm bothered by the silence.

Mya hasn't spoken since we left. I expected her to still be in mourning over Connor. I expected her to still be upset over Julius getting kidnapped. I expected her to be angry or frustrated that Jupiter and Bunny split. But I did not expect her to be silent.

The silence is new and surprising and confusing. The only explanation I have for it is our almost-hookup. We were *this* close to having sex, just a few scraps of clothes between us.

Maybe she wasn't ready for something like that. Maybe I pushed her too hard. Maybe walking into Jupiter so soon afterward has been too embarrassing for her to get over.

Or maybe she blames me for everything and doesn't know how to tell me she hates me now. What if she feels stuck here with me? No friends to run away with, no Julius to come to her rescue, no way to survive on her own. It's just us, and I think that bothers her. I think she regrets everything that happened with me.

That thought makes me swallow. My mouth feels sticky, so I open it to suck in thick, heavy breaths. Then I feel my throat clog with the gritty Arizona dust, and I start to cough. Little ones slip out my mouth at first, but as I continue gulping and heaving, I have to stop walking to double over and hack out the dust as well as a nice glob of phlegm.

When I stand upright again, Mya is staring at me. There is clear concern on her face, but instead of asking if I'm alright, she simply drops her gaze to the ground and presses her lips together.

I sigh. "Sorry."

She doesn't speak.

"Let's take a break," I grunt.

We've been travelling more quickly since being abandoned by our friends, but we've had no progress in finding my family or discovering any real clues on the whereabouts of Mya's father. Our first stop in Phoenix was the events center downtown; as soon as we walked through the front doors, we immediately knew it had once been a shelter. Unfortunately, it looked no different from Orly Center—except these people left bodies behind.

No one survived the attack in the Phoenix events center. The bodies were curled up, huddled in fetal position, hidden behind desks and overturned tables. Dried out and covered in red Arizona dust. The blood was old, the wounds of the dead filled with wiggling maggots. Whoever had come through there had done it weeks ago, so we felt safe enough to loot, search for clues, and move on. I kept a straight face, covering my nose to block out the smell of decay. Mya cried behind me, just trying to keep it together.

We searched the nearest hospital, a movie theater, and even camped out in the sanctuary of a mega church for two days.

Each place was a dead end.

Dangerously close to giving up, I've decided to simply return home. It's a scary idea, to trek across this big city and go back to the place my family used to live. But I simply don't know what else to do, and while the thought is scary, it is also oddly comforting. I mean … I already know my family won't be there. So I'm not blindly walking into a situation that could leave me heartbroken or worse.

Every time I've stepped into an abandoned shelter, I've felt myself tense up, felt my breaths run short, and felt a heavy sweat dampen my brow. There is an everlasting worry stalking the edges of my mind, a fear that is worse than never finding my siblings. It is a fear of finding them dead. Seeing their tiny adolescent bodies strewn across the floor in a lifeless heap, blood trickling from their mouths, their frames thin and starved, or their necks twisted at an awful angle. Just like Connor.

He was not supposed to die. None of us were supposed to die. That's not the happy ending I imagined for this story. But imagination gets you nowhere in the unforgiving reality.

The reality is that I could just as easily find my twin siblings rotting in an alley as I could find them healthy and whole and eagerly waiting for my return. But only one of those scenarios makes it difficult to sleep at night. Only one scenario unleashes the shadow of fear to latch onto my heart, wrapping tendrils of worry around my throat, choking me of my bravery. Every abandoned refugee shelter summons a panic attack that nearly takes me to my knees. I've managed to fight them off so far, reminding myself that I cannot lose my cool around Mya. Not now. But I don't know how much more I can take.

That's why I'm going home; because I know my family isn't there, so I don't have to face any fears or worries of finding their dead bodies in the living room. At home, I can focus on sorting our supplies, doing some looting, mapping out our next target location, and maybe even fixing things with Mya. But to do that, I have to know what's wrong first. Right now, that's a completely different mystery that I don't even want to touch. But I *need* to because this situation won't make itself better on its own. I've got to make the first step.

I kick in the front doors of a local library. This place isn't just great for a break, I think it'll be a nice spot to set up camp for a few days. At least until we're ready to go to my tiny crappy house.

Mya follows me into the lobby, squinting through the dusty afternoon light that pours in through the high windows above us. Once we pass the book return section, we freeze. There's a welcome table set up, just like we've seen in all the other shelters we've visited.

"I wasn't expecting this place to be a safehouse," I mutter, staring at the table.

Mya brushes past me and approaches the stand. Almost everything here is perfectly intact. The welcome table is dusty, but the clipboard and piles of papers are still neatly arranged, the welcome sign is legible and sways in the ghostly wind that drifts through the large empty space. Even the chairs are pushed in.

"What is this place?" I blink around the room, turning a full circle. It looks like a shelter—just like all the others—but it's in such great condition, I almost don't believe it.

There are no overturned tables, no piles of debris or bullet casings left behind. It's scary to see a shelter so clean because it makes me wonder ... Why is it empty?

Clearly, no looters or soldiers got to this place. So why was it abandoned?

Mya must be thinking the same thing because she abruptly leaves the table and rushes for the main library. I figure she's searching for bodies, but she isn't moving blindly. Mya pushes through the heavy double doors with a grunt and marches with a purpose. She ignores the activity stations, moves past the quiet study section, and never bats an eye at the abandoned backpacks piled up in the fantasy/sci-fi section.

I quicken my steps behind her when Mya turns a sharp corner, but as soon as I turn the corner, I nearly walk into her. Mya is frozen, eyes wide and unblinking as she stares ahead. I trace her gaze and my mouth forms a perfect little O.

We're in the children's section of the library, but between the short, kid-level shelves are tents and cots. Each section is separated by a hanging sheet, allowing privacy for the clusters of tents, just like at Orly Center.

"This is where they slept," I say into the quiet.

My voice seems to snap Mya to attention, she physically startles and then holds up a wrinkled sheet of paper. I hadn't noticed it clutched in her hand before—I guess she took it from the welcome table. She's staring at it now, eyes darting through the words in rapid motion. Then she glances up and hastily makes her way through the aisle on our right.

We weave through three tent clusters before she stops again. This time, she doesn't stare at what she's found, she glances over her shoulder at me.

"What is it?" I whisper, and for the first time since I kissed her, Mya speaks.

"Your family."

I rush forward into the little camping area; a large white sheet gives them privacy, and as I reach to snatch it down, I see a patch sewn onto the fabric. It says one word—one *name*. **Nikols**. My last name, one unique enough that I know it belongs to my family.

I stand there in the empty tent, staring at everything, not really knowing where to start. There's a large backpack in the corner, a pile of dirty clothes, and what looks like a box of junk. Probably goods they'd collected over time. But there are only two places to sleep; the dirty cot in the middle of the room, or the sleeping bag unrolled beside it. I'm glad they didn't have to sleep on the hard floor, but two bedrolls are not enough for four people.

It might be enough for one adult and two small kids, however. Danya and Dinara are both small for their age; they could've squeezed into the sleeping bag together or cuddled up in the cot. Since the name on the sheet says Nikols and not my stepfather's last name, I'm going to assume if there was only one adult here, it was my mother.

No matter who it was, they aren't here now.

The tent is completely empty, like the rest of the library. And judging from the layer of dust on the sleeping bag and the dirty stiff clothes, I'd say this place has been empty for a while. Likely months.

"Why..." I whisper, dropping to my knees.

The dam inside me breaks and I feel all of my emotions— my worry, my fear, my frustration—flood into my mind, into my heart. The weight of it all bears down on me and I see my vision blur with tears.

We'd come so far. We'd fought so hard. Only to make it to an abandoned shelter—again.

"Why?" I let out a warbled sob, not caring about Mya seeing me fall apart. I'm in too much pain to care right now. All I can do is crawl to the pile of dirty clothes and clutch the tiny shirt I see there. "Why do we keep walking into dead ends?" I blubber. "We've been so close—"

"Are you kidding me?" Mya steps beside me, and despite the snappiness of her question, her voice is actually calm and almost soothing. "This is not a dead end, Adrian. You've found proof that your family was here." She holds up that wrinkled paper. "The name Nikols is registered as a family of four—"

So my stepfather was here... My thoughts interrupt Mya's voice, but I don't need to hear the rest. I've already got the gist of it. I need to get it together and stop feeling sorry for myself. This is not the outcome I've wanted, but it's better than what I had before. Still ... It just hurts.

"I was so close," I mutter, sitting on my butt and running a hand through my shaggy hair. "I'm so tired, Mya."

To my surprise, she sits beside me. "I'm tired too."

I get the feeling we aren't talking about the same things right now.

"I'm sorry," I blurt without thinking. The confession shocks us both, but Mya is surprised more than I am. She turns to look at me with her eyes wide and then she recovers with an embarrassed smile.

"I'm the one who is sorry. I reacted to that whole thing like a child, giving you the silent treatment. You didn't deserve that."

I shift beside her, inching slightly closer to her. Our thighs touch. "What made you find your voice now?"

"Finding your last name on that sheet of paper. It made me realize there are much bigger things going on than my own childish emotions." She looks at me seriously. "I'm sorry, Adrian. I never should have pushed you away. You're the only person I have right now—but that isn't why I'm sorry. I'm sorry because you honestly deserve an apology. You've always been there for me, but I just now learned to appreciate it because there was no one else here to distract me. I've been so awful to you."

I nod, resisting the urge to reach over and take her hand. I squeeze the little shirt I'm holding instead. "I took advantage of you, Mya."

She chuckles. "That whole situation was all me. I never should have let things get that far, and then when they did go there, I couldn't stop it. It took someone else nearly walking in on us for me to realize how far gone I was."

"You weren't far gone," I say, shaking my head. "You were following what you felt."

"But what I felt wasn't in alignment with what God wants for me, Adrian. I don't get to act on every desire I feel. There is a standard I live by, and it requires sacrifice."

"Even the sacrifice of love?"

She pauses, and I wonder if I might have used too strong of a word. I'm talking about myself right now. I love Mya, but

251

I'm not entirely sure what she feels for me other than a desperate need to replace Julius.

She sighs. "Yes, even the sacrifice of love."

"That's asking for a lot."

"It isn't anything more than what God gave us first."

I raise an eyebrow and she smiles sheepishly. The uncomfortable look on her face makes me sympathetic. It must be so hard for her to talk about God right now, after she let me strip her clothes away and dry hump her on the floor. But she's doing it anyway, determined to get back in alignment. Or whatever.

I don't understand it. I don't even *want* to understand all the effort she puts into her faith. But I do respect it. I've tried having faith and it hasn't worked out for me. It takes a strong person to believe in the face of trouble, to believe when everything is stacked against you, including your own mistakes and sin. But Mya's doing it, and maybe that's the greater message here. Not her perfect behavior, but her constant belief that God still loves her. Despite her terrible mistakes.

"God gave us Jesus, His only begotten Son. The one whom He loves more than eternity could describe. He sent Him to earth to die for us. That's the greatest sacrifice of all time, and nothing will ever compare to it." She takes a deep breath. "So, yes, I am willing to make that sacrifice. Because it was first made for me."

"Mya..." I stare at my leg rubbing against hers. She doesn't seem to notice our proximity. "I'm sorry."

"You've said that already—"

"No." I shake my head. "I'm sorry for more than just pushing myself onto you. I'm sorry for coming between you and God."

She snaps her head toward me, and her eyes instantly fill with tears. I feel so crappy now. How could I have made her cry *again?*

"I'm sorry!" I say again, but she cuts me off.

"No, you haven't done anything wrong!" she blurts, wiping her tears.

"But ... You're crying."

"These tears aren't sad." She sniffles. "It's just ... that might be the kindest thing anyone has ever said to me."

It feels weird that such an apology would be considered a nice thing to say. I have no idea how to even respond to that, so I don't. I just sit in silence as Mya wipes her tears. She doesn't say anything for a long while, but she doesn't leave me. Doesn't even scoot further away. We remain right there, side by side, leaning on each other. Holding each other up.

It's strange, until now, the silence between us has felt stifling. Almost overwhelming, like it was slowly driving me crazy. But now it's comfortable. I welcome the silence like a warm blanket, let it wrap me up and hold me tight. The quiet doesn't feel so stony anymore. It isn't a wall between me and Mya, now it's like a bubble, filled with all the things we've wanted to say to each other for a long time now.

I hear the words in Mya's sniffles, see them in the shy smile she offers once her tears have dried up. I hear her apology and her kindness and her desire in the tiny laugh that spills from her full lips when I bump her shoulder with my own. She leans against me, and I sigh, hoping she hears my silent words too. My own apology, my own weaknesses, my own confusion.

She does hear them, and for the first time in our complicated relationship, I think she accepts them. She accepts that I'm not Julius and I'm not going to be his replacement.

I'm not her desperate second choice, I'm a person with real feelings and emotions too. She accepts that it's okay to enjoy me as myself. Not as her rebound guy or as the next best thing.

She accepts that it's okay to like me at all. That being close to me isn't a betrayal to Julius. Because Julius isn't here anymore. And maybe he never will be again. And that might hurt, but eventually, that'll be okay too.

Mya finally breaks the silence. "We're going to find your siblings."

"And your father," I say gently.

She nods beside me. "Adrian?"

"Yes?"

"Let's camp here for the day."

"Okay."

"Is that okay?"

"It's perfect, Mya."

26

Caesar

When I open my eyes, every part of my body aches. My head throbs as the daylight nearly blinds me. Pain pulses through my temple and knocks on my forehead. I feel the sharp sting behind my eyes, like something is trying to crawl out of my face. But squeezing my eyes shut brings me no relief.

The rest of my body feels like it's been tossed around like a ragdoll. My ribs hurt, my arms are sore and tired, my legs feel heavy and cumbersome. I slowly begin wiggling my extremities, just to make sure they're still functional. My left leg is in a boot. I tilt my chin down to peer through my watery eyes at it. A big black boot covers my foot, preventing me from rotating my ankle.

My memories storm in like a flood and I gasp as I see myself falling off the roof of a building in slow motion. I'd stepped on an empty bottle and lost my footing. I groan, reaching up to touch my head. I'd whacked it on the cement and knocked myself out. There's a thick bandage wrapped around my head, clasped at my temple, just above the ear. I start to pick at the bandage, but someone's voice stops me.

"Don't!"

I glance up to see Dr. Brown entering the room and my eyes widen. I hadn't even noticed I was in a *room*. Last thing I remember is being on a run with Raven, then falling down. But now I'm lying in a bed in a wooden cabin with two windows, a bedside table, and a chair for someone to rest in. Judging from the open book left in the chair, I'd say Dr. Brown had been sitting there earlier. But for how long?

How long have I been passed out—and how did I get here?

Dr. Brown runs to the side of my bed. "Don't touch the bandage. The doctor said you had a concussion."

"A concussion?"

My worry must be written on my face because Mya's dad gives me a reassuring pat on my arm, which hurts. He says, "Don't worry, you're going to be fine."

"I don't know what happened—"

"Some memory loss is common with a concussion." He nods.

I do remember what happened… I just have no clue how I ended up back in *Eternus*. But I keep my mouth shut because if I tell Dr. Brown what really happened, he's going to know I tried to leave. I'm not sure how he'll react to that.

Thankfully, he answers my question without me even having to ask. "Raven dragged you back here all by herself. She's been too overwhelmed to properly recall all the events."

If I didn't hurt so much, I'd grunt and roll my eyes. I haven't known Raven for long, but she's a one-note girl—and I mean that in a flattering way. Tough as nails and so direct it almost makes me uncomfortable. If there is one thing Raven is *not*, it's *overwhelmed*. Which means she's lying to Dr. Brown and anyone else who questioned her.

She's covering for me...

I swallow and wince at the dryness in my throat. Dr. Brown startles and turns toward the door. "You must be dying of thirst! I can grab some water for you, and the nurse too! What am I doing?" He wrings his hands like a nutty character in a movie. "I need to tell everyone you're awake! This is a miracle!"

Not really. I've got a concussion and a twisted ankle, I'd say this is a minor inconvenience, if anything. But I don't say that aloud. Christian people tend to view every good thing as a miracle. I'll let Dr. Brown have his moment of joy.

He stops and looks at me with nothing but love and concern on his face. "Everything is going to be all right, son. You're safe now. God's got you."

I glance down so he doesn't see the guilty look on my face. Maybe this isn't just a moment of joy for Dr. Brown. He was really worried about me. He genuinely cares for me. And I got myself hurt by selfishly stealing supplies and trying to leave.

"Thanks for caring, Pops," I say quietly.

He beams from ear to ear, and I don't know if it's because I thanked him or because I called him *Pops*. He's pretty much the only father I've ever known, I honestly can't think of a better thing to call him.

"Let me go grab that water," he says happily.

"And food?"

His grin widens. "I think lunch will be ready soon. We're having roasted pigeon and vegetable soup!"

He bounces out the door before he can see me grimacing. I have never eaten pigeon before, but I suppose this is the best we can offer when the entire world is at war. I'm just glad it isn't roasted rat. Or cockroach.

I settle into my cushiony bed with a deep sigh, but before I can truly relax and figure out what the heck is going on, my door opens and someone else enters.

I expect it to be a nurse or Dr. Brown with that water, but I'm shocked into silence when Raven stands at the end of my bed. She's wearing cargo shorts and a baggy t-shirt, her afro hair is pulled up into a nice puff atop her head, and her pierced eyebrows are furrowed in anger. She folds her arms and glares at me. In that moment, I realize how toned she is. Running and hauling supplies for miles every day has given her a strong, muscular body that makes it very easy to understand how she was able to drag me back to Eternus all by herself. She'd already done that once with her sister, I'm not surprised she was able to do it again.

"Talk," she says. It's one clipped word, spoken quickly and with enough force that I obey without question.

"I fell off a roof."

She takes a step closer to the bed. "Right. You fell off a roof because you thought you saw soldiers and you wanted to get a better look. So you climbed up there to scout and lost your footing."

I think right now is a very wise time to simply nod and agree.

"That's the story I can tell Captain Hughes who's coming to my tent this afternoon for another round of questioning. Or I can tell him the unfiltered version of the story."

"What's in that version?" I ask cautiously.

"In that version, I find you in the back of an alley with your backpack stuffed full of supplies—supplies that you stole and

258

tried to run off with. But you're so much of a failure and an idiot, you couldn't even get away from someone who *wasn't looking for you* without screwing it up. How's that version sound?"

I stare down at my blankets, feeling uncomfortably hot now. Despite it being February, it's still relatively warm in Arizona. Or maybe I'm just sweating from my nerves. Raven is smart. And she knows what she's doing. If I'm not careful, she will rat me out.

"Why are you covering for me?" I say.

"Why'd you try to leave?" she counters.

I don't speak.

"Seriously, Caesar. You stole supplies and tried to run off." She pauses, and as her gaze shifts away for half a second, I see what she's truly feeling right now. Not just anger, but sadness. "You tried to leave me there."

"It wasn't personal."

The look on her face makes me feel like it *is*—to her at least. I won't be prideful and allow myself to believe Raven did this out of some romantic notion toward me. Our relationship as runners has been entirely platonic, but that isn't to say it was meaningless. From my first day as a runner, I've noticed Raven training like a true soldier. She takes her role here more seriously than any other runner I've seen and has even told me she wants to take over the operation when Captain Hughes gets a much-deserved promotion.

That is why she's so upset right now. Raven doesn't have a crush on me, she's dedicated to me as her running partner. And I betrayed that trust. I've never been a soldier until now, but I've been on a team before. Running track is a different battle entirely, but the fight isn't much easier. I've trained beside my

259

teammates every day, I've sweated with them, sustained injuries with them, encouraged them. I know what it's like to form a bond beyond emotion. A connection that ties you together on a level no one else could ever understand. I hadn't known Raven long enough for that connection to mean something to *me*, but who am I to judge how easily she bonds with someone else? Especially since she'd almost lost her last partner.

I picked the worst possible person to try to abandon. Raven risked her life dragging her own sister back despite being trained to leave your partner when the danger becomes lethal. She ignored that order and saved her sister's life. And then she got partnered with me and ended up finding my unconscious body in the back of a dark alley. I can't imagine the shock and fear she must have experienced. Or the confusion of not knowing how I'd gotten there.

I owe Raven more than an apology. I shouldn't feel annoyed by her attitude or her questioning. I should feel thankful. She might be taking things personally, but she did save me. I had a concussion, without medical attention, I might not have woken up after that fall. Or if I did wake up, I might've been permanently changed. My brain shaken and altered from rattling around in my thick skull.

Raven sucks in a sharp breath, regaining her composure. "If I tell Captain Hughes the unfiltered version of this story, you will be punished for what you've done."

"I know that—"

"No, you don't," she says hotly. "Don't you get it? We are pressed for supplies, Caesar, and you got caught trying to steal. Our secrecy is what keeps Eternus hidden from our enemies— it's what keeps us safe. And you got caught trying to sneak off."

She shakes her head. "The camp leaders could twist this around and say you were sneaking off to meet with enemy soldiers."

"I wasn't trying to do that!"

"I don't know *what* you were trying to do." She slams a small fist on the post of the bed, but she doesn't raise her voice. I'm thankful. There's no telling how thin these walls are. "Our world is at war. That means camp officials and military leaders need to be able to trust you. If they find out you tried to betray us, they'll put you out—or they won't ever let you leave again."

I swallow, praying to God Dr. Brown hurries up with that water.

"Do you understand what I'm saying?" Raven says, eyebrows raised.

I nod slowly. If she rats me out, I could get forced out of the camp or imprisoned. Maybe even worse. These people could kill me if they wanted to. Who would stop them? They've formed their own new country out here and declared me a citizen! I've got to follow their rules if I want to survive now. Getting put out honestly doesn't sound like it would be the end of the world, I was trying to leave in the first place. But I doubt they'd let me go with a bag stuffed full of supplies, or even with the boot on my ankle.

"I still don't understand why you've been covering for me," I say softly.

"And I still don't understand why you tried to leave."

I take a deep breath. "I'll tell you, but only if you promise not to tell Captain Hughes about all this."

"I make no promises."

"Raven," I say seriously, "you just told me they could force me out for this!"

261

"You're just gonna have to trust me."

"While you're holding my livelihood in your hands?"

She makes a nasty face, and her voice comes out in a sneer. "I trusted you."

Touche.

"Get talking, liar."

"Dr. Brown is on his way back."

She shakes her head. "I sent him off to find painkillers for you, but he'll have to sign a waiver and vouch for you. The paperwork may take a while since the circumstances surrounding your need for painkillers are shaky right now."

I take a deep breath. "Alright, I get it. I'll tell you, okay?"

She nods, and I launch into my story.

27

Caesar

I start from the beginning, giving her details about the campus and how everything fell apart so quickly and so painfully. I tell her about Mya and how Adrian always stood at the edge of our relationship, a silent threat I tried my best to ignore. I tell her about staying in Dr. Brown's house, and dating Mya, and falling in love with her. Then I tell her how the relationship fell apart. And how I thought we were about to make up and fix things between us until we heard that whistle from Delilah. I tell Raven how I met Major Banks and was kidnapped by her, then I tell her how I was reunited with Dr. Brown but not my foster mother.

She stands and she listens to everything, not interrupting a single time. She looks patient, even thoughtful, and when I'm finished, she stands there for a while.

I admit, I didn't have to start from the very beginning. I didn't have to give her every detail about the drama with Mya and Delilah and even my doubts about God. But I needed Raven to understand everything I'd been through with my friends so she could see why I was willing to betray Eternus for them.

As I sit in this tense silence, waiting for judgment, I wonder if I got through to Raven. If she sees me as a helpless romantic or a fool.

"I get it," she mumbles, to my relief. "You want to find your mother and your friends and this girl you're in love with."

I nod.

"But there are better ways to do this—"

"No one will help me, Raven."

"Major Banks is in charge of the Search-and-Rescue team. She'll find your friends."

I shake my head. "She wouldn't even let me join their team."

"In her defense, they are selective. And you've clearly proven yourself to be a flight risk."

"So, this is all my fault?"

"Well, *I* didn't shove you off that roof."

I don't even respond to that.

"Why don't you ask Dr. Brown for help? Mya is his daughter, right? I'm sure if he speaks to Major Banks, he might be able to sway her. He's a nice old man, and he's helped Eternus a lot by keeping the generators running. The camp could do him one favor."

"I'm sure they could," I say dryly, "but he isn't going to ask for a favor. Dr. Brown wants to leave everything in God's hands." I groan in anger. "I'm not a man of God. I tried to be, but I can't. I need to *do* something. Sitting around waiting for

God isn't in my blood." Childishly, I add, "He moves too slow."

To my surprise, Raven laughs. It's the nicest sound I've ever heard leave her mouth and it catches my attention immediately.

"What's so funny?" I snap.

She sighs tiredly. "Maybe Dr. Brown is right."

"I doubt it."

"You're just angry, Caesar. And who wouldn't be? The world is falling apart, no one wants to hear anything about God right now. But haven't you noticed that every time you've tried to do something in your strength, your own way, you've failed miserably?"

Of course, I've noticed that. But admitting to it would mean I've got no choice except to let God handle things. And I don't want to do that. I want to handle it, because then at least I know it'll get done. I can't trust God. Not anymore.

"I didn't realize you were religious," I say.

With her knife collection and her eyebrow piercings, Raven doesn't look religious. Then again, neither did Mya before the world fell apart. She used to dress in full goth with heavy eyeliner, platform boots, and ripped jeans. I loved the way she dressed but so many Christians judged her for it, it was difficult for her to make friends. I loved that she never let the harsh treatment bother or change her. She stuck to her fashion and her faith.

Raven bites the inside of her cheek. "I was raised Christian. But I've definitely drifted."

I nod mutely, waiting for her to continue.

"Everything started with this guy."

I almost laugh. Isn't it always some forbidden romance that pulls Christians away from the God they claim to love so much? If that's the case, then who do they really love? God Almighty, or the person sending them cute texts at night?

"His name was Arya," Raven continues. "My mother absolutely hated him, but I just refused to see her point of view on the matter. I was nineteen when I met him, a legal adult. I didn't need my mother's input. So, I moved out."

Sheesh…

"Two years later, the grid goes down. I was living with Arya, but we were in a really bad neighborhood. A place so crappy the National Guard didn't think we were worth an official escort." She laughs bitterly. "We found out via the local news channel that we were to report to the nearest safehouse for shelter. They listed a couple in our area, and we picked a hospital. My sister was staying with us too; all of us packed as much as we could and set out together. But we never made it to the safehouse."

"What happened?" I ask when she pauses for a while.

Raven fills her chest with air, and then lets it out slowly. "We got jumped just two blocks from our house. Some thugs tried to snatch our bags, and we fought back. Arya managed to beat them off, but…" she swallows so loudly, I hear it across the room. "He got stabbed. It was bad—there was so much blood. My sister and I didn't know what to do; we knew we wouldn't be able to make it to the hospital with him like that, so we went back home." She swipes a tear from her cheek. "Arya passed out along the way, and he just never woke back up. For three days, he lay on the sofa with his eyes closed. Breathing. Sweating. Sometimes moaning, I guess from the pain or maybe from nightmares. And then on the fourth day, he stopped breathing. That was it."

"I'm sorry," I whisper.

Raven shakes her head. "I know what it's like to want to save someone you love, Caesar. I even know what it's like to try to trust God to save them for you. I prayed to Him on Arya's behalf. I begged the Lord to spare him. But Arya died on my living room sofa."

I ball my hand into a fist, wondering why God seemed so cruel sometimes.

"God didn't kill Arya," Raven whispers, making me look up in surprise. "Those thugs did. And it's my fault that he died. I was a Christian, but I wasn't like Mya. I didn't bother introducing Arya to the Lord. I didn't *want* him to get saved because if he did, our relationship would have to change."

I completely understood what she was saying. Becoming a Christian meant you couldn't live together anymore, you couldn't have sex anymore, you couldn't do all the fun things grown adults do in their relationships until you got married. But how long would that take? And would it really be so bad if we moved in and then got married later?

Flee from sexual immorality… The Scripture pops into my head in Mya's own voice. We used to have this conversation all the time when I was giving her a headache about the no sex before marriage rule. We couldn't help it that we were surviving under the same roof together, btu when she told me we couldn't live together if there *hadn't* been an apocalypse, I'd gotten angry. And as usual, she'd put me in my place. Biblically.

"The Bible tells us to flee from sin, *especially* sexual sin," she had told me. "Christians cannot live together before they get married because staying holed up with the one person you want to have sex with is the exact opposite of *fleeing* from sin. You are consciously placing yourself in the direct line of fire for sexual sin, temptation, and lust. That's like *volunteering* to work at a strip club and then praying for God to protect you from impure thoughts." She'd patted me on the back. "You wouldn't need to fight that battle if you hadn't willingly run into enemy territory in the first place. That sort of reckless behavior—*knowingly* placing yourself in a sinful or tempting environment—is called testing God, which is also a sin."

At that point, I'd given up the argument altogether.

Raven sniffles, catching my attention again. "Now I regret my stupidity. Now I regret all the fun I'd had because what did it get me? My boyfriend is dead."

"Introducing him to God might not have changed a thing," I say, hating how bitter and angry I sound. "Mya is a Christian, she's made a lot of mistakes, but she's never stopped loving God. She did do the right thing and tried to introduce me to the Lord—but her mother died of cancer." I shrug, though it hurts. "Getting your boyfriend saved would've been nice. But God may not have protected him either way."

Raven remains silent for a long moment, then she says slowly, "You ever think that maybe some people choose to die?"

I blink at her. "What?"

"When I first got here, I refused to go to the camp's church services. After a while, my sister convinced me to give it a try. I broke down crying the very first time I went, and the pastor pulled me aside afterward. When I told her this same story, do you know what she said?"

I shake my head.

"She told me that God had answered my prayers."

I raise one eyebrow, pretty sure her grief is speaking now because last thing I heard, Arya was good and dead.

"I'd spent three days begging God to save Arya as he lay passed out on my sofa. God didn't save his life, but my pastor says He saved his soul instead."

My blood runs cold.

"I don't have the strongest of faith," Raven admits, "but that thought gives me a little hope. Maybe the pastor here is right. Maybe for those three days, Arya wasn't here in this world. Maybe God took him away to visit Heaven and he chose to stay. Maybe Jesus appeared to him and offered him salvation during his deep sleep. And maybe Arya decided it was better to go while he was in God's presence rather than come back here and risk falling right back into sin." Raven sighs. "Maybe the pastor just told me all that to make me feel better, but it's worth some thought. Don't you think?"

I find myself nodding. "It is…"

I think about Mya's mother, how she'd suffered so terribly but had remained faithful through it all. When she finally died, everyone had said she'd lost the battle with cancer. But what if they're wrong? What if Jesus came and got her? What if He appeared to her and told her it was okay to leave, that He had a better place for her and that He would take care of Mya until they met again? I imagine the Lord taking the hand of Mya's mother and leading her from this world into the next with a smile on both of their faces. He could have just as easily healed her, but God is a gentleman, He would've let her make the choice. And only a fool wouldn't choose Heaven.

Mya's mother hadn't lost the battle at all. She's still alive, just not in our world. And her exit had been entirely voluntary. How many other 'tragic' deaths had ended the same way? How many others who are locked in comas spend their time conversing with God? Entertaining angels? Or are in Heaven right now while their body lies motionless and their faithless family weeps.

I stare at my balled fists, still gripping my blankets, and I slowly unfold them. "I've been a fool."

"You have," Raven agrees. "Dr. Brown was right when he said God is trying to save you, Caesar. This is what it looks like when the Lord wrestles you down with His love."

"So, God throws people off of roofs when He wants to talk?"

She laughs, wiping the last of her tears. "God does whatever He must to get the attention of people who refuse to listen."

"So much for salvation being my choice. I fell off a roof!"

"Maybe that stopped you from making an awful mistake. Who knows who you could've bumped into after leaving that place?" She rolls her eyes. "And maybe God *didn't* knock you off that roof. Maybe you fell because you're a klutz who decided to steal supplies and try to escape instead of just trusting God. If you had rested and let God handle things like Dr. Brown told you, you wouldn't be in a hospital bed right now."

I groan in anger. "You sound just like Mya."

"And maybe Mya will say exactly what I'm about to say." She sets her hands on her hips. "God is not going to give up on you, Caesar. Salvation will always be your choice, but you see where your choices have gotten you."

I roll my eyes.

"I'll tell Captain Hughes the filtered version of my story."

My face lights up, but Raven raises a hand to cut me off before I can thank her.

"On one condition…"

"What is it?" I say hesitantly.

"You start coming to Sunday service with me."

"Seriously? You admitted you don't even know what you believe! But you want me to go to church with you now?"

"I don't know what I believe," she admits. "But maybe this is my own opportunity from God to find out." She extends a hand. "It'll be easier to learn together."

I stare at her open palm, not at all wanting to take it. But I know she's right. I know Dr. Brown was right. I know Mya's been right. But I'm stubborn and foolish and I hate admitting when I'm wrong. So instead of saying that I've been wrong and crying my eyes out like a newborn Christian, I just lean forward and hold out my hand.

"It's not like I can go out on missions with this boot on," I grumble.

Raven takes my hand and holds it. "This will be a journey for me too, Caesar. But at least we'll take it together."

28

Mya

We've been at the library for a week now. It's peaceful here. Quiet. Calm.

The place is incredibly well kept, dust being the only intruder besides us. I've kept myself busy going through papers from the offices and the welcome desk out front. Not much information is available, but at least none of it was torched like at Orly Center. Adrian finds more papers with his family's name on them, and I find a handwritten letter from a nearby church offering to take in refugees from the library. Apparently, this place was getting full, and the National Guard had delayed the second wave of evacuations due to enemy raids in a nearby city. The church stepped up and opened its doors, but the letter ends there.

Of course, I didn't expect to find a response letter because that would have been sent and delivered to the church. But I did see an address for the church in the original text; it's located in Koshen, a city in the opposite direction of Phoenix.

When I shared the letter with Adrian, he insisted we check it out. Not only is this the only lead we've got, but Koshen is where Jupiter and Bunny were going. Maybe—just maybe—we'll find them there too. It's a longshot, but I trust that God will work it all out. He has so far.

It might sound weird to hear me talking about God again, but I've been working on getting myself together this past week. That talk with Adrian changed everything. He didn't apologize for kissing me, or for insisting I use him to get over my pain. He didn't apologize for his desperation. He apologized for coming between me and God.

The words had been so precious to me. They'd broken me. Someone else had seen the value in my faith and had apologized for threatening it. That apology reminded me of how much I used to value my faith. And it made me want to value it again. So, I've been in serious spiritual bootcamp this past week, spending time with God, repenting for all the things I've done and trying to forgive myself for falling short of the glory.

I was one of the only Christians in the group, and instead of leading my friends to the Lord and depending on Him for our survival, I acted as a hypocrite and fell into temptation, anger, and self-pity. Jupiter and I spent our time in childish catfights instead of setting an example for our friends. Instead of letting our faith unite us, we weaponized it and used it to judge each other and divide the group.

I can't change the past, but maybe I can make up with Jupiter in the future. Maybe I can find out why she'd changed so much and why she'd begun to hate me so suddenly. Or maybe I'll see her again and realize none of that nonsense even matters anymore.

As far as I know, we both fell victim to our emotions. Jupiter was lost in depression, and I got caught up with lust. Two different emotional states but both of them cause pain, suffering, and change the way you think or behave. Yet, both of them can be defeated by the same God who loves us.

It's funny... When a Christian struggles with depression, the Church sympathizes with them, even shares scriptures and starts prayer groups for them. But if you struggle with lust, the only thing the Church has for you is judgment, anger, and shame.

Jupiter and I both fought a difficult battle and we both lost. We both allowed our emotions to take over our minds, our thoughts, and influence the way we behaved and how we treated others. But my battle is the only one that gets criticized and picked apart.

Good thing my salvation is not determined by the judgment of others. God is still with me, and the Blood of His Son, Christ Jesus, has washed me clean. I am not perfect, and I know I'll continue making mistakes on this journey, but this week has been a huge step in the right direction. We're in a library, so I've been able to read the Bible every day and even pick up some Christian study guides by some of my favorite pastors.

I thank God for this new opportunity. For using Adrian, of all people, to inspire my faith again. I hate to admit it, but I don't know if Julius would have done that. With him, my faith had always been an issue. A fight. I'd had fights with Adrian about God too, but this was different. His words had been sincere. And ever since then, we've found common ground.

We share food and talk during our meals. We clean up our living spaces together and joke about whose area is neater (it's always Adrian's). Before bed, Adrian picks out a book and he unrolls his sleeping bag as I read. I love that part of our day; taking advantage of this great library, getting lost in our books like the world outside these walls isn't filled with hatred and death.

Adrian always picks something from the Christian fiction section, a habit I've noticed but haven't commented on. When it's time, we'll talk more about his faith. For now, I just thank God for the authors we've found who've openly included their faith in their work. It's given me the opportunity to share what I believe in with Adrian through the stories we read together.

Apparently, Adrian used to love reading before all this. He says it helped him escape the awful world he'd lived in with his abusive stepdad and his lazy mother. I enjoyed reading too, but only because it was fun. I never thought there were people who *needed* to read. Needed a dose of fiction to help them cope with reality,

Adrian's rolling out his sleeping bag now, sighing as he flops onto his back and closes his eyes. "You ready?" he asks, voice a lazy drawl.

"Of course." I reach for the book and unfold the dog-eared page. We finished a cozy Christian mystery two days ago, now we've been working our way through an incredible Christian fantasy. Adrian says it's gotten too romantic for his tastes. I completely agree, but we both hate leaving things unfinished so we're powering through it as best we can.

Maybe that's what we're doing now. Trying to power through the confusion swimming between us. Trying not to leave things unfinished. The last time we were alone like this, I ended up half naked on his tent floor. But things have changed. A lot.

I'm not dating Adrian. His presence is warm and welcoming, and I can't imagine finishing this journey without him. But ... I don't know if I'm ready to move forward with him. I don't know if I *should* move forward with him. Accepting the fact that Julius is gone does not mean I have to find a new boyfriend.

The crazy thing is... Adrian knows this. He knows how I feel and he's still here. He'll always be here, but he's made it clear that he's fine being here as a friend and that's what's made this scenario so much easier for me.

I stare at him as he lies there, hands folded behind his head, his firm chest rising and falling with his even breaths. He hasn't had a panic attack since we got here. We still haven't talked about them, but maybe we don't need to. Maybe this peace between us has been a good thing in more than one way. Adrian isn't worrying about his family as much anymore, so some of the anxiety has lifted. It makes sense that the attacks would subside.

A tiny part of me would like to believe I played a part in soothing his nerves, but I won't be so selfish and give myself that credit. Especially since I've spent most of my time making mistake after mistake.

But God has forgiven me... I remind myself as I begin to read. It's only been seven days, but I'm determined to make each day with God count from now on. Besides, it took only six days for the Lord to create the earth, and then He rested on the seventh. One week with God is more than enough to open my eyes. I made countless mistakes and then my own friends abandoned me before I woke up and realized I was destroying myself, but I've finally woken up. Better late than never.

One thing I've learned on this journey—God can still make beauty from ashes, even when those ashes are from fires you've started.

My hope now is that I can at least serve as an example to Adrian of what true repentance looks like. Of what it looks like when God refuses to give up on you. And an example that Christians make mistakes too. We aren't perfect by any means, but through faith in God, we strive to become a better version of ourselves each day.

I pause as I reach the end of a chapter in our book. I listen to Adrian's soft breathing and wonder if he's asleep, but his tired voice fills the room after a still moment. "You've stopped."

"I thought I lost you."

He chuckles. "Never."

I know he's talking about more than just falling asleep, but I don't elaborate. Instead, I start packing up the book so I can head over to my own tent. We sleep in separate areas now, for our own good.

"Time for bed?" Adrian cracks open one eye as I stand.

I nod, brushing dust off my jeans. "We've got an early start tomorrow."

"That's right," he says.

We're setting out for Koshen, in search of that church in the letter. We've looted the library for supplies, and we plan to hit up other abandoned buildings to see what we can find. The journey will be long since we'll have to travel in the opposite direction now, but I'm praying it will be worth it. It's got to be.

Maybe we'll be reunited with Jupiter and Bunny, maybe we'll find Adrian's family, maybe we'll even find another lead for my father's whereabouts. I'm bold enough to pray that one day I'll see Julius and even Delilah again too. No matter what, I won't stop searching for them.

"We'll all be united again soon," I say aloud.

Adrian tilts his head back to peer at me from the floor. "Is that what you want?"

"Yes," I answer. But not for the reason he thinks.

When I see Julius again, it won't be to date him. It'll be to apologize. Apologize for setting a poor example of how young Christian women conduct themselves in a romantic relationship. Apologize for not being strong enough for the both of us. For not being able to properly deliver God's message to him. I want to apologize for being a lukewarm Christian because I think my teetering might have caused him to doubt my faith. I taught him that it was okay to be a hypocrite. I taught him that you didn't have to take your faith seriously. All you had to do was say, *I love the Lord*, and not have sex, and that would be enough.

I was dead wrong. And I hope I get to tell him that one day.

I won't even entertain the thought of rekindling any flames right now. Not with Julius or Adrian. My heart belongs to God, it's time I live up to that proclamation.

I glance down at Adrian, unable to overlook the thoughtful emotion on his face. "What are you thinking?" I ask softly.

"That I don't want you to go."

Sheesh...

I swallow. "You know I have to."

"I know."

278

I turn to leave, but he calls out to me, and I pause.

"Mya?"

"Yes?" I turn back.

"Do you say your prayers every night?"

"Of course."

"Do you mention me in your prayers?"

I hesitate. "I do."

Adrian doesn't speak, so I start walking away again, but then I hear his response. His voice is almost a whisper, but the words are clear as day.

"Maybe one day we can pray to God together."

I don't respond, but I don't need to. Adrian lets out a long sigh and then adds in a louder voice, "Goodnight, Mya."

"Goodnight, Adrian," I say, and then, *finally*, I find my tent and tuck in for the night.

We've got a big day tomorrow—a *huge* journey ahead of us—but somehow, I feel like we're rounding the bend. This is the last leg of our race. It'll all be over soon.

"Are You with me?" I whisper, on my knees beside my pallet. "I can't do this without You, Jesus."

Believe me, I've tried. It wasn't pretty.

I don't hear an answer, but I've been talking to God long enough to know that I don't need one for that question. God is always with me. That will never change.

Finish the series...

**Eternus, Book III in the Treachery Trilogy
Coming soon**

More books by Valicity Elaine & TRC Publishing!

Christian Fantasy
The Scribe
Cross Academy

Christian Post-Apocalyptic Fiction
The Barren Fields
The End of the World series
MAGOG saga

Christian Science Fiction
I AM MAN series

Christian Romance

The Living Water

Withered Rose Trilogy

Fractured Diamond

The Woof Pack Trilogy

Singlehood

The Gap

Beautiful Lies

Christian Children's Fiction

Too Young

ACKNOWLEDGEMENTS

You made it through Book II!!! This book was not difficult to write, but it took me SO LONG for some reason! I'm sorry it is shorter than the previous installment, but that is all the story I have for this one. I promise Book III will be better than you imagine. Can you believe it is already time for this series to close its doors? I've just begun to settle in and now it's almost over. But it was worth it, right?

I truly pray you enjoyed the book and I hope you finish the trilogy. Our story continues in **Book III, Eternus**. **Follow me on Amazon** to get updates on new releases, pre-orders, and reduced prices on my books. Also, follow me on TikTok! I love meeting readers and discussing new ideas.

See you there!